To my sons
Andy and Richard

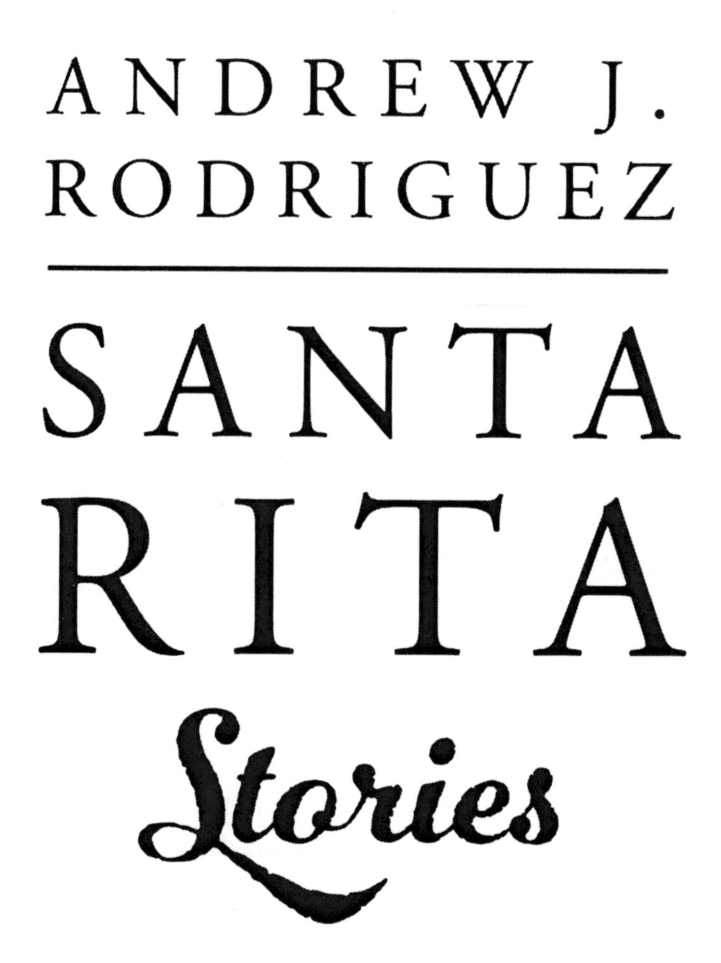
ANDREW J.
RODRIGUEZ
SANTA
RITA
Stories

outskirtspress
DENVER, COLORADO

Outskirts Press, Inc.
http://www.outskirtspress.com

ISBN: 978-1-4787-3698-1

Library of Congress Control Number: 2014909893

PRINTED IN THE UNITED STATES OF AMERICA

CONTENTS

THE CONSECRATION OF EVIL

The story I'm about to relate came from Pedro, a homeless old salt who lived in squalor in an abandoned shack on a dilapidated wharf in the port of Santa Rita, a gossipy little fishing village on the northeastern coast of Cuba.

A born storyteller, Pedro walked the docks each afternoon in search of someone to talk to, and right after dark he returned to his smelly domain to read until his eyelids collapsed.

Early each morning, while dock workers hauled on their bare backs hundred-pound sacks of brown sugar to an awaiting ship, Old Pedro scooped floor residues into his coffee can, added water and dark rum, and sat on the dock's edge, slowly sipping the makeshift brew in lieu of the traditional Cuban breakfast of buttered toast and *café-con-leche*.

The old geezer had an insufferable flaw: a notorious stench that betrayed his presence like skunks their territory. Rumor had it the bearded man never took a shower unless caught in a rainstorm. Yet, in spite of his personal abandon, Pedro was a knowledgeable person who educated himself reading books and periodicals he collected from garbage cans.

I was sitting at the end of the dock one Sunday afternoon, waiting for that big fish to jerk my line, when Pedro approached me and asked if I wanted to hear the story of a long-forgotten incident that once shook our town and rattled the clergy from Santa Rita to the Vatican like a palm in a windstorm.

Itching with the curiosity of a fourteen-year-old boy, I asked him to sit on my leeward side to keep his liquor breath, body smell, and the acrid smoke of a cheap cigar, blowing in the wind.

Pedro cleared his voice, swiped a forearm over his sweaty brow, and started to narrate a most incredible story:

The events I'm about to recall took place in 1879, nine years after Don Patricio Mayor, a poverty-stricken Spanish immigrant, established himself in Santa Rita.

Following years of finagling his way into money, the sagacious refugee managed to stash aside enough cash to engage in a loan-sharking venture, a scheme that made him the town's wealthiest and most influential citizen in less than ten years.

Pride-swollen Don Patricio became so well

known that even the then-Spanish governor, Don Ramon Blanco y Erenas, Marqués de Peña Plata, sent him a personal invitation to attend a gathering of Spanish entrepreneurs at Havana's governor's palace.

Startled by the nobleman's unexpected appeal, the ambitious settler arranged for a set of twin brothers, Jorge and Manolo Campos, to handle simple business matters in his absence. Don Patricio's affairs were in reasonable order except for three past-due loans owed by unscrupulous scoundrels who flatly refused to pay. These he would handle himself.

After carefully studying the thorny dilemma of how to collect the past-due loans without resorting to scare tactics, the wealthy Spaniard, who also wanted to spend a couple of extra weeks visiting the capital and meeting influential bureaucrats, set forth to enlist the services of Juan de Dios Hiriart, a long-standing acquaintance from Santa Clara, a city two hundred kilometers west of Santa Rita.

Don Patricio understood the character of the man he was about to hire. He knew his grit, resolve, and lack of scruples—much needed *virtues* to *negotiate* the collection of hopeless debts.

A notary by profession, Juan de Dios was renowned for drafting fraudulent documents and swearing falsely in court as he saw fit. He frequently stirred up enmities among friends for personal gain, sowing ire where once had been harmony. Losing his temper at the tiniest disagreement, he resorted to threats and verbal abuse to intimidate his opponents.

Hateful of God and the Catholic Church, Juan de Dios cussed the sacraments at every opportunity except in front of priests, and he was as fond of prostitutes as dogs are of tree trunks. But despite being viciously profane, Juan de Dios nonetheless befriended and charmed every priest and judge in Santa Clara, posing as an honorable citizen. Judges sheltered him, even as frequently abused merchants feared his impudence and disrespect for the law. Worse yet, though known for murdering enemies with his own hands, the man never spent a day in court.

A compulsive glutton, Juan de Dios ate and drank liquor as if his hollow core could never be filled, and as an obsessive gambler, he cheated his opponents with the finesse of a magician and the ethics of a thief. Although Juan de Dios surrounded himself with enough boot-lickers to catapult his ego to the clouds, by and large, most citizens couldn't wait to see the hideous man lying in a coffin.

En route to Havana to see the governor, Don Patricio stopped briefly in Santa Clara to meet with Juan de Dios. After an arduous search, he arrived at a white-washed two-story building with a polished brass sign that read:

Office of His Excellency Juan de Dios Hiriart: Upstairs

Both men immediately recognized each other as kindred spirits as well as old acquaintances. Don Patricio's condescending demeanor was difficult if not impossible to forget, and Juan de Dios's body, shaped like a pear, bore a pot belly so large that it hung over his sash. Don Patricio also recalled that the back of the hooligan's head was awfully flat; so flat it looked like a dinner plate.

When Don Patricio explained his predicament to Juan de Dios, the greedy man's eyes grew large. After intense and lengthy bargaining, a contract was reached: Juan de Dios would receive half of the proceeds if he recovered the money and nothing if he didn't.

Thus it came to pass that, carrying Don Patricio's power of attorney, Juan de Dios traveled to Santa Rita to stay with the Campos twins during the *collection* process. No one else in town would know of the thug's mission and ugly reputation.

After coping with pitiless roads for three solid days, Juan de Dios arrived at the twin brothers' household shortly before daybreak. Cautiously greeted by a lethargic housekeeper, he was escorted to a modestly appointed bedroom with various oil paintings hanging on the walls and a large Persian rug apparently lain to mitigate the groaning of a creaky wooden floor. A large window to the East added brightness to the colorful surroundings—the perfect setting for superstitious Juan de Dios, who feared only one thing: darkness.

Following a week of unproductive coercion, blackmailing, and arm-twisting, his ego meanly bruised by the three debtors' mockery, Juan de Dios concocted a scheme to slay them in their sleep while stealing everything of value, for the flat-headed villain was a genius at erasing all evidence of his crimes. And surely judges in Santa Rita would be as easy to bribe as those in Santa Clara, should the need arise.

But life's fickleness was about to settle its score with Juan de Dios, who awoke so sick the morning of the plot he simply couldn't get out of bed.

Doctors and nurses were called immediately to care for him. The twin brothers spared no effort to revive his health, but day by day, Juan de Dios's condition steadily deteriorated. Finally a team of doctors diagnosed him with a rare and deadly disease.

"Light, light!" he continually demanded as the final

darkness drew close. Soon, candles, lanterns, and even torches burned like hellfire in the dying man's chamber.

Aware of his upcoming fate and enraged with everything and everybody, especially God and the Catholic Church, Juan de Dios decided to avenge himself by making believers look like idiots. To this end, he demanded to be buried in a town where he was totally unknown, auspiciously Santa Rita, and to the amazement of both brothers, he urgently requested the presence of a priest to hear his confession and grant absolution.

Suspecting that Juan de Dios was about to cheat his confessor with a bunch of lies, and that a young, inexperienced friar would be tempted to offer him undeserved forgiveness, the twins decided to call Father Pizarro, a wise and respectable priest, time-honored for his astuteness in dealing with society's scum, as well as high-ranking rascals from the underworld. Reasonably fair and compassionate, the friar was also known for his expertise in human conduct and Canon Law.

Walking with a cane and escorted by a gray, hairless dog, the elderly priest showed up at once. Following a brief introduction, he seized a rosary and a little black book from a leather satchel, sat alongside Juan de Dios's bed, made the sign of the cross on the dying man's forehead with holy oil, uttered a short prayer in Latin, took the villain's hand in his, and began to administer the last rites.

"I understand you want to confess your sins, my son. Is this correct?"

"Yes, Father," replied Juan de Dios. "I want to confess all my sins from the day I came into this world, so please don't hesitate to ask me about anything and everything."

"Then tell me, my child." The friar cleared his throat. "Have you ever committed the sin of lust with a woman? And please don't worry about saying the truth. Every man I've ever confessed has done it at one time or another."

"Oh, Holy Father!" The dying man gasped for air. "I am as chaste and uncorrupted as the day I left my mother's womb, and she was the only woman I've ever touched."

"May God bless you," said the priest. "What a pious life have you lived!"

"But Father, I've committed the sin of gluttony after long periods of fasting. More than once I craved lustfully for a drink of water after being exhausted from praying."

"May those prayers elevate you to the company of angels," the priest said, raising his arms. "But what about greed, my son?"

"Please, Holy Father; don't judge me poorly just because I'm staying with these avaricious twins. My visit had nothing to do with the impurity of their souls."

"Then why are you staying here?" posed the friar.

"Because I am on a mission of love and redemption." With clasped hands and clammy eyes, Juan de Dios continued: "You see, Father, coming from a very wealthy family, I offered my entire inheritance to the sick and the poor upon my mother's death. All I have left is enough for basic sustenance, and if I've ever made money from any kind of trading, I've always offered half of it to the Church. But to answer your question; I came to rescue these two brothers from the bowels of hell as commanded by the Archangel Gabriel."

Father Pizarro gasped. "And did you have a chance to meet him as well?"

"His holy image materialized in one of my dreams," said Juan de Dios, tears gushing down his cheeks.

"Oh, my child." The holy man sighed deeply. "May the Lord bless you for being such an exemplary human being and for the privilege of corresponding with an Archangel...especially Gabriel."

Juan de Dios cried out in terror. "It grows dark! Please, Father, I beg you to speed up your confession before it is too late."

"Oh yes, of course. Do forgive me for asking, but have you ever lost your temper?"

"Only against myself after seeing men and women rejoice in sinful endeavors."

"But why blame yourself if you were not at fault?"

"But I was," affirmed Juan de Dios. "When I realized how little I could do to save their souls, I became very angry about my inability to help."

"In God's name, your anger was so justified it doesn't require atonement."

Holding tight to Juan de Dios's cold hands, Father Pizarro posed another question: "Have you ever deceived others?"

"Never!" Juan de Dios bawled hysterically. "In fact, on one occasion, a client who overpaid me for a service never returned to collect the balance. I saved the money and offered it to a beggar with added interest after hearing of my client's death."

Taken aback by Juan de Dios's tears and frantic behavior, the experienced and highly educated friar deemed the dying man's confessions truthful and straightforward. So impressed was he by Juan de Dios's impeccable life that Father Pizarro not only offered him complete absolution but also a burial crypt inside one of the church's chapels.

"Oh, Holy Father!" Juan de Dios erupted into frenzy for no apparent reason. "I don't deserve such honor, for I have sinned in a most hideous way, but since you didn't ask, I lacked the courage to tell you."

"That's why I'm here, my good man. Please tell me what happened."

"I disobeyed my mother once, and also spat on the church's floor. I was ten years old at the time and haven't had a clear conscience ever since."

Eavesdropping behind the door, the twins couldn't believe that a person could lie so unashamedly on his deathbed. Furthermore, they were flabbergasted to witness Father Pizarro's immaculate reputation and longstanding wisdom shattered by Juan de Dios's malicious melodrama. But fearing the wrath of their employer, Don Patricio, they held their tongues.

Deeply inspired by the villain's confessions, Father Pizarro concluded that Juan de Dios was a consecrated man. Determined to spread the *good news* to the world, he began by informing the town priests, who in turn notified the faithful, and soon the entire town was awaiting the impending death of Santa Rita's first and only saint.

Unquestionably contrived by the Devil, Juan de Dios gave up his ghost that very night.

Concealing joy as best they could, the brothers asked Father Pizarro to help with the funeral arrangements. Saddened but not surprised, the old friar began by instructing them on how to observe an overnight vigil worthy of a saint.

Abiding by the friar's authority, the belfry's bells tolled languidly through the night, announcing Juan de Dios's passing, and by daybreak the gossipy town of Santa Rita was totally enshrouded in grief.

Early that morning, Juan de Dios's body, suitably attired in priestly garments, was placed inside a glass sarcophagus and transferred to a hearse pulled by four black horses with black plumage on their heads. Dressed in albs and copes, and bearing crosses before them, a dense retinue of priests and acolytes, headed by Father Pizarro, marched in slow procession behind the hearse.

The funeral cortege grew much larger after crossing Maceo Street, and by the time it reached the church, the rural police couldn't keep the wailing crowds under control.

In memory of the holy man's death, businesses closed for the day and schools sent their weeping students home. Community leaders called upon the city council to issue a proclamation declaring Juan de Dios Hiriart to be Santa Rita's official saint.

To offer the townsfolk a unique opportunity to view and revere their new spiritual model, Father Pizarro had the body removed from the glass coffin to a marble slab across the altar. This gave the faithful a chance to gaze at the corpse, kiss his hands and feet, and pray for their needs.

Since the number of policemen on duty was too small to restrain the frenzied crowds, people pushed and shoved to rip off pieces of the saint's garments for good luck charms. Not soon enough, Father Pizarro ordered the body of Juan de Dios moved into a pinewood coffin and interred in the chapel's holy crypt.

Standing behind a podium and struggling to make his voice heard, Father Pizarro eulogized Juan de Dios. He exalted his virginity, recalled the man's painful tears when confessing disobedience to his mother, extolled his constant calls for light, and spoke of his prayer-induced exhaustion, irrefutable love for humanity, and the cleanliness of mind and heart demonstrated by the hallowed man throughout his entire life, proving once again that God works in mysterious ways.

Father Pizarro convinced the populace of Juan de Dios's sanctity to such a degree that following the interment, every man, woman, and child fell on their knees to pray for miracles to materialize, infirmities to disappear, pains to be assuaged, and so on.

As instructed by Father Pizarro, prayers were to be addressed directly to God, but on behalf of St. Juan de Dios Hiriart.

In less than a week, the marble slab covering the holy man's crypt was inscribed thusly:

Divine Office of St. Juan de Dios Hiriart:
Upstairs

During the weeks that followed, hordes of devotees stood in lines awaiting turns to light candles and make votive offerings by his grave. They also decorated the chapel with statues and figurines of their newly anointed saint.

Juan de Dios's holiness and the reverence in which he was held continued for months as the entire town prayed to God on the saint's behalf every single day. Miracles occurred, the sick were healed, thieves returned stolen items, the blind regained their vision, dreams came true, and astonishing events incessantly took place.

In a matter of weeks, the news reached the ears of Pope Leo XIII, who tried to suppress it from the public in fear that believers worldwide would try to circumvent the Vatican's intricate canonization procedure by appointing their own saints.

With the passage of time, miracles and healings occurred less frequently, and in the end, the bizarre incident of 1879 mysteriously vanished from Santa Rita's past.

Today, no physical or historical evidence of such events exist because someone at a later date was adamant enough to exhume and dispose of the body, seal the crypt, and destroy the carved marble slab, along with any physical evidence. Even the city council's proclamation nominating Juan de Dios as Santa Rita's first and only saint strangely disappeared—which proves that time and again, humans, when convenient, also move in mysterious ways.

Pedro paused, then asked with marked curiosity whether or not I understood the moral of the story.

I replied that regardless of how wise and knowledgeable a person is perceived to be, there will always be someone else sufficiently wicked and astute to make of him the biggest fool by clouding his common sense.

Pedro replied that such a conclusion for a boy my age made sense, but...that was not the moral of the story.

Dumbfounded, I asked about the lesson to be learned, and he replied:

"The message behind this historic event, young Carlos, is that our Creator answers prayers, whether they are expressed directly, by way of statues, or any method chosen by the believer, as long as they are conveyed righteously and in good faith. For faith, young man, and faith alone, is the intangible energy that links us to a living God."

A Tale of Deception

Walking home from the wharf, I racked my brains, wondering about Pedro's story. Was he telling the truth regarding Santa Rita's first and only saint? Were the story's bizarre events a product of his prolific imagination, or was the old man showing me the dark side of religion?

He'd once told me that faith is the only form of energy that connects us to a Living God. Was faith a sixth sense most of us don't perceive—some sort of extrasensory perception? Was he referring to the same energy that transports voodoo worshipers into a state of trance during their rituals, or was Pedro describing faith in his own philosophical way? The old geezer was always so damn capricious in his conclusions that sometimes the moral of his stories was difficult to understand.

And what about wise and educated Father Pizarro, who acted like a solemn fool after his lifetime experience with human deceptions? Only a dumb priest would've granted absolution to a total stranger who swore that he'd lived the life of a saint and had come to Santa Rita only to save the souls of two minor scoundrels. Wasn't Father Pizarro smart enough to become suspicious? What was he thinking? Why would he jeopardize his impeccable reputation by sanctifying someone who might have come from the moon?

But what troubled me most in Pedro's story was Don Patricio Mayor's ability to become the town's richest man in less than ten years, when my father slaved away day and night to offer his family a decent lifestyle.

Perhaps I should ask Pedro about Don Patricio's magic powers to make bundles of money so quickly, I thought, *and then pass the secret to my dad.*

To satisfy my curiosity, I stopped by the wharf the following day after school. It was late afternoon, and the workers had already left. Half asleep and leaning against a pallet-full of sugar bags, Pedro offered the only sign of life.

As usual, he asked me to sit next to him by tapping on the floor. I vacillated at first, but my question was too important to worry about his unpleasant smell.

After asking him how Don Patricio Mayor made his fortune, Pedro replied:

"My dear Carlos; if you really want to know how he became so rich, I suggest I tell you this man's incredible story right from the beginning."

Following my eager assent, Pedro carried on:

In the city of Granada and across the Alhambra, dozens of ancient caves were and still are occupied by thousands of gypsies. To this date, these itinerant cave dwellers are still considered the nastiest thieves in all of Spain. Can you imagine such riff-raff living at walking distance from the Alhambra Palace and enjoying its magnificent view for free?

Well...it was in one of those caverns where Patricio Mayor, the youngest of fourteen brothers and sisters, first saw the light of day during the spring of 1834.

His father, an illiterate thug, trained every one of his children to cheat and pilfer before they learned to walk, and since this was their clan's traditional way of life, Patricio never saw anything wrong with such an occupation. After all, earning a living by extorting decent, innocent people was an intrinsic part of their centuries-old culture.

But when Patricio reached his forties, greed overtook him. Disgruntled with what he considered a mediocre lifestyle for a thief of his standing, he decided to victimize affluent members of the nobility instead of regular citizens.

He awaited the perfect moment to stalk his first victim, a well-known patrician lady who routinely strolled the Avenida de la Reina, every single day at the same time, rain or shine. Itching for her purse, Patricio gathered enough verve to shove through the slow-moving crowd, knock down the woman, and seize her handbag.

Shaken by the thief's brutality, the elderly lady passed out, and moments later she died on the sidewalk.

Those who witnessed the crime tried to hold Patricio under civilian arrest, but the gypsy mugger was so adept and well trained in his profession that he managed to escape as swiftly as a slimy pig would the butcher's knife.

When word of the incident reached Patricio's father, he forbade his youngest son to hide in their cave in fear that the police would incriminate the entire clan. Patricio ran from one hiding spot to the next until he reached the port of Cadiz a week later.

One night, while begging for food at the wharf, he befriended a Hungarian gypsy who worked as a luggage handler on an ocean steamer. Following his new pal's advice, Patricio applied for work as a dishwasher on the same ship. About to depart for Havana and with no one on board to clean dishes, a desperate head-cook hired Patricio without hesitation.

Three weeks of rough weather turned the voyage into a horrid nightmare for everyone on board. Always below deck and hopelessly seasick, Patricio often vomited on the same pots and pans he had cleaned. Swearing never to be caught again on anything that floated, Patricio arrived in Havana during the summer of 1869, pale, disfigured, and virtually dehydrated.

His first occupation in the capital was that of pick-pocketing—a most lucrative but dangerous pursuit in that city, for in those days the Spanish police tortured common thieves as cruelly as they did Cuban Freedom Fighters.

The only time Patricio went to jail in Havana was for stealing a purse left unattended on a store counter. Flogged twenty times for a first offense, his bloody camisole virtually glued to his skin and forewarned that the next conviction would bring a minimum of forty lashes, Patricio decided to move to a more lenient environment.

Knowing that Cuban insurgents were creating havoc in the countryside, and as a result Spain's militias lacked the manpower to chase petty criminals, Patricio pick-pocketed his way to the agricultural city of Santa Clara.

After two days of scrutinizing the town's streets, alleys, and roads, Patricio profiled his next target: a cigar-smoking, flat-headed man who exuded great wealth, not only because of his garments but by his haughty demeanor.

One morning, Patricio followed the chosen victim to the darkest corner of an old, dilapidated building. Once within striking range, he reached for a briefcase secured to the man's wrist by a chain. Fast as a mongoose, the pot-bellied chap turned on his heels and jabbed Patricio's chin with such force that the would-be thief fell to the floor belly-up and semiconscious. But so impressed was the enigmatic man by the gypsy's crafty style that he invited him to his office for food and brandy. During their short walk, the proud stranger introduced himself as Don Juan de Dios Hiriart.

After a lengthy exchange at his disorganized and messy workplace, Juan de Dios offered Patricio the position of "personal assistant." In addition to good pay, "friendly women" were also available free of charge. The boss's only condition: Patricio must learn to dress and behave like a gentleman, for in his judgment, "Even the most nefarious undertaker looks reassuring when properly attired."

Hungry, penniless, and greedier than ever, Patricio accepted the job. But with the passage of time, the new employee grew so jealous of Juan de Dios's ability to create wealth that he demanded three salary increases in less than a year.

Intimidated by his avariciousness, Juan de Dios fired the "assistant" and told Patricio to leave town or face horrible consequences. Knowing that Juan de Dios settled scores in the most hideous ways, Patricio left Santa Clara and arrived a week later in Santa Rita.

Famished and exhausted, he stopped by the town's only church to beg for food, a jug of water, and lodging for the night. Saddened by the beggar's pitiful appearance, a young friar offered Patricio a couple of used garments, dinner leftovers, and a cot in the sacristy.

Anxious to rekindle his old profession, Patricio went on the prowl again, but unless he robbed the church's coffer or the city's few well-off citizens, his earning potential was poor at best in a small fishing town like Santa Rita.

In view of these limited prospects, Patricio took a job at the town's slaughterhouse. Responsible for washing the walls, floors, hooks, and axes, and for dumping excrement, guts, and rotten remains in a sea cove nearby, Patricio worked fourteen-hour days, seven days a week, for meager pay, and to save on food he often ate chunks of raw meat behind his boss's back.

In less than a year, the determined gypsy had saved enough cash to buy a tired old horse and a two-wheeled cart. These he used to haul sick and dead cattle away from local farmers and open fields ahead of the vultures, at no cost. In cahoots with his boss, Patricio secretly delivered decaying loads of meat to the slaughterhouse during the night, and the next morning the establishment was processing cheap, grisly carcasses, ultimately sold to crooked butchers in the poorest parts of town.

Getting paid by the pound, Patricio made enough money to build a smokehouse and purchase a sausage stuffer, a meat grinder, and a mixer. He was about to start his own sausage-making business on the side. Having learned the trade's dirty secrets from a Granada buddy of his, Patricio used the cheapest cuts of beef, meats from sick and dead horses, and if none were available, stray dogs, rats, and cats to create his savory recipe.

First he brought the meat to a paste, then added flour as filler, saltpeter for preservation, beet juice to give a natural red color to a hideous-looking mix, and lots of garlic and salt to cover up the finished product's revolting taste. After stuffing the mixture into pork intestines, he smoked them overnight, and by morning Patricio had the most appealing sausage links this side of Spain. His loyal clientele: poverty-stricken families and Santa Rita's shoddy food establishments.

But it so happened that early one morning, the rural police stopped by the slaughterhouse unannounced to investigate whether the death of an entire family of six was due to rotten beef eaten the day before. In those days, it was virtually impossible to blame a single ingredient for causing food poisoning, so the criminal investigation eventually fizzled. But Patricio, fearing he might not be so lucky the next time, quit delivering spoiled meats to the slaughterhouse and instead applied his energies exclusively to sausage-making. Although his products were even more noxious than plain rotten beef, his business thrived.

Once Patricio had saved enough money from his wicked venture, he set out to change his image in order to attain his life's dream of power and money. He ordered numerous high-quality suits and accessories from the town's finest tailor, called on the best barber for daily shaves and weekly hair trims, and moved from his grimy cubbyhole into a newly built house, the rent for which was next to unaffordable. Finally he hired a young, ebony-black African woman of statuesque figure and striking personality as his personal cook and assistant. The lady was responsible for sponge-bathing Patricio every other night and for keeping his hands and toenails polished and grime-free.

When at last the greedy thief had acquired the faux demeanor of a Spanish nobleman, he audaciously placed this sign on the front door:

Don Patricio Mayor: Financial Counselor to the Royal Bank of Spain

The reinvigorated cheat began to attend Sunday masses and to donate money left and right. So when he asked the priest to introduce him to Santa Rita's most venerable citizens, the friar, who considered Patricio the most honest, hardest working man in town, presented him to Maria Caballos, a dejected widow who had recently lost her disabled and very wealthy husband to yellow fever.

At once Patricio had exquisite red roses, along with plagiarized love poems dedicated to Maria, delivered daily to her door. To gain control of the widow and keep competition at bay, Patricio escorted Maria to social gatherings, never missing a chance to be seen together in public, and since—according to gossip—Patricio had a considerable fortune deposited in the Royal Bank of Spain, rumors that he was chasing after the widow's wealth never materialized.

Most of Santa Rita's single men were courting her favor, but Patricio's youthful appearance and charming personality ultimately won the widow's heart. With sharpshooter's precision and the patience of a clam, Patricio methodically set Maria Caballos's trap. From then on it was a matter of persistence on one side and stupidity on the other.

When the right opportunity arose, the phony entrepreneur asked the widow for a substantial amount of cash to be deposited under her name in the Royal Bank of Spain. He promised the money would be used as collateral for high-quality loans made to selected Havana merchants by the bank. Moreover, Patricio guaranteed he would soon triple her investment.

Trusting her new beau to the point of insanity, Maria Caballos gave him the money without a signed agreement, for she claimed, "There is no room in our hearts for true love and written contracts to coexist."

Patricio grabbed the cash, kissed her on the cheek, and never saw the dim-witted widow again.

To emerge as a victim, that same night Patricio complained to the local newspaper that he had found Maria in bed with another man. He also accused her of instigating a plot to steal his fortune.

Even though the publisher didn't dare print Patricio's claims without further evidence, he made certain the conniver's allegations reached every single ear via the town's grapevine. In a matter of hours, everyone in Santa Rita was reviling *despicable Maria*, who cried miserably for days until she left town in shame to live with her daughter in Havana. To the townsfolk, honest and compassionate Patricio Mayor was the innocent victim of a love affair with a serpent in disguise.

Interestingly enough, Patricio had been sexually attracted to dark-skinned women all his life. Only God knew whether he hired his African maid to fulfill a long-nourished fantasy. Either way, he exploited her many connections with cooks, nannies, and housekeepers by paying them decent money for revealing their employers' peccadilloes and dirty secrets.

After recording these transgressions in a diary, Patricio began to offer shadowy loans to prominent citizens in urgent need of cash. These transactions were sealed only by handshakes. No papers, no witnesses, no signatures. The desperate borrowers paid ludicrous usuries for what came to be known as "Confidential Loans from the Spanish Crown." The caveat: If debtors didn't pay Patricio on time, he would sell their personal and most intimate secrets to the local newspaper, thus destroying their character and reputation for the rest of their lives. Luckily, the celebrated financier never had to pull the plug on any of his victims.

Thus it took only nine years for Patricio to realize his dream of becoming one of the island's wealthiest and most reputable bankers. And this is how the benevolent and philanthropic Don Patricio Mayor became such a widely respected citizen in the entire country.

"Well, son." Pedro looked deeply into my eyes. "Would you like to hear the moral of the story?"

"Not this time, Pedro. You see, with the twenty cents I still have in my pocket, I'm going to buy Dad a small bucket of freshly shucked oysters as a surprise."

"And then what?" Pedro asked.

"Then I'm going to hug and kiss him."

"And then what?"

"Then I'll tell Dad how much I love him, and how proud of him I am."

PEDRO'S STORY

In matters of education my parents were very demanding, especially during finals.

Throughout this hectic period I was expected to walk straight home from school; no fishing, no playing, no friends, and no visiting Pedro—for according to them, it was the old geezer's negative influence that made 1954 my worst academic year ever.

In an effort to boost my intellectual output, and to ensure I grasped my ugly predicament, Mom confronted me as I was leaving for the last day of school.

"Carlos...before you take off so eagerly, I want you to sit tight and listen to what I have to say."

My stomach in knots, I sat on the kitchen counter.

"The reason you've been attending this private school"—she fixed me with that icy, menacing look of hers— "is because of its academic reputation. Yet Dad and I are so disappointed with your grades we've been seriously considering a summer tutor."

"No, Mama, please don't. I promise—"

"Please let her finish!" Father yelled from the bathroom.

"On the other hand," Mother continued, "in recognition of good behavior, and because this was the only bad year you've ever had, we're willing to postpone any drastic measure, as long as you spend two hours a day for the next three months reading Martí, Darío, Balzac, Kipling, and so forth."

Reluctant to play second fiddle, Father zoomed back to the kitchen.

"I also have something important to say." Dad lowered his bifocals to the tip of his nose. "While this may sound irrelevant to a fourteen-year-old," he began, "I want you to fully understand the consequences of generalized ignorance."

"Must you barge in like that?" Mother snapped, hands on her hips.

"I'm sorry," Dad said humbly. "I got carried away."

"Apology accepted," Mom replied with a hint of a smile on her face.

All in harmony, Father continued.

"From now on, son, every time you read the paper, watch movies, listen to the radio, friends, teachers, and to Pedro in particular, try to carefully separate fact from fiction, and excellence from mediocrity. Also make a point to seek truths and discard myths, so as to steer clear of rapacious manipulators.

"You must also remember that dealing with today's reality will help you cope with tomorrow's disappointments, and as I've always said: successful and happy lives are generally rooted in common sense and a well-rounded education. Simply put, my boy, *stop dreaming and get with it!*

"I will, Dad, I p-promise."

But my passions for nature and the outdoors were so intense that in order to enjoy them freely, I routinely faked deep interest and enthusiasm during and after every sermon...and it always worked. This time was no exception. The notion of fishing at the docks while listening to Pedro's stories, playing marbles with friends for nickels and dimes, and diving into shark-infested waters to impress terrified girls, energized my budding macho-image to such a degree that I lost all sense of reality.

Besides, I learned much more from Old Pedro about human frailties and valor, handling disappointments, and even love than I ever did from *La Comédie Humaine*, *The Decameron*, *Don Quixote*, *The Prince*, or even Malaparte's ugly, nerve-racking *Kaputt*.

Santa Rita's skies were of the deepest blue on Saturday morning, and it was hot...beach-bum muggy, to be precise. What a perfect day to start summer vacation, catch fish, visit Pedro, and mingle with neighborhood girls.

The instant Father released my fishing gear from his closet, I ran to the store across the street and bought enough bait to last all day. Then I whistled, hopped, and skipped all the way to the docks.

After waiting over an hour for a bite that never struck, I asked the dock-master for suggestions.

"It's been kind of quiet during the last two weeks," replied Arturo, one of the most corpulent men in Santa Rita. "I suggest you grab a net and catch mackerels instead."

"Oh," I said, crestfallen. "I didn't bring one."

"No problem," the hefty man replied. "I'll let you borrow mine."

"That's very nice, Arturo. But let me try two more casts before imposing on you."

"You're not bothering me," he said in a squeaky voice that belied his girth. "Besides, you're part of us."

I puffed up with pride. "Thank you."

Swiping a forearm over his sweaty brow, the super-sized man drew near.

"Did you know we had to take Pedro to the hospital last week?" he asked.

My mouth dropped open and a surge of cold

sweat oozed down my spine. "No. What happened... is he okay?"

"One of my workers found him unconscious on the floor. He called the doctor, who diagnosed him with severe food poisoning and rushed Pedro to the hospital in his own car."

"What then?"

"He stayed three days at the old people's clinic."

"Where is he now? Will he recover?"

"Pedro is doing fine, though it's short of miraculous he's still alive, but he hasn't left bed since. Now he's writing farewell letters because he thinks he's dying."

"Has he been eating?"

"Better than ever." Arturo beamed widely. "Me and my workers have been bringing him food every day. No more rum, sugar, and coffee for a while. No one can live on booze alone."

Afraid of becoming nauseated, I'd always avoided visiting Pedro's living quarters. But this time there was no escape. I asked Arturo for directions.

"See that smokestack protruding from the roof toward the end of the wharf? That's Pedro's kerosene stove. Walk all the way to the back of the wharf until you find an eight-foot-tall particle-board divider. That's the partition that separates Pedro's shack from the rest of the warehouse. To the right of the divider there's a plywood plank he uses as sliding door to his domain. Knock on it, say loudly who you are, and he'll open it for you."

"Mmm...and how are the conditions inside?" I asked guardedly. "I mean...is it dirty? Does it smell?

"Well, son, what's dirty and foul-smelling to one person might be cologne to another, you understand?"

"Yes, Arturo...I think I do."

"Then take your chances and pay a visit to the old man. I'm sure he wants to see you...before he dies."

After Arturo's suggestion, I gathered enough courage to knock on Pedro's makeshift gate.

"Who the hell is there?" he bellowed.

"It's me, Carlos," I called softly.

"Oh yes, of course. Let me get dressed to open the door."

After a couple of minutes, Pedro slid the wooden plank aside.

"I have awful news for you, son," he said with a long and gloomy face.

"What is it, Pedro?"

"Did you know this might be the last time we see each other?" he asked in a weak voice. "No one believes me, and everyone laughs when I say it, but my old rusty ship is about to conk-out...sooner than you might think."

Except for a seemingly phony frail voice, the old

man looked healthier and cleaner than ever. I gave him a dubious frown.

"But please, sit down!" He gestured grandly to a folding chair. "Dios mio, I'm so delighted to see a young face for a change!"

The room was surprisingly clean, and its décor so imaginative that I virtually ignored Pedro's plea for attention. Hundreds of heavily used books, periodicals, and old magazines stood piled up row after row from the floor to the top of the partition, and along three concrete walls from the floor to the shack's tin roof, thus giving a false impression they were buttressing the ceiling.

Pedro's dwelling must have measured at least sixteen by twenty feet. Plenty of sunlight trickled through a glass-covered opening in the roof, and a lightbulb dangling from the end of an old dusty wire hopefully produced enough light for him to move about and read by at night. The kerosene stove Arturo had pointed out was so clean it shone like pewter, and the half dozen pots and pans that hung from screws imbedded in the concrete wall sparkled like polished silver.

Toward a corner and suspended from a protruding five-foot-long lead pipe, six coat hangers displayed Pedro's scanty wardrobe. Also imbedded in the concrete wall, two rusty nails propped up his only pair of dilapidated boots. A couple of folding chairs, a termite-infested desk with a cracked glass top, an old cot cushioned with layers of blankets, a large pillow, and a seldom-used washbasin, made up all of Pedro's furnishings.

But what surprised me the most was Pedro himself: shaved, his salt-and-pepper hair brushed and neat, and the smell of rosewater in the air.

"When I die," he said faintly, "I want my body and home to look impeccably clean for a change, and my coffin must be—"

"Who's the beautiful girl in the photograph?" I purposely cut him short.

"Ah. She was the love of my life...and still is." Pedro sighed ardently. "Alicia died very young, along with my baby boy."

Pedro had a child? A wife? I thought, amazed. *Perhaps he wants to die to be with them.*

"How old was Alicia when she...?"

"You're what—fourteen? So she was only five years older than you. And I was twenty-eight at the time," the old man replied. "Would you like to listen to that story?"

"Y-yes, of c-course!"

Maybe because I rarely confronted the possibility of dying young, a choking sensation seemed to grip my throat, and when Pedro slung his arm around me as a sign of friendship, it felt as though he was passing me a lethal current. I suddenly became so concerned with death assailing the young that I wasn't at all sure I wanted to hear the story of Pedro and the beautiful woman in the portrait.

What a morbid way to spend my first day of vacation, I thought. But then my curiosity about Pedro's youth got the better of me, and I settled down to listen.

"Have you ever heard of the Pedraza family?" Pedro asked, sitting across from me.

"Of course I have. In fact, Julio Pedraza is one of my schoolmates."

"I'm fully aware of that," said Pedro. "Did you know he's the grandson of Don Roberto Pedraza, the man who hung himself thirty-three years ago from a jacaranda tree? May God save his soul!"

How does he expect me to know about someone who killed himself so long ago? But there he goes again, talking about death, and I hate it!

"Are you sure Julio is from the same Pedraza family you're referring to?" I asked.

"Of course he is. I've been following their doings ever since Alicia died. Believe me; I know more about that destructive bunch than I do about fishing for a living."

"I don't think Julio is destructive," I said. "But he's very quiet and doesn't talk much. Our teacher said his mother forbids him from mingling with other students."

"I also knew that. So do you want to hear my story or not?"

"Yes, Pedro. But only if you stop bringing up death and dying."

"I promise not to mention them unless absolutely necessary," said Pedro, narrowing his eyes in recall.

Born in 1860, high and mighty Roberto Pedraza was the only child of a Spanish nobleman and a Cuban socialite. Raised like a prince whose wishes had to be fulfilled at any cost, Pedraza grew up as though our planet orbited around him.

As a young man, he spent several years studying philosophy and art at La Sorbonne University in Paris. In that city he met Lucille Bouvier, a French aristocrat. They fell in love and married upon graduation, settling in Havana within a year.

Financially supported by Pedraza's father, the couple had plenty of money to live lavishly and eventually send their six daughters to Havana's most prestigious school for señoritas. Truth be told, Pedraza wasn't worth a dime as an art connoisseur, much less a family provider.

Upon his mother's death, Pedraza inherited a huge cattle ranch ten miles from Santa Rita. As the ranch was the family's most lucrative asset, they moved to our town from the capital to keep an eye on it.

Pedraza was an eccentric and bitter man, often tormented by depression. He visited the ranch only on Mondays or when absolutely necessary. Otherwise he either went hunting alone or stayed at his Santa Rita home, exuding vinegar.

Ruling with an iron fist, the man went so far as to bar his girls from leaving the house unless accompanied by Nena, a sergeant-like governess imported from Spain; and to abide by her husband's wishes, Lucille hired a tutor to keep them from mingling with the *public school common folk.*

As you can imagine, the family rarely ventured out except when sitting on their veranda before dinnertime—the homeliest girls sticking out their tongues at pedestrians, Pedraza and his wife swinging on padded rocking chairs, their backs facing the street.

Excluding those who had to lick their shoes to survive, everyone in town despised the pompous man and his family.

For better or worse, I was the only student in class who risked passing by their house on the way home, and that was because of my crush on Alicia, their most beautiful and intelligent daughter. Gazing at this angelic creature from the corner of my eye became the sweetest of treats. But though I whistled soft tunes and expanded my chest as I went by, Alicia simply ignored me. Alas, the less attention she paid me, the more I worshipped her beauty.

After weeks of trying different lures, Alicia finally noticed me...and smiled. Ay, hijo mio! Her aqua-colored eyes shone like precious gems...and those lips! Well, what can I say? They were simply divine!"

All absorbed, I asked Pedro if he smiled back.

"Of course I did." He sighed ardently. "And when I got home that day, Mother must have noticed something unusual in my expression, because she asked why I was walking like a blushing zombie with an unbuttoned coat in the middle of winter."

"Did Alicia pay more attention to you after that?"

"Not quite," he replied. "It rained for an entire week, and the temperature got so cold they stayed indoors for some time."

"Come on, Pedro; I can't wait to hear how you two finally met."

Pedro closed his eyes for long. . .very long moments, then resumed his tale.

My family was very poor, and I had to work after school to help put bread on our table. Employed by a pharmacy as a delivery boy at the time, I managed to stash aside enough cash to register at a Havana law school later in life.

But as fate had it, the drugstore owner suddenly died. And that—well, that changed my life forever.

When the pharmacist's son arrived from Havana to bury his father and dismantle the business, he realized I needed money to help support my family. Reluctant to let me go without work, he convinced Pedraza to employ me at the ranch or elsewhere.

Pedraza owed the deceased druggist a multitude of favors, so he hired me to pump water from an underground cistern at home to a tank on the roof every day after school, and on weekends I would tackle errands and do repairs as needed.

"And that's how you met Alicia, right?"

"Hold your horses, son," Pedro retorted. "At least let me savor this part of the saga without interruptions!"

I held my horses—with a sheepish grin.

The first day I showed up for work, Nena, the governess, made sure the children, especially Alicia, remained out of sight. Aware of her beauty, Nena kept the girl under her thumb while I was around. As far as I was concerned, having Alicia within reach not only compensated tenfold for the loss of income from my previous job as a messenger, but made me desire her even more.

One day, Nena received a message from her brother in Spain, informing her that their mother had fallen ill and had three months to live. Against Pedraza's will, Nena boarded the next ship to Europe.

At the same time, Lucille also had to go to Havana to solve a crucial legal issue regarding her husband's inheritance. Simply put: Pedraza was the only adult family member left behind.

Detesting housework, much less caring for his daughters, Pedraza pleaded with Teresa, the cook, to take over the governess responsibilities in exchange for some old clothes and a set of blankets. His offer accepted, Pedraza stayed at the ranch throughout Lucille's absence.

My first weekend assignment at the Pedrazas' was to unplug a kitchen drain no one else could fix. Luckily, that was the day Teresa chose to fry dozens of yucca sticks for dinner. *Ay, mi madre,* those fritters smelled so good, my mouth watered and my stomach groaned like an old wooden floor.

Either attracted by curiosity or by the appetizing smell, Alicia surprisingly appeared in the kitchen, and when she saw me, her hands flew to her mouth in wonder; then she greeted me with a smile. That's how Alicia and I met."

"And what was your reaction?" I asked, eyes wide.

"My lips tingled to the beat of a pounding heart while I melted like a candle at the kitchen sink," Pedro pronounced, forgetting his infirmity.

"Confused as to what to do next, I gently kissed her delicate hands. To this day, I still recall the scent of her smooth velvety skin. It was love at first sight!

We both sighed in unison.

"The only person with a heart at the Pedrazas' besides Alicia was Teresa, who insisted Alicia and I sit at the kitchen counter to taste her fritters and get to know each other," Pedro said with a sad smile. "That woman must have enjoyed the moment so much she kept feeding us yucca sticks while keeping a protective eye on the surroundings.

"Alicia and I talked for about an hour. She was social, articulate, and very educated. I was sort of shy, untraveled, and ignorant of topics I hadn't studied in school. We discussed our likes and dislikes, favorite music, her flute lessons, my fishing techniques, and much more. But when she asked me where I lived and what my father did for a living, I blushed like a ripe tomato. Suddenly I felt about six inches tall."

"And why did you feel so diminished?" I asked Pedro.

He eyed me as if the answer should be obvious. "Because I didn't want one of Santa Rita's wealthiest girls to know that I lived in the poorest part of town, and that my dad made fishing nets for a living. I was afraid she'd consider me inferior and out of her league, you understand?"

I nodded.

"But I felt much better when, back at the sink, I overheard Alicia asking Teresa to keep under wraps everything she'd seen or heard. The kind woman not only agreed, but suggested we meet again the next day to taste a *dulce de leche* dessert.

"The following morning our conversation became more intimate. Alicia inquired if I had a girlfriend, and I replied no, not yet, and when she asked if I liked to dance, I praised her beautiful eyes and cheerful smile instead of answering the question.

"Startled by my compliment, Alicia left the kitchen without a word. But thank goodness she appeared later with a lovely collection of pastel paintings.

"'I want to know what you think of my landscapes,' she said, laying the album on the counter.

"As I leaned forward to examine her artwork, we

got so close together my temperature rose, but when I felt the sensuality of her breath, my boiler virtually exploded. I felt even more captivated by Alicia when I understood that she wasn't a bit concerned over my social and economic status.

"Thanks to Teresa's generosity, Alicia and I met every afternoon for the entire week, and though it might seem impossible, I always finished my work assignments.

"Sad to say, our hush-hush meetings ended the day Pedraza came home from the ranch to welcome Lucille, who arrived from Havana in spite of bad weather.

"On my way home that day, I realized that none of Alicia's sisters had ever entered the kitchen to scrutinize their new pump-man or sniff at what went on behind their backs. As you can imagine, I found their conduct awfully strange."

"Strange," I agreed in a whisper.

"At the Pedrazas' dinner table that evening, his oldest daughter, Fermina, also known to neighbors as Fat Fermina, stood up to accuse Alicia of 'making love to the *servant boy* while Teresa watched ecstatically their entangled nude bodies swaying on the kitchen floor.'"

At that my mouth dropped open. "What happened then?"

Pedro's eyes sparked with fury. "When Fat Fermina finished her jealous accusation, Pedraza asked his other four girls to corroborate or deny their sister's allegations. Partners in crime, they supported Fat Fermina's claim by offering their own erotic versions of the lovemaking scene. Worse yet, none of those monsters ever showed the slightest remorse for assassinating Alicia's character and dignity in front of their obnoxious father and submissive mother. Nothing but sewage came out of those vipers' mouths. What a tragic night!"

Pedro paused to choke back tears.

"With the rage of a bigot forced to defend his dark convictions, Pedraza banged on the table and roared for Teresa, who came in trembling like an aspen leaf. Numb with shock and grief, her eyes popping at the spectacle, Teresa swore that Alicia and I had done nothing more than talk and hold hands. Pedraza stood up to punch the woman's face for lying, but she ran away from the house, never to return.

"Furious at Alicia, and irritated by the cook's audacity to quit without warning, Pedraza seized the innocent girl by the braid and dragged her into his bedroom, hurled her head-on against the floor, tore off her clothes, and with a horsewhip, lashed her entire body until he was out of breath. Then, pounding his fists on the center of his chest, Pedraza accused Alicia of dishonoring his illustrious name, fell to his knees, and prayed for her eternal damnation.

"Shocked, humiliated, and in excruciating pain, Alicia cloaked herself in a blanket just a lucky second before Pedraza actually kicked her out of the house for good."

"That man was an animal!" I exclaimed furiously.

"Worse than that, boy...much worse, and my story isn't over yet!" Pedro said, tears welling in his eyes.

"It must have been the year's coldest night when Alicia showed up at my house, begging for warm clothes, a place to spend the night, and someone to nurse her open wounds.

"Sobbing incessantly, she promised never to become a burden to our family because 'Sooner or later,' she said, 'my sisters will repent and clear my name, and Father will welcome me with open arms, begging forgiveness.'

"But that didn't happen. Those girls were a mean bunch of piranhas poisoned by vanity, jealousy, and vitreous envy.

"Terribly upset at the sight of her, my dad rushed to the police station and filed battery charges against Pedraza for assaulting his daughter with criminal intent; but the chief replied it was a domestic dispute in which the father had a right to discipline his child as he saw fit. In other words, Pedraza was too powerful for the police to intervene.

"The next day I woke up at the crack of dawn, and in total darkness went after Dad's rifle before riding my horse to Pedraza's ranch. He wasn't at the caretaker's house and the ranch looked deserted, so I checked the toolshed but found nothing. Then the well, the mess hall, even the outhouses. At last, when I reached the stables and saw the back of Pedraza's head protruding behind a stall, I aimed my rifle at the center of his neck. What a perfect target! Then someone knocked me out from behind with the back of a machete."

I gasped.

"I was taken unconscious back to town and left to rot on a sidewalk two blocks away from home," Pedro continued. "After a Good Samaritan splashed my face with a bucketful of water, I realized all I had left were a bloody head and a note in my pocket. The horse and the rifle were gone."

"What did the note say?"

"*'If you want to die of old age, stay away from my properties, or I shall have your head cut off.'*"

Pedro nodded. "And he would have, too. Nowadays, I thank the Lord every night for keeping me safe and for preventing me from killing the bastard." He faced the ceiling with his eyes closed for a moment, then resumed.

"Since my parents and younger brother welcomed the idea of Alicia becoming part of our family, they offered her the room previously occupied by my deceased uncle. Can you imagine a wealthy señorita who had enjoyed every luxury known to man, now cooking, doing laundry, cleaning house, feeding the chickens—suddenly living in poverty? But she did this with no complains, and within a couple of months, our love and affection had grown to the point that I asked her to marry me.

"In mid-May, only four months after her ghastly experience, Alicia and I took our marriage vows in a simple ceremony in Santa Rita's church. Only my immediate family and dear Aunt Rosa, the seamstress who designed and assembled Alicia's wedding dress, were present.

"What about the wedding night?" I pried, blushing, but more curious than embarrassed.

"Pedro gazed into the distance with a rapturous smile. "Alicia looked so stunning I felt all the stars from heaven were mine to keep."

I asked Pedro how he could afford a honeymoon.

"To tell you the truth, I used some of the money I'd saved for law school to check in at the Gato Negro Hotel for a week. As I'm sure you know, the old inn still stands behind our wharf."

I frowned. "How could you spend seven days

locked up in a hotel that offered nothing except watching fishing boats and houses on stilts?"

He looked amused. "First of all, son, it was a sobering and peaceful experience to know that flies and mosquitoes were our only links to the real world."

"Okay, Pedro, but what else did you do?"

"We marveled at the multicolored wakes left by fishing boats at sundown, walked the docks, and measured the ebbing and incoming tides with our own hands. And every afternoon we opened the windows to soak our lungs and hearts with the sensual, humid, delightful scent of the onshore breeze."

"And what did you do after dark?" I prodded.

Now he grinned fully. "We contemplated the colorful majesty of the sunset and enjoyed the full transparency of Santa Rita's night skies."

"Come on, Pedro, quit being so modest and tell me the rest!"

"We made love to each other until our hearts collapsed. Is that what you wanted to hear?"

I smiled...and the old man blushed.

"Listen, boy; I'm sorry, but I don't want to continue," Pedro grumbled as his joyful memories suddenly seemed to have wilted.

"But it wouldn't be fair to leave a kid floating in Limbo," I complained, arms crossed over my chest.

"You certainly don't look or act like a kid," said Pedro. "Who taught you to ask such adult questions?"

"My parents," I answered. "And you."

"Me? How can a homeless drunkard teach you that sort of thing? Oh, what the hell...just keep on listening while I keep talking!"

I settled down in my hard folding chair.

After our wedding, I quit school and went to work as an apprentice welder in a metal shop. My life was so complete I honestly didn't see a need to continue my education.

Two months into our marriage, Alicia became pregnant. Needing more money to support a family of three, I started to work extra hours selling train tickets at the railroad station.

Four months into her pregnancy, my mother realized that Alicia's belly was abnormally large. Alarmed, she took her to the town's midwife to ensure her gestation was normal. But both came back with worried looks and teary eyes. The lady, who also worked as a pediatric nurse for the local hospital, claimed that Alicia wouldn't survive a normal delivery, and that a miscarriage was more than a possibility.

Scared of the outcome, I suggested taking her to a Havana gynecologist—a relatively new specialty in those days—but Alicia was in no condition to withstand the protracted train journey to the capital without endangering both of their lives; and besides, I couldn't even afford a one-way ticket.

On the brink of an impending tragedy, our family and close friends suggested the possibility of bringing a Havana specialist to Santa Rita to confirm Alicia's diagnosis and take a course of action. Our dilemma: we needed a substantial amount of money to find the doctor, and to pay for his lodging, traveling expenses, meals, and rather large fees to cover at least a five-day absence from his main practice.

Rosa, the seamstress, volunteered to ask the local bank for a mercy loan; my father offered his life savings; and I pledged to make monthly payments to whomever loaned us the money, even if it took the rest of my life to pay it off. In real life, however, no one had ever heard of a mercy loan, and Dad's life savings weren't large enough to even consider.

As a last resort, Alicia volunteered to ask her father for assistance and to use his influence to convince a qualified doctor to take the case. Without alternatives, Alicia went to visit Pedraza the next day."

"Listen Pedro," I said at once. "I have a bad feeling about what's coming, and how difficult it'll be for you to continue, so if you want to stop, please do so now."

"If you promise to share these experiences for the sake of others," Pedro avowed stoically, "I shall finish my story."

I nodded solemnly.

When Nena opened Pedraza's door, her jaw almost fell to see my pregnant wife standing in front of her.

"Young lady," she stuttered in shock, "If I w-were you, I'd l-leave this house b-b-before Don Pedraza discovers it was you wh-wh-who knocked on the door."

"This is my rightful home," Alicia stated firmly, "and I won't leave it until my father and I have a talk. Go tell him that his pregnant daughter needs immediate financial assistance to save her life and that of his first grandchild."

"I c-certainly will, señora...if you insist," replied the pallid governess.

"Yes, I do insist! Please hurry and convey the message."

Alicia waited at the doorsill until Nena returned from Pedraza's office, paler than a chalk stick.

"Don Pedraza said you either leave this house immediately or he'll *kick your fat belly out like a garbage bag, even if you bleed to death.* I'm sorry, child, but those were exactly his words."

Furious at her atrocious father, Alicia tried to push Nena aside to enter the house. The governess, much stronger than the expectant girl, blocked her way in to avoid a tragedy.

"My dear child," the stocky woman implored, "please forgive my forceful manners, but in God's name and for the sake of your child, I beg you to leave immediately."

"But I have a moral and legal right to demand—"

"Yes my dear, I'm fully aware of it," Nena replied, "but Don Pedraza is capable of doing exactly what he said...and much more. In God's name, please go back to your husband and in-laws and forget your father."

The intense emotional shock this caused Alicia soon began to take a toll, and by the time she returned to us, my dearest love was suffering severe back pains and loss of blood.

To prevent a looming tragedy from occurring, my father borrowed a neighbor's horseless carriage to take Alicia to the Casa de Socorros while my mother went after the midwife.

By the time we arrived at the emergency room, Alicia, in agonizing pain, had taken on the pallor of a cadaver, which brought me to screams of desperation and tears of wrath. I was so distraught that my little brother had to drag me outside to calm me down.

In a matter of minutes, the midwife entered the room, followed by my mother and the local surgeon—a medical practitioner who didn't know where to start and for what reason. Frustrated by his own incompetence, the physician blamed the lack of suitable equipment for his inability to control the bleeding.

Time passed, and when the skin of my beloved Alicia started to show a yellowish hue, then a bluish-gray, I jumped on her bed, crying and kissing her as if my love would bring back her lively colors.

Shortly thereafter, Mother and Father tenderly pulled me away from her. Only then did I realize she was gone, and ever since that moment the entire universe has never been the same.

"I'm terribly sorry," I said to Pedro, pressing his shoulder. I couldn't prevent the tears from spilling from my eyes, but he sat still, his expression stone cold.

"After that," he continued at last, "I lost my will to finish an education or embrace a new beginning. All the colors of life had faded to black and gray.

"Lacking the willpower to snap out of such a miserable void, I found much needed numbness in liquor.

I was thankful for having a supportive family, but nothing under the sun could alleviate the pointless loss of a lovely wife and child.

"Within a year, the influenza epidemic also took my parents. My brother moved to the capital in search of a better future, and I continued to exist like a zombie and work like a robot at the metal shop. My loved ones gone, I devoted my energies to making sense of man's existence, finding meaning in his sufferings, and establishing an undisputable definition of good and evil.

"In order to achieve my self-imposed mission, I quit work, deserted friendships, cut off most links to the past, and moved to this wharf across from the old Gato Negro Hotel to lean on my sweet memories for spiritual comfort."

Pedro gestured with a wrinkled hand, like a king indicating the breadth of his kingdom. You see, boy, from this filthy hole of mine, I've been able to find solace in the colors of the sea, and serenity in precious solitude.

"In pursuit of answers to life's contradictions, I've read the works of prominent philosophers, stargazers, mathematicians, poets, writers—even books written by notorious experts who claimed to possess the wisdom of the ages, yet knew nothing of the past. I've also studied the world's religions in the deepest detail and virtually devoured whatever came my way concerning the meaning of truth and the pursuit of happiness from the time of creation.

"I've read everything there is to be read, drunk all the liquor my liver could handle, and purged myself from every mind-cluttering temptation to be found in the banal things of the world."

"But Pedro," I ventured, "the question is: Are you happy with the answers?"

He narrowed his eyes at me. "Quite the contrary," he replied. "The more I read, the less I know, and the more I know, the less I understand. But of one thing I'm certain: Regardless of how badly you think life treats you, turn your face around and you'll find someone even more miserable than you." He wagged a bony finger. "Don't let this cliché mislead you, though, for its only purpose is to deceive fools with a sense of achievement."

I nodded sagely, though I wasn't sure I knew what he meant.

"Tell me, Pedro; why did Pedraza commit suicide?" I asked.

"I thought you didn't want to talk about death," the old man replied with a twinkle in his eye.

"That's true, except in this case!" I said at once.

"Then I shall tell you." Pedro continued.

"In 1923, ten years following Alicia's death, a

ranch worker found Pedraza's body hanging from the jacaranda tree in front of the family mansion. No one in Santa Rita knew for sure why he'd killed himself. Gossip had it his wife Lucille had caught him having an affair with an Asian woman. The town's paper blamed his suicide on financial losses and mental problems. But I knew from a housekeeper friend of mine that Pedraza was going mad after suffering unremitting nightmares for the past ten years.

"According to my friend, Pedraza frequently awoke in the middle of the night to the sound of a woman's voice accusing him of murder, and that the voice sounded exactly like Alicia's. These recurring nightmares were so dreadful that Pedraza would awaken the entire family, yelling profanities at a woman named Teresa. My friend also said that Lucille often called her in the middle of the night, asking her to bring Pedraza a clean sleeping gown, for his was drenched in sweat."

"What happened to the rest of the family?"

Pedro shrugged. "Lucille caught smallpox and died, and the disease left her skin so disfigured her coffin was closed for viewing. Of the five remaining daughters, three ended up in a Havana insane asylum. Genetically cursed by nature, Fat Fermina and two of her sisters suffered from depression so severe they had to wear straightjackets to stay alive.

"Pedraza's youngest daughter, Camila, joined a nunnery dedicated to helping mental patients, and Claudia, the clan's most pompous, married during her late forties—a wealthy rancher named Alberto.

"Barren because of age, Claudia and Alberto adopted a child they named Julio to keep the name Pedraza alive for generations to come. As you can see, Claudia is the adoptive mother of your schoolmate, Julio Pedraza."

"That's very sad!" I said to Pedro. "I feel so sorry for him."

"You can always assume," Pedro said confidently, "that there will be a dark motive behind every move undertaken by a Pedraza family member. Luckily your friend Julio is not a blood relation to the clan. But Claudia's egotistical influence on Julio once again confirms that the devil continues to thrive in Santa Rita."

INVITATION TO THE DANCE

If 1955 was my worst academic year on record, our school's summer vacation must have been the rainiest in Santa Rita's history. I spent most of my time reading books and playing poker for nickels and dimes behind my parents' backs, while my much-coveted outdoor life shrank to fishing and riding my bike, drenched by rain.

I also kept an eye on Pedro, who continued to do well despite his obsession with dying. On the whole, the old man was back to drinking cheap rum, searching garbage bins for cigar stumps, and reading compulsively. I could only hope that he was taking advantage of the frequent downpours to bathe and launder his famously stinking clothes.

Once back at school, I was determined to improve the previous year's grades whatever it took, so I sacrificed most of my free time for the sake of academic achievement. My grades were so outstanding during the first two months that Mom and Dad, concerned about the lack of sunshine impairing my body's ability to absorb calcium, insisted I spend more time playing outdoors.

One surprise followed another, and in mid-November a postcard from my gorgeous classmate and elusive crush Veronica arrived in the mail. What joy! It was an invitation to attend her upcoming *fiesta de los quince*, a traditional sweet fifteen birthday party, as her escort. The big bash was scheduled for New Year's Eve at the Spanish Community Center. I was so ecstatic I felt I was walking on air.

But if I accept, will I have enough time to fulfill my academic responsibilities? I pondered with trepidation. *Will this year's grades continue to improve? What about Chucho, her usual boyfriend?*

Despite my fears, the sweetly scented invitation was so tempting I decided to meet with her early the next morning before class.

Leaning against the school's brick wall shortly before dawn, I awaited the sight of a particular slender young woman crossing the park on her way to school. In due course I saw her coming my way, moving with the grace and panache of a flamenco dancer: *Veronica*. Her lightly tanned skin, luscious lips, and delightful chocolate eyes colored her finely carved features, all enshrined by the halo of her opal-black hair.

As she drew nearer, my wildest fantasies escaped. I fancied pressing my body against hers during dance rehearsals, our cheeks rubbing gently through soft musical passages. I imagined the touch of her sweetly scented hands, reveling in their aphrodisiac fragrance. To keep my secret fantasies under wraps, I forced myself not to ogle, but surreptitiously followed her every movement. By the time she reached me with a smile in her big brown eyes, I was glowing with excitement.

I cleared my throat. "*Buenos dias*, Veronica."

"*Buenos dias*, Carlos," she replied, flushing a sexy pink. "Why are you here so early? Are you okay?"

"Of course I am. I just wanted to thank you for the invitation before school started."

"That was very kind of you." Veronica sighed deeply. "You have no idea how much I'm anticipating that party."

"B-but what about Chucho?" I asked, trying to sound casual.

"Don't worry about him," she said. "I wouldn't have invited you unless he was out of the picture."

I nodded, giving my tie a tug. *What is it about this girl that sets me ablaze every time I hear her voice?*

"Chucho never bore ill intentions toward me," she continued, "but since all he cares about is boxing and bodybuilding, I simply told him to go worship himself in a mirror, and leave me alone.

"How did he take it?"

She shrugged. "He was crushed. I saw it in his face."

I could hardly blame him. But thrilled by the upcoming celebration and its romantic *possibilities*, I pushed Chucho from my mind and promised Veronica I would attend rehearsals on time, wear the required formal attire, and turn into nothing short of a waltz king.

In every city and town in Cuba, the most common excuse for teenagers to spark up a gathering was to rehearse for a "sweet fifteen" party—a ritual no family with a fifteen-year-old daughter would dare miss, whether affordable or not. The *fiesta de los quince* offered the pretentious and flamboyant a-once-in-a-lifetime chance to make a social statement in which everything from the sublime to the ridiculous was possible, and it gave the poor and underprivileged a unique opportunity to go all out, according to their means. The popular celebration marked the beginning of an era in which the newly anointed grownup would be allowed to become engaged to be married and line up priorities. All subject to parental approval, of course.

In short, as of that magic moment the celebrant was expected to think and act as an adult without the real benefits of such standing.

These debutante balls were all similar in their format: A Viennese waltz danced by father and daughter, followed by fourteen couples, marked the beginning of the event. In modest circles a radio or record player sufficed, and in higher spheres Hollywood productions were not ruled out. Rehearsals took place way ahead of the party, and every single rehearsal usually ended in another elaborate bash.

According to Santa Rita's unwritten laws of good and evil, I should have told Mom and Dad about Veronica's invitation first, but decided to wait for fear they would water down my soup by criticizing her parents for hosting a Cinderella-like event when they were people of modest means, or by arguing over renting a tuxedo versus buying one I would eventually outgrow, or by asking me to memorize the chapter on escorting debutantes from Amy Vanderbilt's *Complete Book of Etiquette*, and eventually my ears would burn following Dad's worn-out lecture on the social and emotional consequences of going too far with a respectable girl—or worse yet, crossing the finish line.

In fact, after listening so many times to the same sermon, it finally took root in my brain:

"Every decent, well-bred boy needs to understand that the petals of a rose are to be admired, caressed, and even passionately kissed, but when descending downward along the stem in opportunistic pursuit of pleasure, its thorns will painfully remind him of the disastrous consequences he's about to face for lusting at such a young age."

Nearly all parents in Santa Rita sheltered and disciplined their children to prevent sexual improprieties from staining the family's moral reputation. Girls didn't seem to mind the many restrictions imposed on them—at least as far as I could tell. I, on the other hand, detested my folks for being so pushy when they knew I had enough sense to deal with most teenage issues.

Inextricably woven through its time-tested traditions, Santa Rita's most treasured values were the Catholic Church, and lifelong commitments to marriage and family. Men were respected for their chivalry, character, and determination, and women for their virtue, beauty, and sense of compassion. At a very young age we were taught to respect our elders, look after them, and procure their participation in our daily lives. Whether archaic, argumentative, or simply helpless, older people were rarely considered burdensome, and they were treated with the dignity and gratitude worthy of their standing. Nonetheless, I wasn't about to give my parents an additional excuse to lecture.

Everyone I knew welcomed my new assignment as Veronica's escort, not because they liked me, but because Chucho was widely known as a big-headed bully who had learned boxing only to display his machismo in front of women. He'd been expelled from the school's boxing team for punching his opponents below the waist, and for stuffing his gloves with lead sinkers.

Once, when the hefty seventeen-year-old captain of the wrestling team challenged Chucho to a fight in retribution for being called a papa's boy in front of his *novia* (girlfriend), the wrestler ended up in the emergency clinic with a broken nose, bloody lips, and purple eyes.

Later, a group of Chucho's former victims gathered at the corner of Alameda and Calle Martí to teach the bully a lesson for all time. Carrying empty sugar bags filled with cobblestones of all sizes, the young avengers hid behind empty barrels stacked in rows of three on the sidewalk opposite the path that Chucho generally used on his way home from school.

As soon as the bully crossed the fateful street and reached the sidewalk, the mutineers became unglued and all hell broke loose. In the blink of an eye, the hardware store window was shattered by a cobblestone the size of a fist. The entire windshield of a nearby milk truck was pulverized after being hit by a rock as large as a grapefruit. An elderly woman and her five-year-old grandson took cover inside the barbershop, followed by a couple of horrified nannies pushing their baby strollers.

When the police arrived, five adults were arrested, the younger kids sent home, and the town's ambulance (formerly a bread delivery truck) emerged to rush blood-stained Chucho to the nearest clinic to endure as many stitches as he had hairs on his head.

In spite of his ruggedness, the humongous boxer was an honor-roll student who rarely prepared for exams. And perhaps because I managed to keep my distance from the King Kong bully, he had never picked on me...at least up to then.

Since I felt more at ease discussing my personal issues with Pedro, I visited him on Saturday morning.

He must have fallen asleep after a drinking bout last night, I reasoned, after finding the old man snoring on a heap of turbinated sugar bags, cigar stump clasped between his jaws.

"Hey, old man, wake up...we need to talk!"

A waft of Pedro-smell assaulted me as he squinted and stretched.

"And must you wake me up so early?" he muttered, his voice raspy.

"So early?" I said. "It's already ten o'clock! Besides, how many times have I asked you to spit out those turds before falling asleep? One will choke you to death someday!"

Oblivious to my pestering, Pedro searched his pockets for a match to rekindle the salivated stogie. Finding none, he wrapped the mushy morsel in a frayed handkerchief and stuffed it into an old leather pouch he kept in his back pocket for emergency use.

"In my world nothing goes to waste, regardless of size, much less a cigar," he said proudly.

After helping prepare his early fix of Cuban coffee, brown sugar, and Bacardi's Añejo rum, I sat with Pedro at the dock's edge with our legs dangling out. The day was crisp, the fishermen had vanished beyond the horizon, and my eyes itched following a restless night.

"What's up your sleeve this morning, young man?"

"Truthfully, I don't even know where to start...it's complicated."

"Quit scratching your head and spill it all out!" Pedro said, crossing his arms over his chest.

"I just wanted to discuss a series of issues with someone I trust."

"You are very smart to consult the old oracle first," Pedro said solemnly. "After tracking Santa Rita's heartbeat for years, I'm acquainted with the dirty laundry of each and every family—the feminine inclinations of so-called macho-men, the hidden peccadillos of the young and old, and the frustrations of lethargic young men and women who find themselves floating in their own monotonous stew without compass or direction, always waiting for an act of God to catapult them from a mediocre life of ignorance and boredom into a meaningful realm, where determination, hope, and meaning supersede lost time, useless matter, and wasted space, and where all flowers bloom year round and roses have no thorns."

I nodded sagely, though in truth I hadn't quite expected, nor followed, such a pronouncement.

"Hmm," said Pedro. "You don't seem to be too impressed with my wisdom today. What's wrong?"

"I'm sorry, Old Man; but I have too many things in my head."

"Then go ahead and unload. I'm here for you."

I told Pedro about Veronica's unexpected invitation, her sudden breakup with Chucho, my true longing for the girl, and the fact we'd known each other only a couple of months. I assured him that no one else knew of my yearning, and that I needed advice on how to achieve three goals: avoid embarrassment, demolish the bully, and hold Veronica in my arms.

Eyes fixed on mine, Pedro asked why I was so afraid of embarrassment.

I replied that if Chucho wanted to regain his stained macho image with Veronica, he'd probably start by crushing me to pieces, and that alone would be humiliating.

"Don't worry so much about events that might never occur," said Pedro, his voice as calm as the water at our feet. "Make Veronica look nice at the party. Act like a responsible young man, and no one will point a finger at you. As to the narcissistic idiot, I'll show you how to defeat and embarrass him in front of his cronies."

Pedro gently tousled my hair. "But first, can I ask you a personal question?"

"Ask anything you want," I replied.

"Have you ever wished you could pull up Veronica's skirt?"

Stunned, I replied that such a thought had never crossed my mind.

"That's because your libido is still in stage one," Pedro said matter-of-factly. "You see, the longer you rub skins with a girl, hold her hand, kiss her lips, and dance so tightly people see one body with two heads, the closer you come to stage four—and that's what concerns parents the most. Stage four."

He paused, making sure he had my full attention.

"As you know, the sexual mores concerning women are deeply imbedded in Cuban culture. I can't determine when and why they became so entrenched, but our men have revered, honored, and admired virtuous women for centuries."

"But don't you think such beliefs are slowly becoming obsolete?" I asked.

Pedro shook his head briskly. "My dear boy. Every civilized society must preserve its moral values and traditions or it self-destroys."

"My uncle says tradition is what we resort to when issues are not based in reason."

"Not necessarily!" Pedro replied vigorously. "For centuries we have regarded women's God-given right to remain virgins until marriage in the highest esteem, and while such values have no definite reasons to exist, they have helped our culture survive the ravages of time. Are you with me so far?"

"Only to a point," I replied. "I still don't know how to achieve my three objectives."

The old man sighed and gazed out to sea. Then he twisted back to me and jabbed a finger toward my chest.

"Look at it this way, boy: If women were easily

available to satisfy men's primeval instincts, ethical integrity would become passé, and society would sink to a state of moral anarchy in which humans conduct themselves like beasts.

"I'm sure your parents understood the virtues of true intimate love and didn't taint them with the trappings of promiscuous sex. Had your mother reached stage four with a bunch of men prior to your conception, would you have considered her ethically competent to teach you morality and physical restraints?"

"Of course not," I replied.

"When passing these old teachings to your descendants," Pedro emphasized, "make sure they understand the difference between passionate love and lust for passion; for love, in its purest form, is the everlasting spiritual fire that dwells in the hearts and minds of devoted couples."

Pedro eyed me up and down. "Mmm, what's wrong, boy? Am I so boring you're falling asleep?"

"It's not that, Pedro; I simply can't associate my problems with your fancy speeches."

"That's all right son." Pedro nodded sympathetically. "It'll be fine, so long as you've understood half of what I've said."

"Just don't treat me like a nincompoop," I retorted. "Quit tossing poetry and complicated language around, and then I'd learn something."

"All right, young man, in that case I'll call a spade by its name: Given that the cravings of our flesh generally lead us to pleasure-seeking rather than self-control, I sometimes wonder whether a young señorita—in this case Veronica—and you, of course, could respect these old mores if the setting is perfectly suited for having sexual intercourse."

I gaped at his frankness. "Aren't you grossly overstating the situation?"

"Hell no, I'm not!" Pedro shouted. "I'm simply trying to prevent you from fathering a child with that girl, or any girl for that matter."

"For the love of God, I'm just talking about an innocent relationship between a boy and a girl."

"Damn it, son!" Pedro pounded on the wooden deck. "When a man and a woman are physically attracted to each other, nothing of a sexual nature will occur out of innocence. And you know damn well what I'm talking about! I'd bet everything you know about human sexuality came from discussions with your buddies, and perhaps a little pornography here and there. Have you and your parents ever discussed these topics?"

"Are you kidding? My dad would be so embarrassed he'd be stuttering throughout the lecture, and there's no way I'd ask my mom about stage four situations, *comprendes*?"

"Yes, of course I understand," Pedro said kindly.

"Can I ask you an isolated question?"

"My life is an open book." Pedro gestured grandly. "If you don't mind discussing your three objectives later on, go ahead and ask."

"What should a boy my age do when an older woman tries to seduce him?" I asked on a whim.

"Your old oracle firmly believes that a boy your age simply shouldn't mess around with older women, period."

"But what's wrong with sex at my age if she knows how to avoid pregnancy?"

"That's not the point," Pedro said with a grimace. "After reaching stage four with numerous men, these loose cannons tend to become manipulative and insensitive to the feelings and emotional needs of their young prey. If one tries to seduce you, decline with good manners, for honorable men should always treat women with respect. Besides, boys your age—in spite of what you and your buddies may salivate for—are neither emotionally nor mentally ready to engage in sexual shenanigans with these loonies, lest in the end you'd rather keep the bitter end of the rope as a souvenir."

Pedro took his hat off to scratch his head. "But why are you so concerned about having sex with older women?" he asked. "Have you been approached by any of these tramps? Have they asked you for money? Tell me the truth. I need to know what happened."

"Calm down, old man! No one has tried to seduce me. Besides, this place is full of workers trying to eavesdrop on our conversation. I've asked you because my former friend Pancho got involved with a twenty-seven-year-old woman, and he almost died as a result."

"How old was he?"

"Two years older than me. But he fell head over heels for this mulatto woman who'd recently broken up with an older man. Captivated by her charms, Pancho left home and moved in with her."

"At sixteen? What a shame." Pedro sighed long and deeply. "I feel sorry for his parents...and for the young man, of course. What happened afterwards?"

"Her previous lover broke into the house one evening, and at gunpoint ordered Pancho to leave Santa Rita for good or he'd blow his brains out. Pancho moved back in with his parents, but refused to leave home for fear he'd be killed. After he missed the finals and therefore graduation, the entire family moved to Santa Clara, never to return."

"A miserable ending for everyone." Pedro shook his head.

"Do you mind if I ask another unrelated question?"

"Go right ahead," Pedro said, opening his palms.

"I'd rather spend my leisure time delivering answers than doing nothing."

"How did you avoid stage four while dating your girlfriend Alicia?"

"Ah, now we're talking!" Pedro exclaimed. "Well, it was very simple." He rolled his eyes in wistful recall. "When my temperature rose, or a strong craving for stage four triggered my basic instincts, I proposed a short walk, or simply talked about topics alien to love-making."

"What if you both got overexcited after dancing too close?"

"Then I suggested fast rhythms to minimize fondling, or if I knew beforehand that a stage-four scenario may be at hand, I wore my pants backwards."

Pedro's remark detonated in me such an explosion of laughter I had to hold my sides to keep them from hurting.

"Why are you laughing so viciously?" he demanded. "Aren't you smart enough to understand my words, or are you cackling like a witch to make a fool out of your old friend and the woman he loved?"

"I'm sorry, I didn't mean to—"

"Don't worry, boy. I'll fire back before you know it."

Rubbing his hands mischievously, Pedro spoke at the top of his voice: "Being more astute than most kids your age, I imagine you've kissed a girl on the mouth before, haven't you?"

I flushed scarlet. "No, never. But will you please lower the volume? You're embarrassing me in front of these men."

Oblivious to my wish, Pedro continued. "When you do, make sure it is performed exactly by the book...that is, if you want to be known by every woman as the macho man in town."

I replied softly, hoping he would take the hint, as several dock workers had turned to eavesdrop. "My buddies and I believe there is nothing to kissing a girl—that kissing is kissing."

"You and your buddies are downright ignorant!" Pedro cried even louder. "Kissing a relative good morning or goodbye is one thing. Launching a woman to the gates of heaven is another. Therefore, I strongly suggest you listen to the voice of wisdom before messing up your first romance, okay?"

"Please, Pedro; you're talking to me, not to the whole town."

"To do it correctly," Pedro blared, "a kiss must be a slow, irresistible seduction. First, you must gather the girl by the waist, just like in the movies. Look deeply into her beseeching eyes and move your lips closer and closer to hers...but slowly, boy, very slowly. Once you are a whisper away, stick your tongue inside her mouth and move it around as you would on a lollypop...then suck her delicious lips and savor that moment when the heart stumbles after a perfect kiss. Do you know what a perfect kiss is?"

"No, and I don't care, so shut up!"

"Well, if curiosity ever takes you over, the perfect kiss is the one you feel all the way down to the soles of your feet!"

Concluding his flashy tirade, Pedro grinned in triumph. "What's wrong, son? All of a sudden you're shining like a ripe tomato. Did I make you uncomfortable?"

"You know you did." I mumbled.

"Then so be it, young man. Now we're even."

I may have been mortified. But I also took a moment to memorize Pedro's instructions about kissing. When my temper had cooled off, I asked him for the best way to woo Veronica without making a fool of myself.

"First, don't be so concerned with what people think. Simply tell the girl you were so pleasantly taken by her invitation, you'd like to become better acquainted. If she sneers, backs away, or refuses for no good reason, chances are she is not taking you seriously, and if so, cool your jets, step off the cloud, and remain strictly social.

"But if Veronica seems receptive and blushes for

no good reason, suggest a place where the two of you can meet and talk. To me, the park across from school seems perfect for the occasion."

"Where do I begin? What do I say?"

"There you go again!" Pedro looked down on me. "Don't plan so much and use your instincts. Start by admiring what she's wearing, no matter how ugly. Praise her personality, but don't overegg the pudding. If Veronica wears a ring or watch, delicately take her hand in yours and commend her good taste. Observe her demeanor, facial expressions, and body language for clues as to where she's leading you.

"And remember; to avoid drooling in her presence, don't stare deeply into her eyes."

I grew hopeful. "Are you by chance leading me to stage two?"

"Absolutely not!" stressed the old mentor. "But remember: Your heartthrob is a little older, has more experience, and could very well be using you to lure Chucho back."

While Pedro's words may have been well intended, the possibility of Veronica being deceitful constricted my throat.

"On the other hand," said Pedro, using his index finger to draw a heart in the air, "let's be positive about the girl and assume she fell in love with you after finding your curly hair and thick eyebrows irresistible. Sick and tired of dating an ape, she decided to enhance her social image by choosing a handsome escort like you instead."

It was time for lunch, and I stood up to leave.

"Please, sit down." Pedro tapped on the wooden deck. "We still haven't plotted the demolition of Chucho...remember?"

"That's right, I almost forgot."

"Then the time has come to make a plan."

"Come on, Pedro, only a boxing champion can bring that savage to his knees."

"Oh no, my boy, you're completely wrong!" The old man shook his head briskly. "If you listen to me and do as I say, King Kong will be licking your shoes in no time...I promise."

"Pedro, if you're about to loud-speak another kissing-like joke, I'd rather go home and eat lunch."

"Don't be so dramatic and listen to your sagacious old friend."

I settled back down on the dock. "Okay, man...I'm all ears."

"Since Chucho was banned from the boxing team for cheating his opponents," Pedro said, "using a bit of *creativity* to defeat him should be considered an act of self-defense in any court of law. The caveat, young man: You must be willing to cheat."

I didn't care much for the cheating part, but I kept my ears open.

"To begin with," said Pedro, rubbing his hands in joyful anticipation, "Chucho will want to fight you in a public place. So take along your baseball bat and set it where you can reach it."

I nodded apprehensively.

"Since I'm sure your opponent will invite his *female fans* to the event, make him swear loud and clear never to retaliate, regardless of outcome."

Another nod. *Where is he going with this?*

"Once he's done swearing, Chucho will hop, skip, and jab to impress his audience and intimidate you. The minute the fight begins, imitate his hopping and skipping, but stay away from his punches, unless you want to end up in the morgue. From then on, focus on his loins and forget everything you've learned about the sport."

"On his loins, you said? Are you kidding?"

"You heard me. As soon as you detect an opening between his legs, leap toward his crotch, grab his genitals with your left hand, and smash them with your right fist. Once the bully bends over in agony, kick his nose until it bleeds, and to finish the job, pull him down to the floor by his ears.

"From his fetal position, Chucho will curse you, your mother, and every ancestor from the time of

Adam. Grab the bat and swing it furiously in front of his face to show you're insanely capable of anything."

"What if he stands up and chases after me?"

"Then toss the bat and run like hell. In your particular case, however, running away will be construed as an integral part of your survival instincts and not an act of cowardice. Furthermore, watching your rival contorting painfully on the floor will sweeten your ego like good ol' rum and molasses. If you do as I say, he'll be in no condition to chase you."

My self-confidence in high gear, I stood up to leave, but again, Pedro yanked on my arm.

"Shift your props into reverse and listen. We still haven't discussed the most difficult problem: Veronica in your arms."

Pedro took a deep breath, scratched his head, and spoke uncharacteristically quietly: "There are some disturbing issues regarding Veronica's family you must know."

My eyes widened. "What are you trying to say?"

"I'm very sorry to disappoint you," said Pedro, his unsteady hand trying to light up a fresh cigar. "But Veronica, her parents, and Chucho are Jewish."

That was it? "And who cares?" I asked.

"You should, because the obstacles that seemed to begin and end with the bully might worsen with her folks."

"Pedro, you've got to be kidding me."

"Sorry, but I'm not. If the two of you reach the age of seventeen dating each other, her Jewish traditions will supersede matters of the heart."

"What do you mean by *supersede*?"

"If at that age or beyond, a romantic relationship continues to flourish between you and the girl, the remote possibility of their daughter marrying a gentile will set off an alarm for Papa to demand a breakup, or Veronica will face disownment. What's more, he might come after you as well."

"But only a bigot could be that nasty with his own daughter," I said. "Besides, if I don't mind their traditions, why should they care about mine?"

"Because theirs have been deeply rooted for centuries, and their religious beliefs are inconsistent with yours. If a culture so firmly embedded in world history was so strong it maintained its identity for thousands of years, it was because its followers had enough courage to defend their faith at any cost."

"So you're implying that Jews only marry their own, correct?"

"That, or you must convert to Judaism."

"Then what my uncle said about tradition was true."

"Again, not necessarily," Pedro said soothingly.

"But like it or not, you must respect their beliefs and who they are."

I began to pace in a circle on the dock. "You know, Pedro? I'm so upset by the hurdles thrown in the paths of misunderstood teenagers by obsessively religious parents, and by intellectually possessed tyrants like mine, I wish I was old enough to leave home, and if I ever have kids, I'll let them do with their lives whatever suits their fancy. Parents and older folks are so full of hang-ups, they refuse to accept the prevailing trends of modern societies."

"Really?" Pedro fixed his crinkly eyes on mine. "Then why in hell must you squeeze advice from an old prune like me?"

He took my shoulder and gave it a quick shake. "You know something, kid? If I were you, I'd go home, eat lunch, and learn what a cold shower can do to straighten you up."

That night I told my parents about Veronica's invitation, Chucho's role in the affair, the reasons she'd left him, the fact I didn't know how to waltz, the tuxedo issue, and finally my longing for the girl.

While I was explaining, Father didn't lift an eye from the newspaper once, and Mother kept crocheting like a busy termite munching at Pedro's wooden desk. Nothing bothered them until the word Judaism came out of my mouth.

At that, Mother took off her glasses and regarded me with a grave expression. “I can buy you a tuxedo, show you how to waltz, and still find ways to help you achieve good grades,” she said, “but if I were in your shoes, I’d invent a darn good excuse to turn down her invitation.”

That night I slept with a tumult of dreams, as if I’d had Pedro’s nightly measure of rum.

I’d learned in school that on November 27, 1871, the Spanish government executed eight innocent Cuban students for allegedly scratching the tombstone of a Galician newspaperman. Ever since the country gained its independence from Spain in 1902, public and private schools across the nation had commemorated the massacre by giving pupils the day off to join in patriotic events.

On the Monday following Pedro’s lecture on promiscuity, kissing, and Judaism, students in Santa Rita observed the holiday. That morning, the phone rang louder than ever.

“Buenos dias, Carlos; this is Veronica from school.”

I dithered at the sound of her voice. “Oh...er, hello, Veronica.”

"Sorry for calling so early, but I have a favor to ask."

"Just tell me what you need, and I'll be glad to help," I said eagerly.

"Can you drop by my house sometime today? Father positively wants to meet you."

"Am I the reason he's staying home?" I asked, already filled with dread.

"Absolutely not," she replied. "He's taking the day off to finish pipe repairs. Do you know where I live?"

"Not exactly, but I can write it down."

Searching the room for pencil and paper, I tried in vain to invent an excuse to cancel the visit. Meeting her old man face to face would definitely be mentally and emotionally exhausting.

Will he ask me to memorize Moses' laws, plus lay down his own? Will he frighten me with threats, such as, Thou shalt not betray me by holding hands with my daughter, and if ye dare kiss her lips, I shall torment you with fire and brimstone?

Holy mother of God, what am I doing?

"Sorry to keep you waiting," I mumbled, back on the phone.

"I'm sorry for imposing on you."

"It's no imposition at all. I'm so excited to meet your parents and especially your dad, I can hardly wait!" I promised to be at her house before noon.

I chose my most conservative outfit for the occasion: black pants, no shorts; black shoes, no Keds; a long-sleeved shirt; and Brylcreem thick on my hair. On the way out, I told Mom where I was going.

"Don't come back saying I didn't warn you," she said with a skeptical shrug. "And if they invite you for lunch, please practice your best behavior, okay?"

"Are you kidding? There's no way I'll be staying longer than I have to. This is torture!"

In spite of dark pants and long sleeves, the day was cool enough to ride my bike without breaking a sweat. The only moisture between the shirt and my skin was a cold stream of perspiration dripping down my spine. Except for my nicely groomed hair now messed up by the wind, I arrived at Veronica's looking rather groovy.

Whitewashed throughout, the two-story house was the only one on Second Avenue surrounded by a six-foot-tall wrought-iron fence. The upper floor opened to a Seville-style balcony, jam-packed with potted petunias. Underneath, two lonely rocking chairs stood in the midst of a sixty-foot-wide veranda, and to the right, a swinging loveseat hung from the ceiling by a chain.

Three wooden steps and a cobblestone path led from the veranda to the iron-fence gate, and on both sides of the path, flowers added needed color to the bleached ambiance.

I rang the bell twice, but no one answered. I waited.

Suddenly a woman opened the front door, and a hefty Doberman Pinscher catapulted from the door-sill to the gate. Growling ferociously, his shiny fangs in full display, the menacing animal flaunted the breed's elegance and determination.

Wearing a discolored headscarf and a white apron, the overweight, yet agile woman chased after the dog until she had him by the collar. I thought she resembled a *Life Magazine* photo I'd seen, of Russian women plowing beet fields during communist domination. Panting for air, she introduced herself as Olga, Veronica's mother. The dog under control, Olga opened the gate and ushered me into the house.

"*Por favor,* señora; you're not letting him loose, are you?" I asked with trepidation.

"You shouldn't be afraid of our puppy!" she said harshly. "Togo can be a little intimidating at times, but for the most part he's affectionate and extremely protective of the family, especially our daughter."

"Mmm, I see...I believe she's expecting me?"

"Yes, she is. Veronica spent all morning reluctantly helping her father repair our water supply. Now she's up in her bedroom, changing outfits. But please come inside and have a seat. I'll tell my husband you're here." She paused. "By the way," she added, "don't shake hands or embrace any family member in front of the dog, or he will attack you." She pointed to a leather sofa. "Benny will be in shortly."

Togo subdued, Olga dragged him out of the house through the kitchen exit.

What about Veronica? I thought, disappointed. *Why didn't her mother tell her I'm here?*

Sitting on the large sofa, fidgeting and biting my nails, I waited over forty minutes for Veronica, Señor Benny, or even Olga to show up, but no one did. Stunned by their lack of good manners, I sank deeper into the couch, assessing my surroundings.

Hanging on the wall to my right, a contemporary oil painting looked so chaotic, I wondered why anyone with a sense of aesthetics would buy, much less display, in his own home such a dizzying piece of art. Underneath it, a shiny silver menorah stood in the center of a rectangular table, and to my left, a five-inch bronze Star of David hung above the doorsill.

Overflowing with cigar butts, a colorful onyx ashtray stood in the center of a coffee table in front of me. A series of cheerless family portraits from the nineteen-twenties seemed to complain about an awful stench exuding from the ashtray.

Perhaps they should step out of their picture frames, set the stinking butts on fire, and use smoke signals to announce the upcoming encounter between the master of the house and a young man infatuated with his beautiful daughter.

Nothing in that house reflected any welcome, except the Jewish icons and the wildflowers blooming alongside the cobblestone path. The iron fence was overstated; the ubiquitous white paint, including the veranda's floor, denoted serious austerity; and the bizarre painting to my right bordered on the diabolic. Even the dog's belligerence was incompatible with hospitality of any kind.

Eventually, as I peered through the living room window, I noticed a stocky man in his early fifties unbolting the backyard gate. He shared some of Veronica's features, except his skin was rough and heavily tanned, while hers was peach-soft and exquisitely brunette. Barking viciously at an imaginary intruder, Togo trailed him all the way to the kitchen door.

"I've said no twice!" the sturdy man yelled. "Sit and stay until I tell you."

Within seconds, my ears caught the sound of running water from the kitchen sink.

He's washing his hands, I thought. *I must be next!*

At long last, he strode into the living room. "I'm

Benny, Veronica's father. You must be her friend from school."

"Si, señor, my name is Carlos." I stood up and shook his hand. "It's a pleasure to meet you."

"The pleasure is mine," Benny replied in a deep, resounding voice. "Do you mind if I sit next to you?"

"Not at all," I replied.

Benny yanked a soiled handkerchief from his back pocket to pat at his sweaty brow. "My apologies for taking so long," he said humbly. "I didn't mean to be rude, but our cistern is old and took hours to clean."

"That's okay, señor. Surrounded by so much beauty, I didn't notice the passage of time."

"How wonderful!" he exclaimed. "I've always held modern-art lovers in the highest esteem."

"Thank you for your kind words, Señor Benny."

"You're very welcome, young man. As I'm sure you know, I'm fairly interested in having a private tête-à-tête with you." Benny, scrutinized me as I replied.

"I'm fully aware of that, señor."

"So that you know, I've always expressed myself with the minimum amount of words," he continued, "so if you don't mind, let's skip the nonsense and tackle the issues at hand before my daughter comes down the stairs or my wife opens the door."

Tackle the issues at hand? What is he talking about? I felt baffled, but held my tongue.

"Before we discuss your possible involvement in Veronica's party—" Benny tapped the table to make a point, "—I want you to know that this social event means much more to me than to anyone else."

"Excuse me...?"

"It's all very simple," Benny stated. "Veronica looks forward to dancing, dressing for the occasion, eating cake, and having fun. My goal is to elevate the family's social status by impacting Santa Rita's high and mighty.

"Now don't get me wrong," he said, forging a smile. "I don't intend to knock tradition or pick holes in my daughter's dream. The dance must go on, and it should become Santa Rita's most memorable gala. But to ensure absolute success, I've told my dearest daughter to get rid of her boyfriend."

"But Señor Benny, Veronica told me she broke up with him for other reasons. She never said you forced her to do it."

Benny banged on the table. "Then she lied to you! After our last argument I issued her an ultimatum: kick Chucho out, or face cancellation."

"What was her reaction?" I asked, crushed.

"She ran upstairs and locked herself in her bedroom, furiously banging on the walls. Honestly, I never thought her capable of throwing such an atrocious temper tantrum. Also Olga, the most naïve and impractical mother on Earth, told me this morning that Veronica missed him. For goodness sake, what's wrong with women these days? How could she pick such a Quasimodo look-alike?"

"I know it's hard to believe, Señor Benny," I mumbled.

Agitated, Benny carried on. "As a result of multiple disagreements on both sides, my relationship with the family has soured. Veronica's joyful anticipation has vanished, and my *clever* wife refuses to admit our vulnerability for inviting Santa Rita's upper crust and the newspaper editor. I've warned them about these carpetbaggers coming in pursuit of gossip and stains—the editor spreading his usual venom; the others, climbing on our flaws to soar above the heap."

Tense with resentment, Benny threw up his hands. "The reason I wanted Chucho out of our lives is because he is a notorious intimidator who lacks good manners, especially with forks and knives. His parents are very poor, have no class, and his sister was recently confined to a mental institution.

"Even if Chucho's mother finds him a tuxedo that fits, her son will still look like a shaved gorilla. That alone is bound to turn our gala into a zoo, and our family into the town's laughing stock. Can you imagine if the editor published pictures of both families in social interaction? I couldn't bear to see Veronica and that brute waltzing to the 'Blue Danube' in front of an élite audience. Only death by hanging could be more degrading."

I treaded carefully. "Have you ever met Chucho's father?"

"Absolutely not!" Benny shook his head bitterly. "I refused because he's a rough-edged laborer with the personality of an insect and the education of a cork."

I leaned forward as if to share a confidence. "To tell you the truth, señor Benny, I've never liked Chucho either."

"No one does!" Benny exclaimed. "That's why I gave Veronica forty-eight hours to find me the most decent and handsome schoolmate to replace him at the ball. Unlike him, you are a well-mannered young chap with a spotless reputation and a family above reproach. Better yet, you and Veronica on the dance floor will be like Fred Astaire and Ginger Rogers, gliding to a Strauss waltz. What a solid display of elegance for a small town like Santa Rita!"

"But señor...I'm not Jewish."

"Who gives a hoot?" Benny pointed at the silver menorah. "God and tradition have absolutely nothing to do with my determination. The pride and joy of elevating our status far beyond the common folk is all I care for."

All of a sudden, Benny winced as though he couldn't bear a startling thought. "On the other hand," he said, "it'll be an absolute disgrace if the two of you fall in love with each other. But then, why worry about such a ridiculous proposition, don't you agree?"

"Of c-c-course I agree."

"Incidentally, are you a Roman Catholic?"

"No, I'm just Catholic, and so is my family."

"Aren't Catholic men supposed to exert as much influence over their wives and daughters as I do?"

"Not that kind of influence!" I replied categorically.

"That's because you're a boy." Benny laid a patronizing hand on my shoulder. "But let's pretend your sister had fallen in love with a widely known failure, precisely when Santa Rita's upper crust was determined to crush your family's reputation. As her brother, what would you have done to save the girl and the family from total humiliation?"

"Under the circumstances, I'd go to the nearest dock, borrow a boat, and go fishing."

"I'm not joking, son," Benny hissed in my ear. "Admit that you'd be doing the same to your sister as I'm doing to my daughter!"

"But Señor Benny, I don't have a sister. Besides, what makes you think the town's social climbers will elevate you, just because Veronica and I make a good looking pair? By now, half the town must know the truth behind her breakup with Chucho. Won't hiding the facts damage your reputation even more?"

I took a deep breath and forged on. "Honestly, Señor Benny—and please don't take this personally—but acting like an arrogant bully could very well be Chucho's way of achieving the same objectives you're so passionately pursuing. He's an underdog too."

Visibly embarrassed by the similarities, Benny frowned. "A strong premonition tells me that Veronica hasn't spilled the beans yet, but if she loses her cool as she often does, she'll do it in a heartbeat."

"Veronica may not say anything," I ventured. "But señor, what if the truth is all over town on account of Chucho?"

"In that case we'll sue him for defamation, then bribe the newspaper editor to publish that his family is undergoing mental rehabilitation for sociopathic disorders." Benny brightened. "As a matter of fact, the situation could become so sticky that in order to prevail, I suggest you and I work together as a team."

He slowly pulled a wallet out of his pocket. "On behalf of our future association, please allow me to make you an offer."

An offer? What is he after? "Oh no, Señor Benny;" I assured him. That won't be necessary!"

"I know that. But would you turn down an incentive of one hundred pesos a week, plus the luxury of coming out in the news dating a beautiful girl?" Benny wiggled his wallet before my eyes.

"Aren't you placing an enormous responsibility on a person you don't even know?" I said, trying to leap out of the loop.

"I don't have a problem with that, as long as you realize that I'm in debt up to my ears and there won't be a penny more."

"But—"

Benny held up his palm and continued. "For starters, your most important assignment will be to keep Veronica bouncing happily but with her mouth shut between now and December 31st. You shall report her state of mind directly to me, so I know whether Chucho's absence is making her feel depressed, angry, or even vengeful, and if so, you and I should take immediate action to remedy the situation before another explosion takes place.

"Most important: If she continues to meet with the bully behind my back, I shall be the first and only one to know. If Veronica criticizes, insults, mocks, or tries to stain my image in order to save Chucho's reputation, don't hesitate to report her transgression, even in the middle of the night. Fitting together bits and pieces of information will help us decide whether the party should go on or not, and if cancellation is in order, I shall do it without misgivings."

Benny nodded firmly, then rubbed his hands as if scrubbing them clean. "I'll talk to Veronica this evening and point out exactly where she stands regarding the dissemination of private matters. Oh, and before I forget: you and I will meet at least once a week to compare notes and make sure we're on the right track. Also, since the end justifies the means, please don't feel too shy or intimidated to romance and cuddle up to Veronica. But heed my warning, young man. Once the party is over, so are the romantic overtones. You simply go home with pockets full of money and absolutely no memory of Veronica beating in your heart."

"What would you do if she falls in love with me?" I asked, feigning concern.

"I'll suffocate her infatuation in no time. But for now, let's quit making foolish projections and instead, keep our minds and hearts aiming at the most fabulous event ever to take place in this stinking village. If you're smart enough to accept my offer," he concluded sternly, "make sure your lips are sealed... *comprendes?*"

"I understand, señor. But you must realize that

I still need to consider the repercussions," I replied with concealed bitterness.

"Of course I do," Benny said, faking a smile. "Talk it over with your pillow and please call me first thing in the morning. You know my number."

He stood up to leave. "Shall we shake hands?" he said grandly.

Ashamed of my involvement in such a scam, I stood up and reluctantly shook.

Perhaps I should tell Veronica the kind of bastard her father is. Then again, she's also far from being an angel.

"Are your hands always so cold?" Benny asked.

"Only when I'm nervous, or sick to my stomach."

"Would you like to join us for lunch? I have plenty of Alka-Seltzer." Benny's cheerful smile stretched from ear to ear. "Please stay and share the best matzo ball soup on the island. Besides, what a great opportunity for you and Veronica to start making plans."

"I'm sorry, Señor Benny." I reluctantly looked into his glassy eyes. "Today is my grandmother's one hundredth birthday, and we're celebrating it at home in less than an hour. Mother baked the cake and Father bought her a present she's always wanted to have."

"And may I ask how important can any present be to a senile one-hundred-year-old woman?"

"Well, señor, Grandma has always wanted to carry a Colt .45 revolver in her purse."

"A what?" Benny asked, flabbergasted. "Aren't you afraid to give an absent-minded woman such a weapon? Sorry, but I think your father needs to have his head examined."

"You may not believe it, Señor Benny, but Grandma is far from senile. She claims there's a middle-aged man in Santa Rita she wants to shoot between the eyes before she dies."

Benny shook his head briskly. "Your father is very irresponsible! Perhaps I should notify the police."

"Don't worry, Señor Benny. Dad will load Grandma's gun with empty shells. He doesn't think she deserves to go to jail for killing such a wretched, pitiful man."

I left the home of my beloved convinced that her father's obsession with social climbing resulted from a widespread struggle for social supremacy fostered by Santa Rita's pretentious *nouveau riche*. These status seekers alienated themselves from the townsfolk by emulating the lifestyles of foreign societies as imagined, for despite their conceit, most lacked the financial resources to travel abroad, or the education to appreciate cultural values beyond Santa Rita's coastline.

The following morning I called Benny and told him that my parents categorically refused to see me involved in a family feud. I also suggested he call Dad if he had any questions.

Seriously offended, Benny loosed a barrage of obscenities and derogatory remarks about my manhood over the phone. He shredded my parents' integrity and called Dad a solemn idiot for letting a senile hatemonger carry a Colt .45 revolver inside her purse.

In retrospect I realized I should've hung up the phone immediately, but Benny's semantic repertoire was so colorful I decided to listen, and share the new vulgarities with my pals later on.

Truth told, I hadn't related to my parents my experiences at Veronica's, nor did I tell them of my phone conversation with Benny the following day. I simply decided to keep the entire saga to myself and allow Dad to sink his nose deeper into the morning paper, and Mom to crochet large and meaningless pieces ad infinitum. And I wasn't sure they would appreciate my quick-thinking resourcefulness, given that the story of Grandma's birthday and the Colt .45 revolver was improvised on the spot to escape entrapment.

* * *

Despite avoiding eye contact with me during the following school week, Veronica collected enough courage to call me on the phone Saturday morning.

"Carlos; I owe you an apology," she said softly. "A big one for that matter. But I couldn't gather enough nerve to express in front of others the embarrassing situation in which I find myself. It is very important we meet privately."

"Why?" I asked tersely. "Do you want me to find you another fool?"

"Oh, please don't say that. There's much more to this epic than you think, and this is why we need to talk."

"Listen, Veronica, I don't want to know more. The irreversible truth is that you lied, and your devious father took me for an idiot."

"Please give me a chance. You won't regret it. I promise!"

"All right," I said after a prolonged pause. "What about the banyan tree across from school in about an hour? The park is deserted on weekends, and hopefully no one of interest will be around."

The banyan tree was Santa Rita's most treasured landmark. Soaring skyward next to the Catholic Church on the hill, the three-hundred-year-old natural marvel covered an area so large it had become a meeting place for lovers making up and making out, and for those in search of peace or protection from the rain. Widely spaced under its twisting branches, twelve wooden benches basked in its generous shade, and on one of them I sat with mixed emotions, waiting for Veronica.

At exactly two-thirty she showed up, riding her bike.

As she dismounted the breeze picked up, and her fluffy white blouse fluttered in the wind, hinting at her perfectly formed breasts. If Veronica's figure was flawless in school uniform, in tight jeans she was simply magnificent. Her face was lightly made up, and the sunlit moisture running down her cheeks made those voracious red lips more sensual than ever. Seeing Veronica in a sexy outfit for the first time was a bit too erotic for an adolescent to dismiss.

"Wow! You look so feminine!" I said, despite a broken heart.

"Thank you, but I don't deserve your praise."

She lowered the bicycle's kickstand and regarded me with somber eyes. Besides perspiration, her hands were soiled with grease from adjusting the bike's chain on her way over.

I stood up and held out my spotless linen handkerchief. I didn't know whether shaking hands, kissing cheeks, or simply offering my hanky were appropriate ways of greeting a girl under the circumstances.

"No, thank you," she said visibly nervous. "I'd hate to stain it with my dirty hands. Besides, I'll cool off under this tree in no time."

Veronica was so irresistible I couldn't avoid dabbing delicately at her face and neck. I also took her hands and cleaned them the best I could.

When Mother sees what I've done, she'll have me use toilet paper to blow my nose from now on.

Veronica folded the handkerchief and slipped it into my shirt pocket, then seized my hand and led me to the cleanest bench. We sat facing each other. I felt my private parts stirring and moving from stage number one directly to number three.

"I came to apologize not only for lying to you, but also on behalf of my insensitive father," Veronica began. "No one, absolutely no one, deserves to be treated the way you were. I am deeply sorry."

"Sorry?" I said tightly. "How can you justify lying to me so blatantly?"

"I didn't have a choice, believe me." Veronica reddened with embarrassment. "So that you know," she continued, "I eavesdropped on the entire conversation between you and Dad, and regrettably there were no pleasant surprises. What you saw and heard defined my father for what he is—an unscrupulous social climber who's full of hot air and doesn't know when to quit.

"Mother and I are also indebted to you for refusing to play his game and more so for taking a stand against bribery."

I merely shrugged and waited.

"Not everything Dad said about Chucho was true," Veronica went on. "He never liked him, in fact hated him with a passion. What's more, after mailing the invitations and spending a fortune on what he called a tribute to his social and financial achievements, Dad coerced me with a series of pretexts on why we should rid ourselves of Chucho and his family. Then he tightened the noose by threatening to cancel the entire party, and sure enough I had to give in."

I may have been moved by her beauty, but not by her story. "I'm sorry to say it, Veronica, but the way you treated Chucho and his family was demeaning and unfair."

"I totally agree, and I deeply regret it. But a woman becomes fifteen only once in a lifetime, so other than her wedding, this is the only celebration a Cuban girl wouldn't dare miss."

"Tell me more about you and Chucho."

"I will; but first you must understand that in spite of what people think, we've never been romantically involved."

"Then why did you throw a fit of anger in your room and the next day tell your mother how much you missed him?"

"I didn't throw a fit because I missed him. I lost it because I felt tired of being handled like a commodity. It was a desperate cry against Dad's macho tactics, and my only way of expressing anger and frustration for shackling me to his Victorian mores, when it came to dating other boys."

"You wanted to date other boys besides Chucho?" I asked.

Veronica nodded. "Chucho was never my boyfriend," she said. "He and I have known each other from the time we were toddlers, and we've been playmates ever since. Despite his reputation as an arrogant boaster, I've always admired his superior intelligence. We watched movies, played cards at my home, flew handmade kites, and did much more to kill time and have fun, but we never kissed or showed the kind of passion novios do. And he was always willing to help wherever needed, especially with homework. Like it or not, Chucho is the smartest guy in school. He's like a brother to me."

"Huh," I barged in. "But you let everyone think he was your boyfriend so no other boys came near you. Chucho protected you from any other suitors."

"That's exactly right," Veronica affirmed. "And

until recently, that was perfect for both of us. But now we both want to date other people for real. In the meantime, though, Chucho has been so generous to Mom and me that in spite of being treated like trash by my father and driven out of the party by me, he generously decided to save the day by attending rehearsals and dancing to the opening waltz with me. After the celebration, we will go our separate ways."

Against my will, my heart beat out a glimmer of hope.

"Incidentally," Veronica added, "my mother once said that Chucho was a good example of why we shouldn't judge people by their looks, or wines by their label."

"Your mom was absolutely right," I replied. "I know an old man who smells like a skunk, looks like hell, drinks like a distillery, swears like a swine, and yet...loves me like a saint."

Veronica sighed deeply. "I wish most boys would be as sentimental as you are."

"Have you met other Jewish kids?" I asked, feeling suddenly ill at ease.

"Of course I have. Most live in the country, and the ones nearby are either too old or too young for me." She waved her hand as if brushing them away.

I had no reply, so we sat quietly for a moment.

Then Veronica asked, "Would you like to know my father's punishment for my pitching the fit?"

"I didn't realize he would do such a thing," I replied.

"Wait till I tell you. The day you came to meet him, Dad had me clean the entire cistern from eight till noon to ensure I wouldn't be ready to greet you when you arrived. My hands and nails were so black with muddy soot and I smelled so bad it took me a couple of hours to clean and paint my nails, take a shower, put on a nice clean dress, and be ready to welcome you to our home—but guess what? By then you were already talking to him. That's how he disciplined me."

"That's not discipline," I exclaimed. "That's revenge!

"Given Dad's mentality, his only reasons for *celebrating my birthday* so lavishly were to launch himself into the opulent world of Santa Rita's illustrious rich, and as an added bonus, rid his family of Chucho and his *dysfunctional* clan." Veronica choked back tears.

"What made him change his mind and accept Chucho?" I asked.

"When you refused to participate in his plot, Dad found himself alone. Troubled by huge debts, his daughter beside herself, Mother agreeing with me, and you—his last hope—out of the picture, Dad had no choice but to accept Chucho as my escort or cancel the entire show. In simple terms, you had won the battle for Mother and me."

The irony of this outcome did not escape me. "But your dad said he would cancel the party in a heartbeat and without remorse," I said.

"Dad was bluffing. After all was said and done, he couldn't afford to cancel anything."

"Have your feelings for him improved after his change of heart?" I asked.

Veronica rolled her great dark eyes. "Change of heart? Are you kidding? After next year's graduation, I'll be moving in with my aunt Sarah in Havana to attend high school and eventually study law. I love this town, but my only chance to escape Dad's yoke is to focus on a financially independent future somewhere else." Veronica sighed. "I love him dearly in spite of his foolish behavior, but when the time comes to choose my partner in life, I shall follow my heart and make my own decision, and if Father disagrees, well...by then who would care?"

"I'm sure both your parents know of your future plans."

"Yes, they do. Mother fully agrees but lacks the nerve to confront Dad, who insists I should stay home, learn to be realistic, and go to *obedience school*."

I gave her a tentative smile. "I'm sure the obedience school part was a joke," I said. "But what did he mean by 'realistic'?"

"To follow the mission of a Jewish woman, but as defined by him," Veronica replied, her face a mask of bitter rage.

"I suppose you've been attracted to other boys before."

"Of course," Veronica said in a resigned tone. "But I always refrained from getting too close. What about you? Have you ever been attracted to a girl?"

"Mmm...yeah, I think I have."

"Do I know her?"

"Mmm, yeah, I think you do," I answered, red as a rose.

Veronica moved a little closer. "Have you ever kissed a girl like in the movies?" she asked with a hint of a smile on her face.

"No, I've never kissed anyone but family members."

"I haven't either," said Veronica, "and I am older than you. Isn't that sad?" She gazed into my eyes. "Would you let me guess who that girl is?"

"Sure, why not?" I said, quaking in my shoes.

"Is that girl...me...by any chance?" Veronica asked, fluffing my hair.

I could barely manage to speak. "Yes...it is you. But please don't tell anybody."

Veronica let out a sigh, smiled, and pressed her index finger to the center of my chest.

"Will you let me kiss you?" she asked simply.

"W-why?"

"Because I find you very good-looking, and… and because like you, I've never kissed anyone that way before."

"If your father ever finds out we've kissed like in Hollywood, he'll kill me."

"What if we don't tell?"

Oh, my God, I forgot Pedro's instructions. What should I do first?

Drawing closer, her Moorish eyes radiating an exquisite sparkle of vulnerability, Veronica threw her arms around me.

Lowering my lips, I began to kiss hers like in the movies until I recalled Pedro's guidelines.

The heat hung heavy on us as the sweet smell of the sea wafted in the northern breeze. Veronica's breath totally fogged my head.

Our eyes closed, we kissed in a whirlwind of delight.

For the most part, Veronica's *fiesta de los quince* went on as planned, and luckily, nothing derogatory was published in the morning paper. I, for obvious reasons, did not attend the celebration.

In order to keep our unique relationship away from Benny's radar, Veronica and I continued to meet secretly at odd times and in secluded areas. Showing affection in public became mutually dangerous and potentially explosive.

One hot Sunday during spring, I borrowed a row-boat from one of the dockworkers and took Veronica on a voyage to a remote deserted beach. We tanned, played baseball with only one base and a home plate, played catch in the turquoise waters, and finally horsed around in the sand.

By then we'd already gulped lots of coconut water and an entire bottle of cheap wine I had purchased at the dock store. Little by little we drew so dangerously close to stage four that the two of us instinctively decided to avoid *perfect places* from then on.

Veronica and I continued our forbidden but delicious liaison until right after graduation, when she left Santa Rita on a train to Havana to continue her education. Two days before her departure, and for Veronica's sake, we decided in a bath of tears to avoid further contact, especially in writing. After all, it was short of miraculous that no one in town except for Pedro and the Chinese man behind the liquor store counter ever showed the slightest suspicion about the relationship between Veronica and me.

And Pedro was right: When moved by the heart, that first kiss is the one you feel all the way to the soles of your feet.

CHRISTMAS IN SANTA RITA

More often than not, I walked down the hill on my way home from school.

"Buenas tardes, Señor Gomez," I said to the father of one of my friends who was busy sorting out rolls of Christmas lights.

"Good afternoon, young man!" he replied, eyes fixed on the wire mess.

"Are you decorating for Christmas already?" I asked, feigning curiosity. For it was clear to any and all passers-by that the winter ritual had begun.

"Son, it's never too soon to start decking out for the holidays," Señor Gomez replied joyfully. "Besides, the sooner I finish, the longer I have to make home improvements and collect the grand prize."

"Buena suerte, Señor Gomez! I hope you win!" Holding my books to my chest I continued my downhill stroll.

The sun might have risen after eleven months of darkness when the quiet residents of the barrio called La Loma (The Hill) decided to start celebrating Christmas and the advent as early as November. What's more, by the time December of 1955 arrived they'd already reached a collective state of euphoria in which the past was irrelevant, the present was to be enjoyed, and the future—well, never mind the future.

Year after year these middle-class citizens celebrated the holidays by underestimating expenditures, glorifying gift-giving, overindulging in food and drink, and stockpiling enough merrymaking in their otherwise conventional lives to last the entire holiday season.

With the community's cash award of five hundred pesos set aside for the family with the most tastefully decorated home, these party-goers decked out their dwellings day in and day out until exhausted. The most overexcited owners went as far as whitewashing their entire property, while the more lethargic did only the balconies. Many draped colorful wreaths and garlands around their houses, or hung large Christmas ornaments and decorations on the front porch.

The most flamboyant, however, worked at great lengths to make their dwellings look magnificent, bizarre, or somewhere in between, depending on pocket depth and taste—or lack thereof. No one ever knew why otherwise austere, ultra-conservative families like the Gomezes engaged in such over-the-top behavior during the holidays. But by the first week in January, bad moods and fatigue overwhelmed every man, woman, and child in Santa Rita's most unconventional neighborhood.

The rest of town decorated their trees, outdoor bushes, pillars, and stairways in traditional ways, but hung miles of Christmas lights, everywhere they could find an electric outlet nearby. The power demand on the old electric plant was such during December that blackouts occurred intermittently during the night. Pedro had never visited the *Planta Electrica* but he claimed it was energized by a retired railroad fireman shoveling firewood into a gigantic boiler that produced enough steam to spin a couple of old dynamos at ridiculously low speeds—a concept that made Dad chuckle, for he considered the Old Man an inveterate liar.

Like most cities and towns, Santa Rita also had its share of virulent, bitter citizens who derived pleasure from crushing the holiday spirits of friends and foes alike. Even though by late November most whiners had left town to escape the upcoming pandemonium, quarrelsome nitpickers stayed to sprinkle holiday vinegar on every cheerful human.

These sourpusses complained about unnerving

Christmas songs coming from everywhere; boisterous children playing past their bedtime; the blackouts; the excessive amount of garbage piled up on sidewalks, waiting for the trash man to sober up and haul tons of wrapping paper, empty boxes, and decayed leftovers to the city dumpster; and so on. They grumbled when it rained and when it didn't, when it was warm and when it was cold. If their surroundings were perfect, they moaned about each other, and in lieu of others, they groaned about themselves and their miserable lives.

Deeply religious groups formed part of Santa Rita's colorful canvas as well. Few and far apart, these citizens celebrated the birth of Christ by attending mass, eating in moderation, and exchanging meaningful gifts in a civilized manner.

Santa Rita also had two shantytowns that celebrated Christmas in unusually lucrative ways. The largest one followed the Central Highway east toward La Laguna, a muddy body of water used by its adjacent dwellers to satisfy their needs. Most of the time the stagnant lagoon emitted an awful stench perceptible for over a mile, and the only time the odor dissipated was after a heavy rainfall spilled over its banks every form of organic matter and raw sewage to a foul-smelling creek that ultimately defecated the putrid load into the ocean.

The smaller slum was to be found at walking distance from a water tank owned and utilized by the railroad company to replenish its steam locomotives. Situated a mile west of the train station, this favela was comprised of a series of makeshift tents set on both sides of the tracks. While this group of indigents illegally siphoned well water from the tank during the night, the railroad workers refused to stand guard after hours, especially when the water didn't cost the company a penny. Contrary to their Laguna counterparts, and perhaps because of their access to potable water, these beggars looked cleaner and healthier—though still tattered and thin.

Every December 25th, shortly before sunrise, these panhandlers barged into town and knocked on every door, begging for *aguinaldos*, or hand-me-downs. Most residents detested their annual pilgrimage, mainly because it was ill-conceived and also because it created a deep sense of guilt in whoever answered the door. Then again, those who considered poverty a self-inflicted malaise simply opened their door widely, then slammed it forcefully in front of the mendicants' faces.

Trailing these beggars were numerous children, some with parasite-inflated bellies, others with green boogers dripping from their noses and into their mouths and on their shirts. Regardless of how cool the morning was, these little ones came down naked or simply clad in raggedy T-shirts in a most depressing display of neglect and malnutrition.

Since Mother believed the indigents' intentions were to squash our holiday spirits, every year I helped her pack food leftovers, neglected toys, and used clothing, and leave it all outside our front entrance with the sign: Take what you need, but don't knock on the door.

Confronting so many holiday irritants, Father often referred to Christmas as an *expensive state of mind*, but at my age, I didn't pay much attention to his words of wisdom.

Closer to home lived a widely known character, who, unlike everyone else in town, had decided to mourn the passing of his wife Alicia, fifty years before, by designating December as his most miserable month.

In commiseration with Pedro's self-inflicted, perhaps fictitious, grief, dock workers and their families flocked to the wharf during the holidays to pay short visits to the Old Man, who readily accepted food, delicacies, and gifts. In return he would tell a Cuento de Navidad (Christmas tale) to young visitors, if any. As a result, Pedro collected enough free goodies to fill his pantry for at least two months.

As to our family traditions, I shall simply describe them as a series of variations on the same theme.

A week or so before Christmas, Mother and I raked Santa Rita's countryside for branches and twigs of various shapes and sizes; our mission: to trim and tie them piece by piece to a six-foot stem until the conspicuous bundle took on the triangular shape of a Blue Spruce.

To secure the mock-up tree, Mom inserted the bottom of the stem into a bucketful of dirt she would later camouflage with white sheets to resemble snow. I helped her cover the branches with cotton and decorate the tree with our traditional collection of ornaments.

Unlike most parents, mine installed the lights last to facilitate bulb replacement. My task: to check each and every bulb, discard the bad ones, and run to the pharmacy for replacements.

Father shook his head as he entered the living room for his annual undertaking. "Damn it, I hate this job!" he complained.

Mom rose from the couch, clamped her arms around his neck, and gave him a loud smack of a kiss to calm him down.

"Don't be such a grouch!" she said softly. "It'll be over in no time."

Dad shot me a commiserating look. "Did you check all the bulbs to make sure they are okay?"

"Yes, sir, they are all good," I replied in a military tone. "Only three were bad and I replaced them."

Father's annual mission was no fun, and besides, it was unsafe. As soon as the lights were all on, he would veil the entire tree with a hideous American invention known as *cabello de angel,* or angel hair—dreadful bundles of shiny filaments of pulverized glass that if inhaled could damage the lungs. Wearing the kitchen rubber gloves, a baseball cap, and a handkerchief wrapped over his nose and mouth like a *bandido,* Dad cut and stretched these fibers into sections resembling spider webs, then draped the whole tree with the awful stuff until it achieved the impression of being glimpsed from afar on a foggy night. Dad's entire body itched so badly following his assignment he would run to the shower to mitigate the agony of feeling microscopic fragments of glass lodged inside his pores.

"Don't count on me moving a freaking finger next Christmas!" he yelled from the shower every year.

Wishful thinkers with nostalgic imaginations thought ours was the most authentic Christmas tree in Santa Rita—even more realistic than "those artificial ones mimicking giant bottle brushes." But since these friends and relatives had never traveled abroad, or for that matter anywhere, their judgment, no matter how sympathetic, meant absolutely nothing except another proof that beauty is in the eye of the beholder—and ugliness in a man tormented by fiberglass.

On a sad note, the sometimes ethereal appearance of our tree brought to mind grief-inducing memories of Grandpa's body lying on his deathbed with a thin gray veil draped over the pallid face—a twisted tradition followed by Voodoo worshippers and plagiarized by Santa Rita's holier-than-thou crowd to add cryptic symbolism to an already sorrowful setting.

At the homes of the pious, Nativity scenes were considered more relevant than the venerated pine tree. In modest households, figurines were made of clay and *papier-mâché*, and the *crèche* was assembled with straw. In homes with money to burn, statuettes were either imported from a St. Francis of Assisi porcelain outlet in the town of its name, or from Lladro's factory in Valencia, Spain.

* * *

As I was walking down Maceo Street one morning, I found the parish priest trying to remove the front wheel from his old Ford. Sweating profusely, the cleric's hands and face were blackened with soot. Pedestrians greeted the man in black, but no one besides me offered him a hand. Amazingly, it was the first time he had dealt with a flat tire.

"This jack can't go up any higher. What should I do?" He paused, gasping for air.

"There's your answer, Father!" I said, pointing at a hunk of timber lying on the curb across the street.

"What about it?" asked the priest.

"If you lower the jack all the way down, I can jam that piece of wood under its base."

The priest frowned, clearly dumbfounded. "What then?"

I explained patiently. "Then you can pump up the jack until the tire is off the pavement, and the rest is a no-brainer."

The two of us went to work, and in minutes the wheel with the flat tire was off and the spare installed.

"Young man, I don't know how to thank you," said the priest with a sigh of relief. "I wish I had the time to reward you with an ice cream or a soda, but I still have to bless more than twenty nativity scenes all over town, and time is running short."

"And what should we do to have ours blessed as well?" I asked coyly, knowing my mother would be more amused than honored by the gesture.

The influence exerted by Santa Rita's wealthy families on the local clergy was such that they were the only ones in town to have their lavish Nativity scenes blessed by the parish priest. The common folk generally didn't do a thing, for in terms of religious traditions, a simple image of a newborn baby, his parents, and a couple of barn animals were enough to reproduce a créche meant to symbolize poverty and humility.

"All I can do is add your name and address to my list, and God willing I may be able to squeeze in a short visit right before Christmas," the priest told me. "But I can't promise you anything!"

As December 25th drew near, parents traditionally went Christmas shopping to the local pharmacy or the hardware store—the only two establishments selling toys, gifts, and the trappings of the season. Both businesses were owned and operated by elderly couples; the pharmacist and his wife lived on their building's second floor, and the other pair with two cats in an attic directly above their repair shop. Both businesses became *venerated institutions* during the Christmas season, and by chance they were only a block away from each other.

Parents of young children left their presents with the shop owners for storing and packing, and on December 24th, shortly before midnight, they ran to both stores to retrieve their purchases. Also, in appreciation for safe-keeping and gift-wrapping their presents, every parent showed up with a bottle of wine in return.

Most traditional Catholics exchanged gifts on January 6th, the day of Epiphany, which meant that instead of Santa Claus hauling presents on a sleigh pulled by reindeer all the way from the North Pole, they were delivered by three Magi, and not in a sleigh, toboggan, or luge, but on three camels, all the way from the land of the "Thousand and One Nights."

Children receiving presents on December 25th shared their cache with those expecting theirs on January 6th. Lesson learned: Only those willing to share got to play with toys from opposite worlds.

I was twelve years old when my mother overheard a conversation between a younger cousin and me.

"Come on, Pepe, don't be such an idiot," I scoffed at my younger relative who claimed to have seen Santa Claus buying presents at the local pharmacy. "You must have seen someone dressed like him; otherwise how can you be so stupid?"

"Carlos, for the love of God!" Mother yelled as she marched into the room. "Will you shut up and let him act his age?"

As of that day my parents knew I didn't believe in Santa Claus anymore, so expensive presents fell by the wayside. Santa's allowance shrank to a pittance, and I only received *levelheaded* presents, also known to my folks as "judicious surprises."

Following my exposé, I wasn't even allowed to choose gifts. My well-educated parents believed it was time for me to take life seriously and start reading good quality material instead of *chatarra* (junk).

I'll never forget my first Santa-less Christmas, when their so-called surprises consisted of a World Atlas, an engraved Catholic Bible, and a biography of Ludwig van Beethoven. I welcomed my presents with such a long face that the following year I took delivery of a brand new bike, a baseball bat, and no books, for heaven's sake!

But that was the first and last time Mom and Dad slipped. From then on they consistently showered me with books, school uniforms, underwear, and things I needed to have but hated to buy. No more baseballs, bats, fishing gear, or new tires for my bike.

Thank goodness Tio Jorge, the uncle who asserted that tradition is what we resort to when issues are not based in reason, and who detested crowds with such a passion he refused to visit a store or church during Christmas, came to my rescue. Every Navidad he gave my older cousin and me a manila envelope bursting with brand-new bills of the lowest denomination.

According to Dad, Tio Jorge enjoyed watching

our avaricious grins as we frantically counted the same pesos two and three times to ensure each cousin had received the same amount.

My evocation of Christmas wouldn't be complete without mention of Nochebuena—the evening of December 24th, when Santa Rita celebrated the feast of all feasts in anticipation of Jesus' birth. This was the only time of the year when family rivalries tended to smooth out, though they never entirely disappeared. And I was absolutely certain those hard feelings were softened by the sight of food and drink, and not in remembrance of the birth of Christ.

In spite of having a relatively large family in town, our only guests for Nochebuena that year were a couple of characters for whom Mom and Dad felt sorry: the lady next door, and Rivero, a homely young man who ran errands for Dad's apparel shop.

Our lady guest was a modest, unassuming eighty-five-year-old descendant of a wealthy Spanish family that made a massive fortune smuggling stolen slaves from Cuba to the Port of New Orleans during the mid-nineteenth-century. Her parents were so proud of making their fortune with Cuba's powerful neighbor to the north they had decided to bestow on their firstborn daughter the name of "America."

Unfortunately, America's family fortune was lost

during the Great Depression, and the only asset she had left was the little wooden house next door. Worse yet, she had no one to care for her.

A highly educated spinster, Doña America embraced our family as her own. The only creatures sharing her lonely existence were a couple of Amazon parrots she had trained to talk and sing. But no one, including elegant Doña America, ever knew who had taught her youngest bird to whistle after every passing woman, and to make obscene remarks about the size of their buttocks. The classy lady claimed some foul-mouthed joker in South America must have inculcated profanities in the animal.

Mom and Dad felt so sorry for the lonely woman, she became an annual fixture at our Nochebuena dinner table. In fact, Doña America used to be my short-term babysitter during the tender years when Mom and Dad went to retrieve my Christmas presents from the pharmacy and the hardware store.

Rivero, our other Nochebuena guest, was disowned by his family, mocked by the ignorant, and hated by most village idiots, who thought they'd be elevating their status by stepping on a feeble human being like him.

At age nineteen, Rivero already had a prominent hunchback due to severe scoliosis of the spine, and to make his life more miserable, his face was disfigured after a drunkard poured battery acid on it in retaliation for his allegedly spreading gossip about the drunk's teenage daughter being pregnant out of wedlock. The attacker was condemned to a twenty-year prison term, but Rivero's face remained so scarred it resembled that of the violinist from *The Phantom of the Opera.*

But of all of Rivero's misfortunes, the most tragic ensued from a birth defect the family considered Satanic in nature. They believed Rivero had been born a eunuch as punishment for transgressions committed during his previous life in Purgatory.

Unfortunately, Rivero's condition persisted for life because his empty-headed parents had refused to let a surgeon correct the abnormality at a very young age. Their reasoning: "Whatever spells Satan cast on him shall remain unchallenged, or the Devil will curse the entire family forever."

With such a mentality, or lack thereof, his Devil-worshipping parents should've been the ones condemned to scorch in the bowels of hell in retribution for crimes committed against their innocent son. I'll never forget Rivero's tragedy, the lessons learned from his good nature, and my father's admonition: "Ignorance is the vilest degradation of the human soul."

Our traditional Nochebuena dinner, and those

of most Santa Ritans, consisted of *puerco asado* (roasted pork); a Santa Rita-style guacamole salad (pineapple chunks tossed with olive oil, sweet vinegar, and avocado slices); *yuca frita* (a savory root unearthed and consumed by our long-gone Siboney Indians), fried in pork lard and sprinkled with a *mojo* of lime juice, garlic, and salt; black beans and rice, better known as Moors and Christians; Spanish Rioja wine; and for dessert, a variety of nougats introduced to Southern Spain by the Moors during their seven-hundred-year occupation.

After dinner I always asked Mother to prepare me a container with all the trimmings, including dessert, to take to Pedro. I also added a bottle of wine surreptitiously taken from Dad's cabinet.

On Christmas Day of my sixteenth year I went to visit Pedro, whom I found lounging on a wooden bench, the legs of which were screwed to the wooden pier to keep it from being pushed into the water by nearby rascals.

"*Feliz Navidad*!" I yelled in my approach.

"*Tu también, mi hijo*!" he replied, his voice so deep it sounded like a human woofer.

"Are you sick, Old Man?" I asked.

"Who knows?" he replied. "I might be coming down with something." A smile flickered at the corner of his mouth. "Can I guess what's inside that box?"

"What else but your Nochebuena dinner and a bottle of Rioja?" I said, handing him the container, the bottle, and a corkscrew.

Pedro opened the package, sniffed the goodies, and swiftly uncorked the bottle of wine.

"Thank you, son. I knew you wouldn't forget me, and you want to know something? I haven't had any rum in over a week."

"You've got to be kidding me!" I grinned, hands on my hips.

"I haven't because I didn't want to nauseate you with my boozy breath on Christmas Day. Please come closer, so I can give you a hug."

"I don't think I should," I said ruefully. "You sound very sick, and I don't want to catch it."

"I understand," he said, squeezing my hands. "But please thank your parents for their generosity and wish them a Feliz Navidad as well."

Pedro always wanted to hear about my most recent encounter with Verónica, but this time he was so engrossed with his Nochebuena dinner he didn't snoop at all. In the end, he wiped off his mouth and entire face with the linen napkin, folded by Mother as neatly as she would for any of our guests.

"Well, tell me what you had for Christmas?"

"Shirts, a pair of dress shoes, and three books: *War and Peace*, *Moby Dick*, and *The Three Musketeers*," I replied, flat as a flounder.

"Those are great masterpieces. Your parents certainly know quality; congratulations!"

I just shrugged. "I would have preferred a new first-base mitt, a newer bat, and lots of baseballs."

"Well, son, I can't wait to tell you, there's a big surprise waiting for you." The old man took a long sip of wine at that.

"But Pedro, how many times have I told you not to spend money on me?"

"I didn't...recently, anyway. All I can say is that I've cherished this present for years as my only link to an idyllic past, but since I'm living on borrowed time, and you are my only heir..."

I held up my palms. "Here we go again with your death wishes! Will you stop repeating them in front of me?"

"I'm sorry for troubling you," Pedro said politely. "I didn't realize you were so sensitive to the dark things of life."

"Christmas isn't exactly the day of choice to talk about death and dying," I responded. "Besides, why don't you move out from under that dark cloud?"

"But son, don't you think it's about time you stop acting like a child and learn to cope with reality like a grownup?" Pedro shook an admonishing finger. Then his face came alight as he dangled a paper bag in front of my eyes. "Guess what's inside this sack."

"I have no idea." I stated unemotionally.

"What else but your highly appropriate Christmas present?" Pedro opened the bag and handed me a fist-size box, giftwrapped for the holidays.

"Now, open it up so you can start dreaming." Hands tightly clasped, and with a hint of anticipation in his face, Pedro scrutinized my every movement.

I untied the ribbon and carefully ripped the wrapping paper to open the little box.

My eyes flew open.... An elegant but simple platinum ring with a small diamond on top shone a light of its own from inside the jewel box. My chest started to pound; I didn't know what to say, and I didn't know what to do.

"Would you like to keep the box as well?" Pedro gave my shoulder a joyful shake. "I pray to God you'll marry a beautiful young woman like Verónica someday," he went on. "I know for a fact it might not be her, but you'll find a gorgeous doll who will love you as much as Alicia and I loved each other. This was her wedding ring, and I wanted you to have it."

Now I was in shock.

"Oh, Pedro, I don't think this is right..."

"I don't care what you think, and I won't take no for an answer," Pedro said firmly.

"Mmm...a wedding ring...at my age?"

"No more excuses. The ring is yours. All I ask in return is that you keep this raggedy old man in your thoughts and prayers, and his dissertations deep inside your skull. I always thought you should have it, but decided to wait until you did something commendable and worthy of a mature young lad."

"And what was that?" I asked, truly mystified.

"The moral support you offered Verónica during her embarrassing ordeal, and your courage to confront her selfish and wicked father face to face. That kind of behavior says a lot about your character and spiritual values."

A surge of emotion filled my entire being. Overlooking Pedro's hoarseness, I moved to hug him with all my might.

"Thank you for embracing me, and for being my loyal friend," he said, growing teary.

"Do you think I should start wearing it right away?" I asked.

"Must you be so dense?" the Old Man said, scratching his hat. "That's a woman's ring, for heaven's sake. Keep it in a safe place until you slide it onto your bride's finger someday...whenever that happens, *comprendes*?"

No gift or gesture could have made my impending departure from Dreamland more evident than a wedding ring. I suddenly realized my Pollyanna days were coming to an end, and that was a bit too profound to dwell on.

* * *

Santa Rita's holiday season ended with Las Fiestas de Fin de Año—New Year's Eve celebrations.

So far, I hadn't been allowed to leave home after dark on December 31st. Dad said it was the most dangerous night for the young to hang out among drunkards and hell-raisers.

One of that evening's most hazardous feats was to toss firecrackers under cars in hopes their gas tank would explode. Even though such calamity never occurred, our town idiots constantly pushed the envelope in senseless pursuits of bragging rights.

Businesses such as liquor stores, clubs, and *cantinas* remained open through the night, and some even offered free breakfasts to those who stayed until sunrise. Fist fights flared on account of nothing and the town remained in a virtual state of siege until the rural police had rounded up hundreds of citizens, including some from the La Loma area, and locked them up in makeshift jails all over town.

Fireworks were also sold in unlimited quantities to any buyer, regardless of age. Prices were cheap because these fireworks and rocket launchers were imported from the island of Taiwan by a large Asian community in Havana. During late November, the cargo vessel unloaded the largest part of the shipment in the capital and the remainder in Santa Rita. The Havana delivery covered the city and adjacent provinces, and the one in Santa Rita the island's easternmost cities and towns.

While sitting with Pedro, I had watched dock workers unloading numerous crates jam-packed with fireworks and pyrotechnics into large trucks and train cars. Their job lasted all day and was dangerous; one blunder and the entire dock, along with Pedro, his books, the termite-laden desk, and hundreds of turbinated sugar bags could blow up into the sky.

Santa Rita's local cargo was consigned to a small Chinese community, who purchased and stored in their homes enough explosives and noise-makers for the holidays. These Asians bartered fireworks for meats, booze, and perhaps a girl or two from the Chinese brothel. Cash never exchanged hands, and by mid-December the entire town was bursting with gunpowder.

When neighboring villagers knew the ship had left, our small population nearly doubled with visitors from those areas shopping for fireworks. In fact, a couple of friends and I usually went to visit the Huang family way before the shoppers arrived.

"You same boys from last year, but grown up." Señor Huang greeted us at the front door.

Short of stature, with incisive eyes and a frozen smile, Señor Huang had a Buddha-sized belly that hung over his sash. In his late sixties, he lived in a little house with his wife, twelve sons and daughters, and a bunch of older relatives. Señor Huang was known in town as a wheeler-dealer who knew how to convert junk into gold. He bought and sold everything under the sun, but his most profitable businesses were shark liver oil, bottled, advertised, and sold as cod liver oil, and fireworks during the holiday season.

Since all living room seats were occupied by sharp-eyed relatives, we carried out our business standing up and in a hurry.

"How many firecrackers would you give us this year for every customer we bring?" asked Alfredito, one of my buddies.

"Two for every two pesos customer spends with Huang." The Chinaman used his fingers to make sure we understood.

"This year we'll need three firecrackers for every

two pesos spent." I showed three fingers to make a point.

"You boys greedy, not good...but Huang accepts deal. Now go bring customers. Huang busy bottling Miracle Oil.

New Year's Eve was also known by the young and the young-at-heart as firecracker day. Some parents participated in the fun and others simply observed from a distance.

My friends and I played with gun powder as though it was black sand. In many unfortunate instances, however, rockets exploded while being held, and the victims usually ended up in the hospital with broken fingers, second-degree burns, or a hand in need of numerous stitches.

Our formula for creating havoc during the day was totally harmless as compared to the nighttime activities: After twisting the fuses of three firecrackers together, we placed them under the lip of an empty can of beans with fuses sticking out, set these alight, and in seconds watched the can skyrocket to the heavens. Even though our bragging rights depended on the altitude reached by the container, it was impossible to determine the exact distance covered.

But absolutely nothing could top off the

generalized mayhem brought about by the church's bells tolling at midnight. People with access to noise-making devices such as sirens, locomotive whistles, car klaxons, ship horns, and so on, sounded their gadgets in unison. The climax didn't develop until the last ding-dong was heard, which served as a signal to those who had collected urine in bedside vessels to pitch the brew out the window in order to rid the household of evil spirits. Therefore it was not uncommon to watch intoxicated bystanders being baptized with acrid-smelling pee from head to toe.

According to Pedro, this heretical practice, like so many others, also originated during the times of slavery, as servants rid themselves of curses, jinxes, and spells. But at most civilized homes, including ours, we let our hair down by giving every person in the household a small cup filled with twelve grapes, one to be swallowed after each toll of the church bell. The rite was followed by a toast to the New Year with Sidra Asturiana, an alcoholic apple brew from Asturias, Spain.

Predictably, in less than an hour after midnight our home was empty. Guests if any would have departed, Mother and Father would be in bed, and I'd be in my bedroom, thinking it would take another eternity for the next holiday season to arrive.

Pedro said to me once: "Father Time fools us in

mysterious ways, son. He travels slowly when we're young and increases speed as we age, thus making it hard to understand why time passes so fast the wiser we become."

THE MISER AND THE HURRICANE

In Santa Rita, as in most Cuban towns, people with colorful personalities, weird behaviors, ugly faces, and awkward disabilities were branded with *apodos*—nicknames. Those known for their vices and sins also were labeled. Pedro was known as el Borracho del Muelle (the drunk from the wharf), and Antonio Silva, whose insatiable thirst for money made him the stingiest man in his hometown of Santa Cruz del Sur, as el Tacaño de Santa Cruz (the Miser of Santa Cruz).

Fishing at the docks one afternoon, I overheard a couple of sailors using the name of el Tacaño while arguing about the future path of a tropical storm north of Grand Cayman that was expected to land west of Havana within twelve hours. I tried to fine-tune my ears, but the strong incoming tide and the crashing waves beneath the dock muddled their words, so I couldn't determine the connection between a tightwad and a low pressure area. But this wasn't the first time I had overheard someone referring to el Tacaño when discussing tropical systems.

Curiosity took me to Pedro, who was sitting on a stool, the old remnant of a cigar in his mouth, repairing a fishnet for one of his buddies.

"What are you after?" he asked simply. "Did you get tired of catching fish?"

"Are you joking, Old Man?" I threw up my arms in frustration. "Not a single bite so far."

"You should've known that afternoons are no good for fishing," Pedro said, always the authority. "Plus there's a storm coming in. The fish won't be feeding."

Of course I knew he was right. "Can I ask you a couple of questions about hurricanes?" I asked.

Pedro snorted. "I can't believe you're worried."

"I'm not," I snapped.

"Then what's the fuss? Haven't you been through one before?" His crooked fingers flew as he mended the net.

"I have, but at the time I was only six years old, and all I can remember are uprooted trees, broken branches all over town, and a roof leak directly above my parents' bed."

"Naah...the one you're referring to was only a tropical storm, not a hurricane," said Pedro. "In fact, it deteriorated into a depression after crossing the island."

"In all honesty, I didn't come to ask weather-related

questions, Pedro; I've learned enough of that in school."

"You might think so, young man. But regardless of how much you've learned from books, knowledge of tropical systems is not complete until you get caught in one."

"How many have you experienced?" I asked.

"I've been through dozens of these disasters, and in one the tide was so high, my modest quarters flooded to the top of my desk, ruining all my furnishings plus hundreds of books and periodicals."

"You've got to be kidding me." I crossed my arms over my chest. "And the flood didn't kill the termites?"

Pedro managed a wry smile. "No, it did not, but if you want to know about the worst hurricane ever to hit Cuba and the horror of its aftermath, I shall tell you about the behemoth that hit Santa Cruz del Sur on November 9, 1932. Ranked as a category five, it was one of the deadliest storms ever recorded in the entire world." Pedro sucked all the smoke left in his salivated stump before bucking it away, clearly ready to continue his history lesson.

"Sorry, Old Man, but I only have one question and lots of errands to run before the stores close." I tapped my index finger on my lips to shut him up.

Pedro raised a bushy eyebrow, the same gray as

the sour smoke he released. "Son, you either sit and listen to the whole story, or go back to your errands. We can always talk about hurricanes later on."

My curiosity was stronger than Mom's need for food and supplies, so I asked what I wanted to know: "What is the reason for linking the name of el Tacaño to tropical systems?"

"As always, my son," Pedro said grandly, "you have come to Santa Rita's most reputable soothsayer for answers."

"Come on, Pedro. Save the bragging and tell me the truth. Am I asking a foolish question?"

"No, you're not," Pedro said with a shake of his head. "Your nose for a story is well trained, but in order to understand the connection, I must first relate the story of el Tacaño, *comprendes*?

"Si, señor," I replied.

Pedro narrowed his eyes in recall:

"Antonio Silva, also known as el Tacaño, was born during the early part of this century in the small town of Santa Cruz del Sur to Don Felipe and Doña Sarah Silva, owners of three of the town's five grocery stores, a laundry outfit operated by Chinese immigrants, and the town's funeral parlor, which was eventually managed by Antonio, his wife Lily, and their three daughters."

"How big was Santa Cruz in those days?" I asked.

"Smaller than Santa Rita. Santa Cruz del Sur was as large as it is now; roughly three thousand people, ninety percent of whom depend on the sea for survival. The city had four barbers, three attorneys, two doctors, and two priests. If most citizens lived off the fruits of the sea, the rest, including the Silva family, lived off the fruits of the fishermen. With the passage of time, Antonio's mortuary became the Silvas' most lucrative venture. Profits were so huge that his wife referred to it as the Golden Goose.

"A shrewd but unscrupulous merchant, el Tacaño hired a carpenter to build coffins day and night, just to keep in stock. Apprehensive by nature, he was firmly convinced that sooner or later a major plague or similar tragedy would befall Santa Cruz, and he planned to make a fortune from such a disaster by selling every coffin in his inventory. Furthermore, he would keep neighboring morticians from peddling services in his area.

"Following Silva's instructions, his only carpenter would use cheap pinewood from discarded fruit crates to build the coffin frames, and large segments of cardboard material from unwanted cartons, courtesy of Don Felipe's grocery stores, to form the traditional casket shape.

"In order to strengthen the cardboard sections, the carpenter would brush them with a solution of hot water and corn starch, dry them under the sun, cut them in sections to fit the wooden scaffold, and nail the toughened material to the framework. The top was built using the same method, and it was secured to the coffin with three door hinges on one side and a mortise lock on the other."

"They were locked? Who kept the keys to the coffins after they were buried?" I asked out of morbid curiosity.

"The next of kin, of course," said Pedro. "Not that anyone would ever unlock one. Superstition or not, no family would want to set a spirit free to rise and settle old scores."

"No!" I said, wide-eyed.

"To create the desired deceptive finish," the Old Man continued, "Antonio's carpenter concealed the printing on the cardboard and any pinewood blemishes with black paint. Then he applied putty to cover visible cracks and imperfections before brushing a second and final coat of glossy black paint over the entire piece. These flimsy caskets were sold at outrageous prices to the common folk, and for the well-heeled, one of el Tacaño's daughters, who was taking oil painting lessons at school, hand-painted religious motives on the cover."

Pedro paused to fix me with a piercing gaze."Just imagine the durability of these caskets buried six feet underground in a town that by nature is two feet below sea level."

My eyes nearly dropped from my head at that. "You mean bodies were floating around down there?"

"Young man, I never dug up a grave to find out, so use your imagination. Now let me continue.

"El Tacaño's family was known as reclusive and secretive. No one ever knew of their comings and goings, family conflicts, health issues, and most important, the site where Antonio's paper-money fortune was kept. While the Golden Goose continued to fill his pockets, el Tacaño ensured that no one, including his wife and children, would ever find the hidden cash, and in the event he predeceased them, such fortune would stay intact wherever it lay. Friends and neighbors joked that Antonio, like the Egyptian pharaohs, believed his earthly riches would follow him into the afterlife.

"Eventually, Antonio's hidden treasure became the town's topic of speculation. Some argued he hid the money in empty cans buried beneath the wooden floor of his living room. To substantiate their assumption, they pointed out that Antonio's house, unlike most, was not built on stilts but directly on the ground.

"Others asserted the cash was kept inside a refrigerator buried under the floor, to keep the bills cold, dry, and mildew-free, and those who normally went to bed late swore they had seen him loitering around the cemetery past midnight, thus triggering rumors his money was secreted inside one of the mausoleums. No living creature in Santa Cruz's history has ever incited more speculation than Antonio el Tacaño and his vast accumulated wealth."

"What does he look like?" I asked Pedro.

"Son, I'm sure in a small town like Santa Rita you must have seen Antonio Silva at one time or another. He's short of stature, perhaps five and a half feet tall. His back is severely hunched so he walks with his eyes practically glued to the pavement, hands crossed behind his back. When you see him, you'll notice he carries a brown paper bag that produces a metallic sound as he moves."

"And what's inside the sack?" I asked.

"Some people claim he associates wealth with the sound of metal, so he walks around with a small bell in the sack."

"But the guy is nuts!" I expressed in disbelief.

"Of course he is!" Pedro replied. "He has been *loco* for quite some time." He nodded. "Completely loco. And that's not all. If el Tacaño finds a lost penny, he crosses himself, mumbles a prayer, grabs the coin, kisses it, and into his pocket it goes. If he finds a bent nail, he'll take it home and straighten it up for future use. He retrieves discarded notes, receipts, and all kinds of paper, wipes them off, and uses the cleaner side to write on. He also grabs cigarette butts and recycles them into individual wrappers for personal use. To tell you the truth, I'm stunned he doesn't eat his own excrement to save on food."

"Was he that tight when he lived in Santa Cruz?" I asked, amazed—though I couldn't help but think of Pedro's own frugality with cigar butts.

The old man tapped my shoulder.

"To understand his present-day lifestyle in Santa Rita, I must explain his previous one in Santa Cruz. Unless you need to go run those errands you mentioned?"

I shook my head firmly.

"All right, then." Pedro resumed his story. "In order to keep the household budget near the ground, Antonio coerced his spouse into working for the mortuary as a maid, and forced the girls to assist him with the repulsive chores common to the world's oldest craft. In the end, their meager compensation bounced right back to subsidize the household expenses—such as they were. Except for the roof above their heads, Antonio kept the women intentionally destitute.

"Every Sunday night, el Tacaño gathered his family around the dining room table to scrutinize their personal expenditures. Nothing within the man's domain was sacred. Even the cost of female-related needs was evaluated against a carefully calculated formula, and when a raggedy outfit obviously needed replacement, el Tacaño made sure the piece was beyond mending before authorizing a purchase of an equally or lower-priced garment.

"Furthermore, in order to conceal his financial shenanigans from the tax collector, el Tacaño dealt exclusively in cash. No bank transactions, and no lawyers or bookkeepers involved. He cooked his books and presented them as *faultless* to every government inspector upon request."

"Tell me, Old Man," I asked after a short pause. "If you lived in Santa Rita all your life, how did you manage to know so much about a stranger from Santa Cruz del Sur?"

"Very simple." A slow, lazy smile moved over the old man's face. "In those days I worked part time for the railroad that ran between both towns. Lopez, one of my co-workers, taught me to become a switchman, and upon the engineer's request, the entire crew often stayed in Santa Cruz overnight. During those boring evenings, we gathered inside the caboose to brew café Cubano, share a bottle of rum, and talk until our eyelids collapsed. It was during those gatherings that I learned about the Miser of Santa Cruz del

Sur. But let me continue before I lose track of what I'm saying."

Pedro cleared his throat.

"Prior to the demise of Don Felipe Silva in 1924, Antonio falsified his father's will to become the sole heir of his assets, thus leaving an older brother in Santa Rita absolutely nothing."

"Sorry to barge in, Pedro; but did Antonio bury Don Felipe in one of his fake caskets?"

Pedro shook his head in disbelief. "Funny you should ask. He used no coffin at all for the old man. Instead, in order to keep his huge inventory intact, Antonio used the embalming equipment to pump kerosene into his father's femoral artery, took the body to the countryside, laid it upon a flat rock, and set it on fire. Whatever remains Antonio collected after the explosion, he scattered along the coast."

"Wow!" I said with a whistle. "He fried his own father? Then what happened?"

"El Tacaño was so anxious to take legal possession of his father's assets before Don Felipe's death reached his brother's ears, he exerted ownership even before the last will and testament was officially sanctioned by the probate court. The first thing he did was to replace the grocery store's purveyor with a cut-rate supplier who didn't hesitate to alter the expiration date of food products. As a result,

Antonio sold outdated canned foods, some about to burst; rice infested with rodent pellets; corn and wheat flour contaminated with bugs; and the list went on and on.

"Selling low-quality products at ridiculously low prices to a trusting public, el Tacaño took away a significant number of customers from his rivals, virtually eradicating competition. Soon, the profits from the grocery stores surpassed those of the Golden Goose."

"Did he and his family eat the same stuff he sold to the public?" I asked.

"Not a chance," Pedro replied. "The new supplier delivered Antonio's personal goods directly to his home."

"What about the Chinese laundry?"

"The only reason he didn't interfere with them was because he refused to ruin his own garments by cutting down on detergent. But it didn't matter. In less than two years, Antonio became the wealthiest citizen in Santa Cruz del Sur."

I narrowed my eyes. "When are you going to explain his connection to the weather?"

"Take it easy, son, we'll get there in due time. Now, just as you've heard the most appalling qualities of Antonio el Tacaño while living in Santa Cruz, I will proceed to describe the apocalyptic destruction inflicted upon Cuba's southeastern coast by the monstrous hurricane of 1932."

I rolled my eyes, but I knew I had no choice but to wait while Pedro launched back into his story.

"Initially perceived as a small tropical storm two hundred miles east of Guadalupe, it passed over the Leeward Islands on the last day of October as a ninety-five-mile-an-hour hurricane. Instead of veering north, as most storms do in those latitudes during that time of the year, it turned southwest, and on the morning of November third it swept Punta Gallinas, Colombia, with winds exceeding one hundred and ten miles per hour.

"For the next two days, the storm gained considerable strength while dithering in the warm waters of the Caribbean, and on November fifth, it flattened the Cayman Islands with wind gusts of over one hundred and thirty miles an hour."

Pedro pulled a cigar butt from his shirt pocket, struck a match against the sole of his shoe, lit up the stump, and slowly inhaled its delicious aroma.

"Come on, Pedro, put your skates on."

"Young man, older people need time to organize their thoughts, so be patient."

"But why do it at the most critical moment?"

"Because I also want to teach you endurance and listening habits...that's why."

After a lingering pause, Pedro continued the narrative.

"Packing winds that exceeded one hundred and fifty miles an hour, the frightful hurricane took an unexpected turn to the northeast, and on November ninth, the eye of the storm made landfall in Santa Cruz del Sur. Along with torrential rains, a twenty-eight-foot surge flooded the area as far as the eye could see, and waves measuring twelve feet above the surge changed the topography of the coastline forever. Tragically, the storm not only wiped out the town of Santa Cruz del Sur, but swept away over ninety percent of its population."

"What about damage to Santa Rita?" I asked.

"Only minor...and no casualties." Pedro crossed himself twice. "We had ten inches of rain along with strong winds, but as luck would have it, the vortex passed forty miles east of town as a weakening system.

"Since power and telegraph lines were down, news of the Santa Cruz disaster spread only by word of mouth, and the town of Santa Rita was among the first to take immediate action. In Havana, the government didn't grasp the magnitude of the disaster at first, but it assumed it was massive enough to send military convoys to help cope with the calamity.

"Twelve hours after the news reached our town, a

band of volunteers, including three doctors, two nurses, Lopez and other railroad workers, the church's priest, and myself, boarded the local train with axes, saws, sisal rope, cots, tools, blankets, canned goods, bags to carry casualties, drugs, medical equipment, and much more. A municipal truck loaded with fifty-gallon tanks of potable water arrived at the station just in time, and in less than an hour, the heavy cargo was transferred to a flat car.

"With enough coal to last four days, the faithful locomotive and its two-man crew left Santa Rita by late afternoon. At the time, the engineer's sense of urgency was such that he promised to reach Santa Cruz in less than five hours—a feat that was virtually impossible; a normal run took us seven hours in clear weather.

"Three miles into our trip to Santa Cruz, the engineer began to encounter obstructions on the tracks, but so far they were small enough to crush and keep the train rolling. But as we continued and larger debris began to appear, the engineer asked for a couple of volunteers to sit in front of the locomotive and alert him to dangerous obstructions by blowing a boatswain's whistle."

"Did you accept the challenge?" I asked.

"Of course I did!" Pedro smiled broadly. "But between you and me," the Old Man lowered his voice to a whisper, “I was so scared of falling off the train that I wet my pants.”

“What about your friend Lopez?”

“His face looked ashen, but then it could’ve been my panicky imagination.”

“How often did you blow the boatswain’s whistle?”

“Often—and then Lopez and I would wait for the train to stop, step down, and drag away large pieces of debris entirely on our own. All kinds of obstacles littered the tracks—doors, broken furniture, dead cows, tree trunks, and a large tin roof among other things.”

“What happened when it got dark?” I inquired.

“The engineer slowed down the train to almost walking speed. He knew we were about to cross the bridge over Arroyo Negro (Black Creek), less than two hours from our destination. He suspected the creek would have flooded above its banks, possibly damaging the supporting trestles.”

“How could anyone spot running water in the middle of the night?” I asked, dumbfounded.

“Come on, boy.” Pedro sneered. “When was the last time you saw a locomotive?”

“You’re right, Old Man. I forgot the bright light in front of the engine.”

“Now, what was I saying?” Pedro scratched his hat in recall.

"You and your friend Lopez were standing watch in front of the train," I replied with a hint of sarcasm.

"Oh yes, of course. As the train kept moving," Pedro continued, "a glittery spot ahead became progressively larger. Lopez and I concluded that tiny Arroyo Negro had indeed become a wide, vigorous stream, so again we blew the boatswain's whistle.

"Carbide lamps in hand, the engineer and the fireman climbed down from the engine to investigate the shiny spot. Once we reached the outskirts of the area, I volunteered to walk farther down the tracks to measure the water depth in the center of the bridge, but the current was so strong it wasn't safe to walk more than ten feet.

"The engineer suggested to the fireman that we risk crossing the bridge at a very fast clip. He maintained that with currents so strong, nothing dangerously large could be lying on or between the tracks to cause a derailment; therefore the faster we crossed, the less our chances of tipping over. The fireman agreed, saying he thought that the weight of the locomotive and its affixed coal car would exert enough clutching power to drag the train through the flooded tracks with little or no risk.

"Lopez, on the other hand, observed that without some kind of counterweight, the two cabooses risked being toppled by the powerful current—and could drag the rest of the train with them into the swollen depths of Arroyo Negro. In a nutshell, he worried that the entire train would be at the mercy of the cabooses.

"While our bosses continued the debate, Lopez and I returned to the passenger car, where the priest and a handful of volunteers were praying for God's help in crossing the bridge. Shortly thereafter we noticed that the train was slowly moving backwards. Five minutes passed, and then the engine released a cloudburst of steam, followed by a complete stop. Thank goodness, we thought, that the engineer and fireman had decided to return to Santa Rita instead of trying to cross the questionable bridge over the Arroyo Negro.

"Suddenly, *vooom!* A violent jolt jerked the entire train, followed by an increase in forward speed.

"*That's it,* I thought. *Now let's hope our two heroes have more brains inside their skulls than courage in their hearts.*

"As the train continued to gain momentum, I noticed that every valve in the engine's armor was discharging massive amounts of steam.

"'Look out, everybody!' cried the doctor, hanging halfway out the window. 'We're already crossing Arroyo Negro.'"

"Lopez and I braced ourselves, waiting for those

cabooses to start wobbling and send us all into oblivion. It must have taken nerves of steel for our two chiefs to barrel across the flooded bridge and arrive on muddy but drier tracks without skidding or tumbling. Thank God, Lopez was wrong.

"Thrilled by their success, the engineer continued to blow the whistle until the daring locomotive achieved its highest speed. After two hours of continuous tooting and jolting, our small convoy arrived at the Santa Cruz railroad station, ten hours after leaving Santa Rita and shortly before daybreak.

"The station was a ghostly reminder of things past. The stone building was in ruins, its roof gone and the glass windows shattered. A wrecking ball couldn't have done a better job. The beautifully landscaped surroundings were either buried in mud or under the sea. Fifty yards east of the station, the railroad water tank lay flat on the ground, its fifty-foot-tall steel supporting beams now twisted as if made of rubber.

"Opposite the station, I noticed a forty-foot Royal Palm pierced from side to side by a five-foot-long wooden shaft. A local witness swore he'd seen the flying chunk of timber penetrate the trunk from one edge to the other as if the tree were made of butter. It reminded me of William Tell and the arrow that went through the apple perched on the head of his young son.

"Utterly shocked by the catastrophic landscape, our volunteers stepped out of the train to witness the saddest, most wrenching manifestation of sorrow we could have imagined. Those who, like me, had known Santa Cruz prior to the disaster became painfully aware of the turbulent realities delivered by Mother Nature.

"It was a cool morning, and a group of men, women, and children, most of them still in shock and some totally nude, tried to cover themselves with whatever material they could find among the rubble. In spite of the local warnings, most citizens had been caught entirely by surprise, for no one believed that on such a beautiful evening, a hurricane of that magnitude could assault Santa Cruz when in recorded history no tropical system had ever landed in town.

I vividly remember the fireman taking off his shirt to cover a naked middle-aged woman who was shivering with cold. The lady's name was Francisca. According to Francisca, an unexpected wall of water as tall as a light post had uprooted their sturdy house built on stilts. When the woman regained her senses, she realized she had lost everything of value to the flood—not only her home, but her husband, their four children, and a sister. All she could remember was the moment she grabbed and held onto a chunk of floating timber. She said she'd lost her sleepwear to the current, and by the time her naked body crashed against the top of a brick wall, her house and everyone inside had vanished. In the opinion of many, she must have been gripping a floating rafter, conceivably from her own house, and after drifting semi-consciously for about three hundred yards she reached the structure from which she dangled until the waters began to recede.

"Francisca told us she had been searching all over for bodies that resembled those of her family, without any luck, though she had seen numerous corpses partly buried in mud, as well as limbs protruding from the saturated ground. Like most survivors, Francisca had been in shock for so long, she couldn't even remember her husband's name.

"That morning, our group's consensus was to divide ourselves into groups of four, each searching in a different direction. A rough map of the area was drawn to ensure that in five hours all foursomes would meet back at the station. Each group carried numerous red-colored sticks to mark the locations where cadavers were found.

"Lopez, who was responsible for carrying two buckets full of potable water, bore the containers hanging from a rope tied to each end of a wooden rod, the center of which rested against his neck and shoulders. He would hold the heavy rig secure by spreading his arms along the length of the stick. Two volunteers would search among the rubble and inside crumbling houses for injured victims, and I was to mitigate Lopez's burden by taking over his heavy load now and then, plus assisting the other volunteers. In short, I spent the entire time leaping from one assignment to the next.

"The section of town we covered was essentially a pile of rubble, heavily contaminated with sewage from septic tanks. Water from the aqueduct was deemed unacceptable for human use, and besides, the pump station and filtering plant wouldn't function without electricity.

"The muddy streets already stank of rotting flesh. In the midst of what used to be the busiest commercial zone in town, men, women, and children desperately begged for food, water, and warmth. Moaning sounds and screams echoed from every corner. That awful spectacle impacted my mind and soul for years to come."

Pedro paused to wipe his eye, his expression haggard and haunted. A tear? I wondered.

"Walking further down," he continued, "we spotted a group of five elderly survivors. Like zombies, most seemed to stare into a void. Unfortunately, we learned that these victims had gathered to share their misery and find a lasting solution to their suffering.

These folks couldn't have cared less about our presence, much less our mission. They all seemed to share a state of mind in which submission to mortality seemed far preferable to future confrontations with life. Simply put, they were contemplating mass suicide, and in spite of our efforts to rescue them from such a miserable state, they adamantly refused to follow us."

"But Pedro, why would they want to kill themselves when it was an act of God that saved their lives?" I asked at a loss.

"Son, you are too young to understand their way of thinking; these people had lost their loved ones and everything they'd worked an entire life for, including their homes. They were too old to work, too proud to accept charity, and too cantankerous to adapt to a new environment."

"But didn't they realize they still had a future?" I asked. "Even if what you've said is true, life at any age could be joyful and full of meaning. If you ask my dad, he'll say that attitude is everything in life."

"I totally agree," Pedro reflected with a finger to his nose. "But just like wrinkles develop with age, so can negativity. You see, when people live for too long, chances are they'll despise the present, close their eyes to the future, and curse their inability to recall the past. So with no butterflies to catch or rainbows to behold, they simply sit and wait for their final breath."

I sighed. "That story must be the saddest I've ever heard," I told Pedro. "So what did you do with them?"

"Since our group had so much to accomplish, and time was running short, we decided to leave these stubborn creatures alone and continue searching for victims who needed and welcomed our help."

"Do you think your strategy fulfilled its purpose?"

"Only to a point," Pedro replied. "You must realize we were common people dealing with issues the majority of which were above our heads; but we did the best we could under the circumstances. Did we save lives? Yes, many. Did we offer hope to those in need? Yes, we did, and by five in the afternoon all groups arrived at our meeting point by the train station; ours with sixty-three survivors comprising men, women, and children.

"Upon examination, our doctors on board concluded that some hurricane victims were still in shock and needed treatment; others were suffering physical trauma; and all of them had wounded hearts. So while our lady volunteers cared for women and children, the rest of us looked after the remaining victims, some of whom had to be carried onto the train on improvised stretchers, while others walked in pain or leaned on the strong.

"Inside the passenger car they were offered more water, a generous meal, and blankets to keep them warm."

"And how many bodies did your group find?"

"Our count stopped at seventy-four." Pedro drew a deep breath. "On the bright side, however, countless survivors who were able to walk and move around, joined us in a common quest to lend a hand to those in need. Twelve took over the gathering and stacking of body bags inside a concrete building previously used as a depository for salted fish. These corpses were to remain in place until the proper authorities decided their final destination."

"What happened to the rest of the houses built on stilts?" I asked.

"Since they were closer to the coast, only a dozen or so of about a hundred remained standing, all roofless and all empty. Santa Cruz simply became a flattened muddy area inhabited by ghosts."

"Pedro, please tell me the truth; did you cry?"

Pedro bristled. "To begin with, son, I don't cry easily. At times I felt like tears would come out, but they never did. Even though it was the first time in my life I had confronted human suffering on such a grand scale, I couldn't remember how to cry."

He puffed on his cigar. "So back to the train," he said.

"To allow hurricane victims the use of passenger seats, a group of men, including Lopez and me, crawled into the coal wagon in search of a soft spot where we could spend the night. Can you imagine a group of lucid men searching for comfortable spots inside a car full of rocks?"

"You fellows must've lost your minds!"

"Anyone would in that environment."

"Where did the remaining volunteers spend the night?" I asked.

"Using oakum bundles as pillows, the engineer and his pal held a snoring match on the engine's floor. The doctors and nurses spent the entire night bouncing from one caboose to the next, assisting the critically injured, and the rest simply stretched out under a stinking tree, the smell of which was supposed to repel mosquitoes and other pests.

"Early the next morning, a twenty-car train approached the station from the west, having left Havana the day before. Much better equipped than our group, the soldiers and civilians aboard began the dreadful task ahead. The train carried plenty of drugs, water decontaminating tablets, cots, two flat cars loaded with four small jeeps, army tents, the ever-present body bags, official plans for the relocation of survivors, and plenty of building materials offered free of charge to those who wished to stay and start all over in the aftermath of the disaster.

"In spite of the opportunity to rebuild, our passenger cars were totally occupied by victims who didn't know where to turn, but refused to stay in Santa Cruz.

"The military commander and a couple of bossy civilians from the government train met us to appraise the situation. Knowing we were almost out of food, water, and medical supplies, and that another rescue train was expected to arrive that evening, they asked us to leave before dark so the incoming convoy could use our track. In return they offered us a two-soldier escort and enough food, potable water, and medical supplies for our return trip. So by late afternoon, our fully loaded train was on its way home. By then the waters had receded enough that we could cross the Arroyo Negro safely."

"What happened to the survivors once in Santa Rita?" I asked.

"Luckily, dozens of families from all walks of life were waiting at the railroad station to offer them a hand. Most adults stayed in shelters provided by the church and the Spanish Club. Local families with children welcomed compatible groups into their homes, and the municipal government offered food, clothing, and medical care free of charge."

"And you?"

"Physically exhausted, and proud of my town's generosity in a time of great tribulation, I walked back to my home on the wharf, where dozens of workers anxiously awaited my stories."

"Some things never change," I commented wryly, but Pedro ignored me.

"Within four months," he went on, "the homesick had returned to Santa Cruz to rebuild their lives; another bunch migrated to towns where relatives and friends offered support; and only a handful settled in Santa Rita.

"In the realm of the exceptional, a set of teenage twins had saved enough cash from various undertakings to purchase two one-way tickets to Havana. Those who knew them well said the two boys took an oath to pursue a higher education in the capital in memory of their deceased parents."

"Did you ever hear from them?" I inquired.

"One became a civil engineer and is presently designing bridges in Eastern Cuba. The other turned into a talented musician who today leads his own band—an example of what character and determination can do for those who stay true to themselves and their values."

Pedro gave a vigorous nod and waited for me to nod back to show him I understood the Moral of the Story.

"Before I finish," Pedro emphasized, "let me tell you that seeing people from all walks of life lending a hand to strangers in need was absolutely inspiring. Sad to say, disaster is about the only condition that brings out the best in us."

I nodded again. Another Moral of the Story.

"But hey, Pedro!" I exclaimed, hands on my hips. "You forgot to describe the connection between Antonio el Tacaño and the hurricane!"

"No, I did not," said the Old Salt, eyelids about to close. "But I'm a tired old geezer who can only go so far, so please be considerate and let me finish the story tomorrow."

"I can't believe my ears!" I complained in deep disgust.

"You have no choice," Pedro said firmly. "I simply won't discuss the matter today, or tonight, but *mañana*."

"How can you have the audacity to leave me in Limbo?" I demanded, flushing with rage. "For goodness sake, Pedro, I'm going back home empty-handed because the stores are already closed. Do you understand what that means?"

"It means you're about to face a long sermon as a prelude to a spanking."

"For the love of God, Old Man, how can you be so cruel?" I stared deeply into his eyes.

Pedro shook his head. "I'm not cruel. You are."

"Me? What have I done?"

"You couldn't care less about your old friend's health, that's what."

I leaped up in anger.

Pedro pulled me down by the arm. "And where in hell do you think you're going?" he asked mildly.

"I'm going home, never to return."

"Just cool it, boy. There's no point in acting like a spoiled brat. Please sit down."

Eyes fixed on the floor, I sat as told.

"You know something?" Pedro took a long drink of water from his clay jug. "Again, I was trying to test your patience, which as you see was nonexistent. Of course I am very tired, but to be honest, I never intended to finish the story tomorrow."

"I'm really sorry, Old Man," I muttered. "I know I acted like a brute."

Pedro took my shoulder and gave it a quick shake. "Just make sure your bad manners are kept under control next time, you hear?"

"Yessir, I do."

The sun was about to set, leaves declined to jiggle, mosquitoes wallowed in a blood-sucking feast, and Pedro, tired as he was, continued with the story.

"Among the volunteers," he explained, "was a short man in his late forties nicknamed el Viejito

(Little Old Man), whose face was as wrinkled as a man twice his age. El Viejito was el Tacaño's only brother, and he had joined the Santa Rita volunteers because he was concerned about Antonio and his family, in spite of their betrayal.

"Immediately after our train arrived in Santa Cruz del Sur, el Viejito left our group to search for Antonio. He slogged through mud, puddles of water, blown-away homes, debris-covered streets, and worst of all, points of reference that didn't exist anymore.

"Walking by the cemetery, he identified pine-wood splinters and disintegrating pieces of cardboard from coffins sold by his brother. Decomposing bodies, skeletons, bones, and stained clothing that were to remain inside sealed caskets littered the morbid panorama like a canvas from hell.

"Once in the general vicinity of his brother's neighborhood, el Viejito eyed a raggedy man pacing an area between two fallen trees. Hands clasped behind his back, his curved body bent like a butcher's hook, and sobbing intensely, the deranged man mumbled disjointed words and hummed the same tuneless song over and over.

"As el Viejito approached, he suddenly recognized his brother Antonio. He called his name numerous times. He reminded Antonio of who he was, asked about his wife and daughters, mentioned the mortuary, the usurped grocery stores, the hidden fortune, and a myriad of familiar circumstances in an effort to shake him up, but the man remained unresponsive.

"Hoping to show him something familiar, el Viejito dug into the mud, swept debris, lifted branches, and removed objects such as old tires and tennis shoes, but found nothing recognizable. The sea had flooded the area and the wind had blown with such force it uprooted, scattered, or made pulp of everything in its path.

"El Viejito realized that Antonio's possessions and those of his family were either strewn farther inland or reclaimed by the deep. How Antonio survived, was and still remains a mystery."

"What about the big money?" I asked Pedro.

"Weeks following the storm," the Old Man responded, "word of Antonio's hidden fortune spread like fire throughout the entire island. As a result, gold diggers and treasure hunters—some with improvised metal detectors, others with sniffing dogs, teams with picks and shovels, and even tractors—went after the money. But to this day, no one has unearthed anything worth a wooden nickel, not even signs of an earlier life that Antonio could relate to."

"What did el Viejito do?" I asked.

"Even though he knew about Antonio's falsification

of their father's will, he didn't take revenge. Rare as it may sound, money didn't seem to arouse any kind of greed in the wrinkled man, who in spite of knowing all about his brother's treachery, has taken compassionate care of him ever since.

"Psychiatrists, researchers from the University's School of Medicine, and experts in memory loss and early senility have all examined the man, and the consensus they reached was that the mental and psychological trauma of losing everything he had, money in particular, had triggered a severe post-traumatic mental disorder that led to an irreversible form of amnesia. Even electroshock treatments were applied without significant results.

"On the other hand, after ten years of cognitive therapy, Antonio's mind has improved to that of a three-year-old. He communicates with sounds and hand motions; cries when approaching women, especially young ones; and smiles when he finds coins, pieces of shiny metal, and paper money."

"For the love of God, Pedro. That man should've never been born!"

"On the contrary," said Pedro. "Since God also wants us to learn from the foolishness of others, He sends idiots to fulfill His wishes."

"Are you referring to those known as avaricious money worshipers?" I asked, tongue in cheek.

"Son, you couldn't have found a better example in an encyclopedia."

Pedro stroked his beard. "Now tell me; can you see the connection between el Tacaño and hurricanes?"

"Yes sir, now I do," I replied confidently. "When disaster threatens, people tend to reflect on the possibility of personal losses. But in Santa Rita, el Tacaño's poignant story shows what a greedy, heartless human being misses when the values inside his heart are twisted. He was so *loco* and obsessed with money that he lost his mind upon the loss of his wealth. Sad to say, he never knew the joy of loving, and being loved."

And thus, I realized the tragedy of the miser and the hurricane would always remain on the lips of Santa Ritans troubled by impending doom.

El Amigo Fritz

Our early morning routine rarely changed. At the deafening clatter of an old alarm clock, Mom jumped out of bed to prepare breakfast and boil water for the family to drink during the day. At five minutes past six, she'd be dragging me into the bathroom to shiver under the cold water shower prescribed by Dad to make a man out of me, and by seven I'd be facing both at the table.

"Buenos dias, *hijo*. Are you full of vigor to face the challenges of a new day?" Father would greet me from behind the newspaper.

"Yes sir! There's nothing like a cold morning shower to stimulate body and mind," I always replied, cold and rigid like a Popsicle.

Except for weekends and holidays, the same routine went on word for word until the day Mom and I saw the *The Daily News* unfolded on the table and Father wagging a finger at the editorial.

"There he is!" he announced joyfully. "You'll never guess who won the Nobel Prize in Literature this year."

Mom shrugged, arms crossed over her chest. "And may I ask who the fortunate laureate is?"

"Who else but the Great Ernest Hemingway?" Father declared in a pompous, resonant tone.

"What's the book about?" I asked.

"It is about a fisherman named Santiago, who looks like your pal Pedro!" Dad took a sip of Cuban coffee.

"It must be *The Old Man and the Sea*?"

"You guessed right." Father set the cup back on the table and shot me a knowing glance.

I turned to my heavy-eyed mother. "Mom, have you read the book?"

"No, and I certainly won't. I'm sick and tired of listening to fishing stories." She yawned long and deep.

"But woman!" Dad flushed an angry red. "This is a major achievement! How dare you react so indifferently to one of my favorite novelists?"

Mom snorted. "For the same reason you ridiculed *Anna Karenina* because it was conceived by a Russian womanizer."

"Hey guys!" I exclaimed to avert warfare. "I also have great news!"

"What is it?" Father asked with skepticism.

"Didn't you know today is Flag Day?"

"And who cares about Flag Day?" Father frowned, folded the paper, and left the room grumbling.

"You'd better leave for school right away, son," Mom quietly suggested. "It's starting to drizzle."

"What's wrong with Dad? Why is he suddenly so annoyed?" I asked.

"Don't worry, Carlitos," Mom replied. "He'll soon return as if nothing happened. Dad gets upset when anyone picks on his favorite authors. He must have been a bookworm in his previous life."

I grabbed my duffel bag and baseball cap, jumped on my bike, and began to pedal under light rain. Climbing Maceo's cobblestone street, I spotted my classmate Felito biking downhill at full speed. I waved at him, and in seconds he slid to a screeching stop barely an inch away from me.

"Hey, man," I yelled. "You're driving like a maniac in the wrong direction."

"I'm not that stupid," Felito retorted. "School is closed today and perhaps tomorrow."

"Don't be such a dummy," I replied. "On Flag Day we only get the afternoon off, not the entire day."

"Yep, that's correct, except last night the septic tank blew a hole in the backyard, and poop keeps gushing out like there's no tomorrow."

"You must be kidding." I shook my head in disgust.

Felito clasped his nose. "Why would I joke

about something so stinky?" he said in a squeaky voice.

"Because you've always been a prankster, that's why."

"Why don't you check it out?" Felito leaned his bike on the ground. "And if you feel like helping out, grab an extra shovel, dig deep into the crud, and while you're at it, read the sign that says: Classes to resume on Monday."

"Naah...I'm not that stupid either. By the way, what are your plans for today?"

Felito shrugged. "Nothing exciting. When I told Mother what happened, she told me to meet her at the shoe store because my Keds already have holes. So now I'll be trying new ones all day...and I hate it! What about you? Are you going back home?

"Of course I am, but first I'll stop by the wharf and pay a short visit to my old pal."

"Are you brain-picking Pedro again?"

"None of that. This time I'm surprising him with incredible news."

"I'll bet you a million pesos it's about Hemingway," Felito said, smirking.

"Yes, it is...but how did you know?"

"Dad told me this morning."

"So did mine," I said. "But Hemingway lives in Havana—so why is he so famous in Santa Rita?"

"Hell if I know." Felito raised his bike and pedaled away.

"If you're looking for Pedro," said Don Clemente, the wharf's bookkeeper, "he is probably lounging in his fleapit, waiting for the rain to stop." He continued adding a row of figures.

"Is he sick?" I asked the chubby man.

He looked up at me through his thick lenses, shaded by a green visor.

"Oh no," he replied. "But since his uncle died of pneumonia after being rained on, Pedro won't leave his room until the sun comes out. But go knock on his door," suggested the bookkeeper, returning to his calculations. "I'm sure he'll tell you about the Nobel Prize and his favorite author."

Gee...even this man knows about Hemingway.

Curious as a fox, I stepped inside the warehouse, walked to Pedro's quarters, and knocked repeatedly on his makeshift door.

"Pedro, it's me, open up."

"Damn it, son, just kick it where it jams and come in."

Sitting on a chair that leaned against the wall, cigar clasped between his teeth and a bottle of rum by his side, Pedro grumbled: "Why in hell aren't you in school?"

"Because today is Flag Day," I replied, "and the yard is full of crap, and I wanted to surprise you with the news about Hemingway, but apparently everyone in town including you already knows about it. I didn't think people in Santa Rita ever read his books or had even heard of the man."

Pedro let his chair tip forward and gave my shoulder a quick shake. "First of all, son, thanks for remembering me.

"Now, to satisfy your curiosity..." Pedro paused to slug a mouthful of rum straight from the bottle and wipe off his mouth with a yellowed handkerchief. "Let me begin by saying that most citizens in Santa Rita don't read his books, or for that matter anything of value. Art, music, literature, and history are so alien to their lifestyles, most believe that cultural education is achieved by listening to soap operas and local news, watching silly movies, reading junk, and arguing about politics and baseball on street corners. Alas, to most of these folks, culture is the white stuff added to milk to produce cheese."

He waited a beat for me to nod that I understood.

"What's more, it irritates me to live in a town where its citizens don't give a hoot about the humanities, and this is why mediocrity reigns in Santa Rita. On the other hand..."

"Please, Pedro." I clasped my hands together to

implore him to shut up. "All I want to know is why Hemingway is so well known in Santa Rita."

Pedro shook his head in frustration. "Son, it'll be virtually impossible to describe something so complex if you're in a hurry."

"Can't you just reply to a straightforward question with a simple answer?"

Pedro folded his arms and met my demand straight on. "Okay," he said. "I'll give it a try on the condition that you read the book."

I held up a palm. "I solemnly promise to read *The Old Man and the Sea.*"

"In that case, hand me my water jug and sit down quietly while I wind up my memory. You must realize that unless I add a little water to the tank, my early morning brain is useless."

Pedro uncorked the clay jar, and with closed eyes, slowly drank most of its water.

"Do you want brown sugar as well?" I asked.

"Not now, son; maybe later with a little rum."

Serenely and without uttering a word, I sat on Pedro's old recliner, staring at the ceiling and waiting patiently for his brain to click.

"Hey, Old Man," I said after a prolonged silence. "I'm all ears, but I'm also tired of watching the roof."

Pedro leaned forward to draw my attention.

"Sorry, boy, I didn't mean to be rude. But when

I finish my story, you'll see why Hemingway is the only author known by these provincial idiots, so be patient."

Pedro took a deep breath and held up his index finger. "First of all, I'll define his character as unpredictable, adventurous, and conceited to some degree."

Oh my God, here he goes with another dissertation.

"Nicknamed Papa by friends and cronies, this great American writer was also a newsman and Red Cross volunteer during World War One. Regrettably for future generations, he became part of a large group of writers who were disillusioned with American society, its values, and its pursuit of wealth through war. In fact, it was war that forever left an indelible mark on his temperament.

"Hemingway was an extremely competitive and ambitious fellow who strove to excel in every undertaking. Proud of his works, physical prowess, capacity for drink, experience as a fisherman, and hunter of large exotic beasts, Papa was surprisingly meek at times. In brief, he was a complicated individual who easily collapsed into a teary state of depression for no apparent reason." Pedro made a tragic face.

"Overly pessimistic about the future and disappointed with the present, he could also reach an exhilarating mood when least expected." Now he beamed in contrast. “Papa needed solitude as much as he did the company of friends, drinking buddies, local strangers, and mesmerized listeners. I observed this about him myself.”

“Yourself?” I sat up straight. “You knew Hemingway? How did you come to meet him?”

“I met the Americano by accident, when his yacht needed urgent repair.” Pedro spun his soggy cigar between his teeth. “Henceforth, I can either expand my overview of the writer’s life, or merely answer your question about why he is so widely known in Santa Rita.”

“I’d rather hear about his life in town and his personal relationship with the locals, especially you,” I said at once.

“Then, son, prepare yourself to hear a story beyond belief.”

I settled comfortably in the tattered recliner.

“It all started on a cool February morning, when a messenger dispatched by the owner of El Gato Negro Hotel delivered me a personal note signed by his boss. It basically said: ‘Pedro, please come over right away. An important Americano has docked his fishing yacht in one of our slips and urgently needs a marine mechanic to help save his vessel from sinking. As you know, Rudy’—he was the town’s best mechanic at the time—'is out of town for the rest of the week, and even though you despise this kind of greasy sweaty work, I took the liberty of recommending you as an old salt who knows marine engines inside out.'"

Pedro grinned a little. "He also reminded me that offering my services to the Americano would be a quick way to settle my debts with the hotel bar. He concluded, 'I beg you to come, but please don't act grouchy in front of the well-known man.'"

"Did you go?" I asked Pedro.

"Of course I did," he replied. "I asked the messenger to identify the Americano, and he said the man was a famous writer.

"My excitement was such that I picked up some tools from the wharf's bin and rode to El Gato Negro Hotel on the back seat of the messenger's scooter.

"When we entered the hotel-restaurant through the back door, the owner, Felipe Garcia, introduced me to a tall, heavyset fellow with Santa Claus cheeks and a nicely groomed beard. At the time no names were mentioned except mine, and though I suspected who the man was, I acted as if I didn't.

"The Americano led me to his boat, a thirty-eight-foot fishing yacht built of precious teak and mahogany woods, and as I spotted the name *Pilar* painted on the transom, I knew the mysterious Americano was Ernest Hemingway.

"Once inside the vessel he introduced me in perfect Spanish to Señor Fuentes, his longtime and trusted captain, who showed me where the problem was. Under the scrutiny of both, I descended into the dimly lit engine room, which reeked of creosote, dead fish, and diesel oil, and with a borrowed flashlight I saw that the compartment was rapidly filling up with seawater.

"Back on deck I agreed with the captain's assessment that the problem, caused by a burnt shaft gland, needed urgent attention. I knew the appropriate material to replace the damaged packing gland was unavailable in Santa Rita, and the closest source would be in Santa Cruz del Sur, a twelve-hour train ride departing our station early next morning.

"I told the writer and his captain that by carefully hammering oakum or even old woolen socks into the cavity, I could possibly reduce the seawater leak to allow his bilge pumps to maintain a safe level inside the engine room, but in order to perform such a temporary repair I needed to access the shaft from inside the cockpit.

"'After you, young man,' the Americano said. He held the door with arms extended.

"As I stepped into the cabin, my eyes almost fell

from their sockets and a cold sweat ran down my spine. To my left, a fifty-caliber machine gun was mounted in its tripod, and to my right a bazooka rocket launcher stood on the floor, firmly pushed against the wall. Directly ahead and next to the ladder accessing the forward stateroom, numerous boxes labeled in English contained rounds of ammunition. Tied together with heavy sisal rope, a dozen or so rockets lay on the wooden floor to keep them from accidentally rolling and hitting something. Lastly, three sharpshooter rifles, each with two-stage telescopes, hung from the ceiling next to an assortment of fishing gear."

"Did he notice your astonishment?" I asked.

"Of course he did, and with a sharp sense of humor he scrutinized every step of my temporary repair.

"Once the leak was reduced, the three of us walked to the hardware store to order new packing glands. After calling long distance to his other retailer in Santa Cruz, the owner guaranteed the shipment would arrive in Santa Rita two days later by train.

"'Are you sure the old socks will hold the leak for two more days?' asked Captain Fuentes.

"'Pay close attention to the high water alarm and keep plenty of oakum handy in case of emergency,'

I told him, 'and don't hesitate to call if things get worse.'

"The Americano shook my hand, and with a sigh of relief, invited me to share a bottle of wine with him and Fuentes that I gladly accepted. Once inside his yacht, the captain had me swear not to divulge what I'd seen to anyone.

"At that, the tall Americano turned to his captain and asked him, tongue in cheek, 'Hey Fuentes, are you sure we can trust this guy?'

"'*Naturalmente,* Papa,' Fuentes answered. 'Otherwise we sink.'

"At that moment the American celebrity introduced himself as Ernest Hemingway and told me he and Fuentes were on a secret mission sponsored by the American Embassy in Havana.

"Upon Papa's request, Fuentes opened a lazaretto and gathered three wine goblets that were so fogged they must've never been washed. Fuentes opened the bottle and poured the wine.

"'Let me tell you about our secret mission so you don't get the wrong idea,' said the famous writer. 'As I'm sure you know, Cuba was formally asked by the United States to declare war on the Nazis because of the huge number of German submarines sinking American cargo ships off Cuba's northeastern coast, especially around Cayo Romano, which as you know is only a few miles north of Santa Rita Bay. Excluding the Gulf of Mexico, these U-boats have already sunk over one hundred vessels in this area alone.'

"'What is their main objective?' I asked at a loss.

"This time Fuentes answered. 'To destroy freighters entering and leaving the Panama Canal, crude oil tankers navigating the Strait of Florida, and cotton-filled barges cruising north of Cayo Romano.'

"Papa Hemingway intervened. 'Fuentes and I have volunteered to track down and possibly destroy these U-boats during the night.'

"Have you detected any?" I asked.

"'Not only detected,' exclaimed Fuentes. 'Two nights ago we spotted one surfacing under the full moon at 320 degrees, fifty yards off our port side. I stopped our engine to avoid detection, and as soon as we noticed a handful of sailors climbing to the turret, I turned *Pilar* towards the submarine's starboard beam at full throttle while Papa kept sweeping the enemy vessel with round after round of fifty-caliber bullets. To keep *Pilar* at a safe distance from the U-boat, I turned south toward Santa Rita Pass, and in a half-hour we were inside the Bay.'"

My mouth hung open. "And whatever happened to the sub?" I asked Pedro.

"According to Fuentes, the next morning local

fishing boats discovered a huge stream of diesel oil floating on the water."

"Does that mean they sank the submarine?" I asked eagerly.

"Either that, or the oil appeared by magic." Pedro smiled broadly. "Papa considered Santa Rita a safe haven and its transparent blue waters a fisherman's paradise. He usually brought back large tunas and groupers from his missions, and if he went to the Gulfstream, he often came back with a marlin weighing hundreds of pounds. According to those who knew him well, Papa loved fishing as much as fighting a war. But as it happened, most American locals were outraged at his using taxpayers' money to buy fuel, a portion of which was burned while fishing."

"Did you meet him again?" I asked.

"Only when his boat needed work, which was quite often," Pedro continued. "After our first encounter, Papa started calling me Santiago instead of Pedro because I reminded him of the main character in *The Old Man and the Sea*."

"Wow," I said. "Even then he saw the Old Man in you!"

Pedro grimaced, but nodded.

"How much longer did the Germans keep pillaging our waters?" I asked. "Longer than anticipated," Pedro replied. "A couple of years."

"What made them quit?"

"If you sit quietly and allow my memory to recall distant events, I'll be able to relate with absolute certainty the process by which our people helped kick the Nazis out of American waters."

Pedro gazed at the ceiling. "But first, let's digress momentarily to our century's first decade, World War One, and the mid-nineteen-thirties, when hordes of Europeans from different nations sought political asylum in North, Central, and South America to escape the horrors of warfare in Central Europe and the Spanish Civil War.

"Most refugees came to Cuba from Spain, Germany, and Poland. The Spaniards proliferated all over our nation, and Santa Rita was no exception. Speaking the same language and sharing similar cultural and religious backgrounds, they were easily assimilated in our society. Refugees speaking foreign languages usually established their own closed communities—a distinction that didn't last long because in the end, these exiles integrated themselves by their own free will."

I knit my brows with suspicion. "Where did the Germans settle in Santa Rita?"

"They formed a Bavarian community of about seventy families in Punta del Guincho, five miles east of La Gloria district. Their village was unique.

It had a small but effective infrastructure, its own beer-brewing facility, a church with an astronomical clock, a sausage factory, schools that taught Spanish during the morning, a firehouse, and a garbage collection system.

"These Germans ran errands to and from Santa Rita, and in their broken Spanish always got what they were after. Santa Ritans also visited their community during festivals to buy homebrewed beer, Black Forest ham, sauerkraut, and bakery items."

"But Pedro," I said, confused, "I'm fifteen years old and never heard of such a place—not from you, my parents, or anyone else. Does it still exist?"

Pedro lowered his face in deep disgust. "It isn't there anymore!"

"What happened? Did they learn Spanish and leave?"

"No such thing," Pedro replied. "Something atrocious came upon their village, but we'll discuss that in due time. Now it is important to take another detour and talk about the Spanish immigration."

"Why not continue with the submarines? Why are you switching so quickly from one unrelated story to the next?"

"They're not unrelated," Pedro warned, his face red as a pomegranate, "and if you make another pointless interruption I'll stop and continue another day!" Pedro massaged his brow and continued after a short pause.

"Most Spaniards started with absolutely nothing and through hard work and dedication ended up making money and owning their own businesses. Likewise, professionals such as doctors, teachers, nurses, and so on, made comfortable wages in their careers. Only lawyers found themselves trapped because our laws were different from those in Spain.

"As to our town, the most widely known immigrant was a humanitarian from Madrid whose personality, sense of compassion, and willingness to help the needy were so genuine, he actually opened a soup kitchen for the homeless, organized numerous fundraisers, donated substantially to our church, encouraged public participation in local politics, and within a short period of time had met almost every family in town. Furthermore, his memory was so vast he remembered the names and qualities of every man, woman, and child in Santa Rita. In short, he was looked upon as a genuine role model.

"Talented in various undertakings, the gifted immigrant worked as a telegraph operator for the railroad, a shorthand recorder for the courthouse, and since he was fluent in five languages including German, as an interpreter for local and international shipping companies.

"Since this unassuming chap attended social and political events, friends and admirers urged him to run for mayor, and to this end, prominent citizens circulated a petition to grant Spanish immigrants the right to participate in local elections and occupy public office.

"This individual didn't look like a politician, though. He must have been in his early fifties, but looked considerably older because of his bushy gray hair and wrinkled face. Curiously, the man lived alone in the upper-floor apartment of the telephone company building. He avoided the company of females and never invited anyone to his home, for according to this fellow his house was like a temple in which absolute silence and solitude must reign in order for him to transcend this world into another dimension and intermingle with spiritual beings from far and beyond without interruptions.

"And what did he mean by far and beyond?" I asked.

"Even though his so-called mystical practices sounded wacko, no one ever asked about his far-and-beyond concept or even guessed at the kind of cult he practiced under so much secrecy. Then again, since every individual had a constitutional right to practice his own religious rituals, no one ever paid much attention to his pious eccentricities. Sometimes he disappeared for days at a time, and when asked, he invariably replied: 'I was in the wilderness purifying my soul and doing penance for my sins.'"

"What was his name?" I asked in wonderment.

"The man's name was Don Francisco Fernandez y Fernandez, but since he despised the cacophonic mishmash, the mystical Spaniard asked everyone who crossed his path to simply call him Fritz, which is Francisco in German; no more and no less, he would say, just Fritz. In fact the entire town came to know him as El Amigo Fritz.

Pedro stretched and opened the window to check on the weather. It was still raining.

"I assume that by now, you'd like to return to the German village and the submarine issue, right?" he asked, turning back to me.

"Oh yes, sir. And this time I promise to hold back interruptions." I eyed Pedro to gauge his reaction.

"I'm proud that a sensible boy like you has finally learned to shut up and listen without disruptions."

This being said, Pedro shut the window, returned to his wobbly chair, and began to make sense of his unrelated stories.

"Failing to bring the U-boat attacks to an end, a frustrated U.S. Government donated a dozen submarine hunters to the Cuban navy and trained over fifty crewmen to run a covert operation. Months passed, the assaults continued, and only one German U-boat, the *Reiner Dierksen* U-176, was sunk by the Cuban patrol boat CS13. In spite of the tremendous effort to crush the Nazis' attacks, no further casualties were inflicted to the enemy besides the U-176."

"Where was Hemingway's navy in those days? Was he still active?"

"Evidently, Papa must have gotten tired of his self-appointed *custodian of the seas* mission. I saw him numerous times during the fall of 1942, but he didn't seem to care much about chasing U-boats anymore. You see, Papa got easily bored. He never stopped chasing dreams, new adventures, famous women, camaraderie, and most importantly, a place of total solitude where he could be by himself and write without misgivings. All I knew about Papa in those days was that in early 1943 he took the *Pilar* back to Havana to join his third wife and eleven cats in Finca Vigia—Sentinel Ranch— on the outskirts of the capital. Later on he left his wife and ranch and went to Africa.

"Meanwhile, President Roosevelt was so frustrated with what he called a *tropical malignancy*, he ordered the U.S. Ambassador in Havana to call our then-President Fulgencio Batista to tactfully request that all Germans, except women and children living on Cuba's northeastern coast, be immediately taken to a concentration camp in Isla de Pinos, an island south of Havana.

"Both countries validated such injustice based on intelligence received from different sources claiming that among these hard-working immigrants, some were spying for the enemy and providing food, fuel, and supplies for their submarines.

"Caving in to the Americans, Batista carried out Roosevelt's wishes without the slightest remorse. So in retaliation for what was done to his compatriots, Hitler increased the presence of submarines and the frequency of attacks in that specific area. Cayo Romano and its surrounding cays, so precious to local fishermen and paradise hunters in better times, became a mine field for all vessels, regardless of size, ownership, or flag registration."

"Gee, Pedro; what a terrible nightmare for those families in Punta de Guincho, don't you think?"

"You're absolutely right." Pedro's voice deepened. "That's why the German community eventually abandoned the entire area. All you can find these days are decaying homes covered in sand, and invaded by weeds, sea oats, and giant lizards reproducing at a fast clip.

"Shame and degradation followed these families everywhere, especially when American and Cuban intelligence openly suspected the loyalty of women and children as well. But the true abomination," Pedro intoned at the top of his voice, "is that our country continues to have a murderer like Batista as a head of state!"

"Shut up, Old Man!" I held him by the arm. "If any of his hooligans ever catch word of what you've just said, you'll be dragged to the torture chamber and executed by a firing squad in no time."

"Yeah, I guess I'd better shut up." Pedro sighed deeply, then continued.

"By mid-1943, one of the German hostages in Isla de Pinos wrote an anonymous letter in fluent Spanish to the Santa Rita Chief of Police." Pedro stood up, opened a cabinet door, rooted around for a few minutes, then produced a wrinkled newspaper clipping from that day.

"'Estimado Capitán Alvarez,'" he read:

"'Before we were arrested and falsely accused of espionage, I felt compelled to disclose one event that would have exonerated all of us from charges of treason, but fearing retaliation against my family, I waited patiently for the right moment to disclose the truth. Now that my wife and children live under the care of her Swiss uncle in Havana, I feel morally obligated to release for your examination the following evidence:'

"'One stormy night I took my fishing boat out, longing to return with a generous catch. But the seas were too rough and fish didn't bite, so at three in the morning I returned ashore, wet as a sponge. I pulled the boat to higher ground, and to protect myself against torrential rain, I leaned against one of many pilings supporting a house on stilts. At least it was warm and dry under my temporary roof, and if it weren't for the clicking sounds of a telegraph transmitter, I would have fallen asleep immediately.'

"'Expecting the worst, I crawled in silence toward the source of the noise until I got as close as twelve feet away. My jaw almost fell off when the man's kerosene lamp revealed the vivid image of El Amigo Fritz, transmitting and receiving information to and from the ocean. To ensure this wasn't a mirage or a product of my exhausted imagination, I returned to the same spot the following night, and the next.'

"'*Mi Capitán*, you don't know who I am or where my family is, yet I beg you to keep my letter a secret until the truth is publicly exposed. I hope you will take the necessary steps to ensure our entire German community is exonerated.'

"'It is indeed demeaning to keep innocent refugees in captivity just because they speak the enemy's tongue. We deserve to be released honorably and to receive adequate compensation and public apology from both the American and Cuban governments for impounding without cause a harmless and peaceful community on account of groundless suspicions for crimes they never committed.'

"'Please don't let this letter go to waste. This is our last and only hope for freedom and vindication. Apprehending this traitor and bringing him to justice will turn our nightmare into an honorable victory.'

"'Signed: A wounded heart in pursuit of justice.'"

Pedro shook his head sadly.

"Wow, Pedro, the story sounds more and more like a movie! What happened next?"

"The Chief of Police tracked El Amigo Fritz every night that he disappeared into the wilderness, 'searching for spiritual renewal.' Once two of his officers had witnessed and documented the crime, he requested a search warrant from the local judge to examine the home of El Amigo Fritz inside out for hard evidence of high treason. The police waited for El Amigo Fritz to return from one of his wilderness trips and presented him with the warrant.

"Inside his home, the authorities found so much clutter it looked like a bomb had gone off. El Amigo Fritz kept complete logs of every sunken vessel and the name of every crewman on board. They found transcripts written in German documenting the cargo, country of origin, destination, and each vessel's exact location. He also stored batteries, electric chargers, retractable high-power antennas, and a squelch maker to keep his transmissions impossible to decipher.

"The day our local newspaper and radio station obtained government permission to publish in its entirety this cowardly act of treason, Santa Rita's enraged population fell into a state of madness. A group of men carrying kerosene torches and chanting *death to the traitor* marched to set his home on fire. Cattlemen with loaded rifles climbed upon roofs and other strategic positions from which they hoped to spot and kill the traitor. In virtually no time, every able woman in town was out on the streets, banging on pots and pans and chanting vindictive slogans against El Amigo Fritz, who also used his jobs at shipping companies, the railroad, and the courthouse for easy access to sensitive information he would pass to the enemy at a convenient time.

"The military was summoned to prevent full-blown riots from exploding and to keep El Amigo Fritz safe for deportation. Shackled and handcuffed, the Spanish immigrant was taken out of his house in the middle of the night, under heavy guard, to stand trial in the United States. There he was found guilty of high treason and was sentenced to hang.

"Released from Isla de Pinos, the German exiles received a public apology and generous compensation from the U.S. Government to start a new life. Most families resettled away from Santa Rita, and the few who stayed refused to return to the ruins of their old community.

"Santa Rita's Chief of Police ran for mayor the following year and won by a landslide."

"Gee, Pedro, this must be the most exciting story you ever told." I shook his hand and gave him a hug. "But why haven't I heard it before, even from my parents? How could anyone forget or ignore an episode of such magnitude?"

"Because in a world in which new experiences occur every day, every hour, and every minute, people tend to disregard or forget the most distant events and evoke the very recent, regardless of magnitude. And so, as long as we keep turning a blind eye to important historical issues, humans will continue to suffer equal or worse consequences until the end of time—and this, my boy, has been humankind's most entrenched and devastating curse since the creation of History."

Pedro stroked his beard.

"Son, now that I have finished my dissertation, have you learned any lessons from it?"

"Of course I have. First of all, we should never paint a group of people with a single brush. All Germans are not evil; all Spaniards not good. Second, appearances can be deceiving. In my opinion, Fritz's story was too good to be true."

"Mmm, not too bad..." A smile flickered at the corner of Pedro's mouth.

SHARKS

Unless I had a reason to jump out of bed early, I usually slept until nine on Saturdays and Sundays. But one day Mom barged into my room screaming, "Wake up!" She shook my shoulder, waving the daily newspaper. "I have bad news."

"Bad news?" I asked, half asleep. "What bad news?"

"Your friend Alfredito was attacked by a shark yesterday afternoon."

I sat up, stunned. "Is he alive?"

"He is, by a miracle," Mom said, tossing me the newspaper. "By the time his friends pulled him out of the water, his left leg was mangled from waist to knee. He spent the night at the clinic in severe pain and it took seventy stitches to sew him up."

"What did the doctor say?" I asked, bolting upright.

"The doctor thought that the shark was unaccustomed to human flesh, so it tried to identify his prey in several places by biting him with those blade-sharp teeth before it locked his jaws on him."

My hands shook as I searched the paper, but I couldn't focus on the print. "How was he rescued?" I asked Mom.

"It's all right there," she said, tapping the front page. "His friends tossed him a rope, pulled Alfredito ashore, and asked a nearby lady for her scarf to use as a tourniquet. Their quick thinking probably saved his life. They called an ambulance, but by the time it arrived at the hospital, Alfredito was unconscious. He'd lost a lot of blood, so they had to give him a transfusion, and it took hours for the doctor and his nurse to stitch him up. Some of the gashes were very deep, so they are worried a severe infection could develop. Alfredito will be taking penicillin for a while to prevent that, but according to the doctor, his battle for survival is just beginning."

Mom ruffled my messy hair. "Thank God you're not as stupid as some of these kids. I'm so blessed to have a son who doesn't have to prove his machismo by jumping into shark-infested waters. I shall thank the Lord every single day for your wisdom and common sense!"

Mom's words humbled me to no end.

She doesn't know I'm part of that group and that I've been taking the same risks time after time to impress bystanders, especially girls. Oh, my God, how lucky I am! Thank you, thank you. I promise never to engage in such an idiotic undertaking again.

I decided to skip my morning shower, eat a quick breakfast, try to do some fishing, and by noon visit my buddy at the hospital.

Pedro once said that a fisherman should never be in a hurry and that patience is the heartbeat of the sport. I knew he was right and tried to follow his advice. But this time I biked to the wharf as fast as I could, ran all the way to the end, and sat at the edge. The morning was crisp, fishing boats were trolling out to sea, and around me a group of fishermen were chatting about Alfredito's near-death experience. Every time someone mentioned his name I felt like the dumbest, yet luckiest, creature on Earth.

I had just begun to notice that the gathering of gossipers looked rather unusual that morning when Pedro surprised me from behind, resting a hand on my shoulder.

"Everyone, please listen!"

My legs quivered. *What the hell is he up to now?*

"It is my privilege," the Old Man announced, "to introduce you to one of Santa Rita's most daring shark *provocateurs*." To my chagrin, he raised my hand into the air like a champion. "Gentlemen, please give this young man a round of applause."

"A shark provo...cat what?" A middle-aged Asian I hadn't seen addressed me directly. "Where in hell did you learn such a stupid profession? I can't even pronounce the word."

Pedro's audience roared with laughter.

"Look at my stump," the Chinaman said bitterly. "Do you care to know how I lost four fingers?" He jabbed his truncated hand at me.

Embarrassed, I nodded my assent.

"Years ago," he stated, "while a shark lay dead inside my boat, I was attempting to remove the hook from his throat by unraveling the lead wire inside his mouth when all of a sudden the beast clamped his jaws shut with such force I didn't see my fingers until we opened his belly. The dead creature chopped them off with the speed and dexterity of an executioner."

The man wagged his stump in front of my eyes. "So you listen to me carefully. If you'd rather die of old age, stop teasing these brutes unless you're after their meat to survive. As far as I know, this is the only creature on Earth that kills after being dead. Fooling around in their environment could be the last game you'll ever play."

Either impressed by Alfredito's accident or simply ashamed for standing like an idiot in front of these men, my breakfast of *café con leche* and cereal was already producing cramps.

After the Chinaman's admonition, Pedro piped in, "If anyone else wishes to address my young friend, please do so. I'm sure he'll listen."

I vaguely recognized a young man with a heavy, rather sullen face and a bush of yellow hair falling over his forehead. Disabled from the waist down, he spoke from his wheelchair.

"When I was about your age, I thrived on people's attention so much I performed acrobatic feats in areas frequented by girls. But every time I finished my demonstrations, onlookers simply laughed and walked away.

"One day, though, I decided to keep the audience in awe by stretching a tightrope from our third-floor balcony to the one across the alley, which was owned by my aunt. I would wait for the nearby school to release its female students, and when the area began to crowd up, a friend from below would signal me to proceed with my tightrope walk. I did it for several days without incident. The public went wild, applauding my idiocy and asking for autographs. My ego was about to explode.

"Word of my daring act spread, and the alley filled up with students and pedestrians every afternoon after school. But one day, a sudden gust of wind swept me off the rope. I fell hard on the cobblestone street, which damaged my spinal cord, and I haven't walked since.

"Bigheads like me rejoice in attention and admiration," the disabled man confessed with teary eyes, "and with every round of applause I felt a step closer to fame. Now look at me—a half-man condemned to a wheelchair for the rest of his life and one who must depend on public charity to survive.

"So listen to my words of wisdom, young man: Learn from the misfortunes of fools before you become one. Don't let vanity control your emotions, or adulation to nourish your self-esteem." He nodded modestly to the onlookers' applause.

As Pedro's puppet show continued, I began to feel nauseated. Noticing the pallor on my face the Old Man asked if I was feeling well.

"It's only nerves," I replied. "As I'm sure you know, graduation is coming up soon."

"Then we shall continue." Pedro gestured to a six-and-a-half-foot-tall mulatto from Martinique.

"Evaristo! Why don't you tell our friend about your daily encounters with sharks, and dangers of that sort?"

Proud, well educated, and strong-minded, Evaristo, also known as Evo, was considered Santa Rita's most daring and experienced seaman. To demonstrate he didn't have a scratch on his body arising from his profession, Evo always wore canvas shorts and nothing on top.

The impressive seaman stood up and spoke with a deep French accent.

"Among my various trades I am an underwater arc-welder who repairs the hulls and external components of large ships. Before I descend into the deep, I get into a diver's suit made of heavily rubberized canvas. It usually takes an hour to put on the *buzo* outfit, and two trusted assistants to help me in and out of it. This subaquatic suit has a heavy brass helmet that bolts into its neck, making the full attire waterproof. I can see my surroundings through a couple of glass openings and breathe through a long rubber hose that runs from the helmet to an air pump set on the vessel above.

"For quicker submersion, thirty-pound rubber boots with lead soles are bonded to the suit, and my belt has enough lead sinkers to hasten the descent even more. A derrick-driven chain lowers me down to a maximum depth of three hundred feet by a hook clasped on the helmet, and lifts me back up to the surface. I communicate by means of a rubber tube that will collapse under heavy pressure, so below one hundred feet I'm virtually on my own. In isolated cases the breathing pipe has been cut off by accidental twists or perforated by curious sharks and barracudas.

"In short, every time I dive, my life depends

on the chain, the breathing hose, and the dexterity of workers onboard the vessel. Always aware of the dangers, I usually descend alongside the ship with a basketful of tools and the arc welding equipment. Once the repair area is in sight, I begin my daily assignment, always keeping an eye on the surroundings, the chain, and the breathing hose. When I need to surface, I yank the chain three times to tell the derrick operator to pull me right up."

Pedro raised a hand. "Tell my friend how you keep the damn sharks away."

Evaristo nodded. "Schools of sharks usually surround or follow large cargo ships because they feed on the food and waste thrown overboard. When they approach me I simply hit them on the head with a hammer. This makes them mad as hell, but after a couple of blows the curious creature will leave me alone. As a matter of fact, missions have been cancelled because of their harassment."

Pedro turned around. "Are you still feeling okay, son?"

"Yes, sir, much better." I'd found Evaristo's account more fascinating than terrifying, which must have soothed my anxiety and stomach discomfort.

"Tell young Carlos about your other occupations," Pedro called.

Evaristo pointed to the sky. "Every time there's a

full moon, I jump on my seventeen-foot gas-powered *chalana* to hunt for sharks along with a friend. Once we have six or eight on board, we motor back ashore. Next morning we clean them up, sell their meat, salt and hang to dry what's left, and save the livers for a Chinaman to extract their oil, and the dorsal fins he'll peddle as aphrodisiacs.

"I also own a sixty-foot passenger boat in which I take tourists to La Boca Beach on weekends."

"As a man of multiple talents and skills," said Pedro, "do you mind sharing a few words of wisdom with my young pal?"

A slow, bashful smile moved over Evaristo's face.

"Son, I've been in the diving and shark-fishing business all my life, yet there isn't a single scratch on my entire body caused by a work-related injury. I am widely known as a cautious man, but my prescription for survival is much more demanding.

"For starters, let's recognize that every living creature starts taking risks at birth, yet those who spend their entire lives trying to avoid the unpredictable are, in my modest opinion, out of kilter with reality and fulfillment. I enjoy my different occupations in spite of their dangers because after years of experience, I have learned to apply discipline and common sense to handle my anxieties and fears, and to increase the probability of my safety.

"The similarities between a professional high-wire acrobat and me are that we're both trained to rid our minds of matters unrelated to the actions at hand. We use our years of experience to detect the unfolding of capricious circumstances that may weaken our survival skills." He spoke to the disabled would-be wire-walker. "For example, a professional high-wire performer would not be trying to impress girls, and would be alert for changes in the wind, yes?"

The young man in the wheelchair nodded ruefully.

"Likewise, I pursue my profession with total focus." He turned back to me.

"So, young man: Keep the law of probabilities always on your side. Educate your instincts to perceive situations that demand restraint, and after ensuring all your standards are in place, then proceed with caution. Never allow passion or sentimentality to interfere with these principles, and when in doubt, be very scrupulous about whose opinions you respect—and under no circumstances should you be intimidated or afraid to say *no*."

"Cheers, Evaristo! I didn't know you spoke Chinese so well," one of the men said jokingly.

Pedro rubbed his hands. "Thank you, Evaristo. Thank you, gentlemen. I'm sure our friend will choose to live a longer and healthier life after listening to your experiences and advice. I know he's upset at me for putting him on the spot, but I love this boy as if he were my own."

Once the small group returned to their respective fishing spots, Pedro looked me straight in the eye. "Thanks for sharing your shark encounters with me in the past," he said, "and let's hope Alfredito recovers."

I begged Pedro to refrain from spreading word to my parents, and upon his agreement I gave him a quick hug and left for the hospital to visit my friend.

Poor Alfredito. He looked as if a train had run him over. Sound asleep, half his body under an oxygen tent, lips displaying a yellowish hue, his injured leg bandaged from the knee up and suspended by a chain to reduce pressure and avoid further loss of blood, Alfredito also had intravenous tubes connected to both wrists, one with a blood transfusion and the other with some kind of medicinal water. His mom, dad, and little brother sat alongside the bed, eyes glued on my dearest buddy.

The room was packed with standing friends and relatives. I talked to Alfredito's parents and grandmother for a while, but since he was sedated and sound asleep, I only stayed for a few minutes. When I left the hospital, a haunting sense of loss and apprehension took me over for days.

But Alfredito recovered sooner than anticipated, and an itch to experience new adventures got into my head. This time, however, I was committed to choosing a safe but gratifying way to enjoy the great outdoors.

Ever since I'd met and listened to Evaristo's story, I'd been tempted to join one of his excursions to La Boca Beach. Evo spoke often of his determination to work with the environment, and use his brains instead of his passions, and his trips were widely known as safe; so I knew my folks wouldn't hesitate to stamp their seal of approval, which they did under two conditions: Go with a friend, and absolutely no diving in the channel.

In spite of my excitement, I couldn't wipe out a deep sense of culpability for lying to them about my idiotic shark encounters.

Three weeks later, my friend Felito and I met at the dock from which Evaristo's passenger boat was supposed to depart. It was Sunday, and the pier was packed with awaiting passengers carrying loads of beach umbrellas, chairs, snorkeling gear, insulated chests packed with ice and beverages, and every kind of beach paraphernalia known to God and man.

Evaristo's floating contraption measured sixty feet in length by twenty-five at the beam. It had fifteen rows of wooden benches securely tied to the floor, each extending from port to starboard and intersected by a central path that ran from bow to stern. This restricted passageway would be used by the captain, his two mates, and those visiting the aft head, labeled with a sign on the door. Opposite the head, and printed with the warning: *Engine Room, Do Not Lift,* a plywood plank two feet wide by five in length covered a floor access to the engine room and bilge compartment.

The entire vessel was sheltered from sun and rain by a large canvas top, held in place by numerous wooden rods secured to the rub rail throughout the boat's perimeter. Toward the bow and secured by frayed hemp ropes, four stacks of orange life jackets were ready for deployment. Evaristo sat on a tall barstool toward the front, and to its right a black console held the wheel, two throttles, one radio transmitter, and a multitude of switches. This was the first time I had seen a helm facing sideways instead of forward.

One thing I didn't like was the short distance between the water line and the rubbing rail near the center of the ship. Those who sat at the end of a bench could actually touch the water simply by extending their arms.

According to a written government warning posted on a wall, the vessel was authorized to carry a maximum of sixty passengers, and violations were subject to heavy fines, impoundment, and/or imprisonment. But after observing the number of people waiting to board, I knew for sure that someone would be counting heads before long.

As soon as Evaristo ordered his mates to start the boarding process, the single file of ostensibly civilized people suddenly became a pushing and shoving mob, trying to penetrate the vessel all at once. After the entire horde took their seats, Evaristo counted sixty-four heads, then asked the last four boarding passengers to please identify themselves.

At that, numerous passengers viciously pointed at a family of four as if accusing them of a crime. As it turned out, they had been the last ones to board because of difficulties handling Grandma's wheelchair. What's more, during the boarding melee I had witnessed numerous passengers pushing the disabled woman aside in order to board first. Then I saw a young family member moving the wheelchair to the end of the line to avoid a confrontation.

Except for a little girl crying her heart out in disappointment, the discouraged family left the vessel without resistance. Some older passengers were visibly upset at the sad scene, but most were so engrossed in having a good time they simply couldn't care less.

Evaristo began his routine by starting the noisy engine, then teaching all passengers the use of life jackets in case of emergency, clearly stating that such condition shall be announced only by the captain. He read the latest marine weather bulletin issued by the navy, calling for dangerous thunderstorms and the possibility of water spouts to develop shortly before sunset. Therefore he asked all passengers to be on board at least two hours before the scheduled departure time of five o'clock to avoid bad weather on the way back. All in all, we would have four full hours to enjoy ourselves at the beach.

To my surprise, no one complained about losing a couple of hours to save their skins; but Evo's calm, confident delivery left no room for argument. One of the mates collected the round-trip fare of five pesos per adult and two for children smaller than the length of a wooden stick he carried. Then, shortly after nine, a couple of hands from the pier heaved us the docking lines, and after a maneuver to turn the ship around, sixty cheerful folks were on their way to La Boca Beach.

While underway, Evaristo's boat seemed to handle two-and three-foot swells extremely well, and best of all, the worrisome distance between the water surface and the rubbing rail didn't change much during the voyage. Minutes before eleven we were tying up to a couple of neglected dock pilings at La Boca Beach.

On the opposite side of our derelict dock, a nervous captain was anxiously working on the engine of a much smaller passenger vessel. After elbowing and shoving each other, our disembarking passengers headed for the beach while Felito and I waited to ask our neighboring master if we could be of any help.

"Look, guys," replied the sooty man. "I have the ominous feeling that the engine blew a gasket on our way over."

"And what does that mean?" I asked a mate standing behind us.

"As far as I know," he replied, pointing at the scene, "the engine needs to be disassembled for repairs, and that can only be done in town."

"Why don't you call Evaristo to see what he can do?" Felito asked.

"That's a great idea!" The mate trotted over and disappeared inside our boat.

"Come on, man, let's go to the beach!" Felito pulled me by the arm. "After all, there's nothing you and I can do. Let Evo and his mates figure it out. We don't have much time."

As we strolled toward shore, I vividly recalled how La Boca had looked when I'd come with my parents ten years before. In spite of tropical storms, hurricanes, and tourists, everything seemed to have withstood the test of time—its numerous coconut palms and luscious bushes with wildflowers of different sizes and colors, the tame iguanas large and small pestering for food scraps, and the lack of storm shelters, fresh water, and latrines that isolated this idyllic spot as a forgotten paradise for swimmers and sun-worshippers alike. Peacefully and undisturbed, one could spend hours enjoying the white sand beach, so bright by midday, one's eyes could only view it halfway open.

A Robinson Crusoe sense of isolation permeated my spirit, despite the sixty-plus tourists energizing the area. Notwithstanding the amount of visitors calling on La Boca every year, one never found empty bottles, rotten food, paper plates, or any kind of trash buried in the sand or flying in the wind. Most visitors used their own boat facilities for relief, and those staying overnight brought their own portable potties.

"Stop worrying about the disabled boat and let's go swim with those cuties." Felito pointed to a group of girls chatting by the shore.

"And who said I'm worried?" I asked.

"If not, why are you so silent? Come on, man, let's go do some splashing!"

The scene was so tempting I ran after my friend all the way to the beach and splashed enough water not only to earn the girls' attention but their rage as well. They retaliated by splattering salt-water on our faces until our eyes turned red.

We met the six lively girls and had a great time swimming and horse-playing in the transparent turquoise waters of this unsullied side of our world in which sand felt like sugar and girls smelled of spice.

Time flew unnoticed, and by a quarter to three our mixed group was rushing to Evaristo's boat, where we found the eight passengers from the disabled boat occupying our benches. It transpired that the captain of the stranded vessel had begged Evaristo to take his passengers to Santa Rita, due to the dangerous low-pressure system advancing to our area.

Felito was furious. "If we're allowed to carry only sixty passengers, who the hell is staying?"

The girls pointed to him, laughing. "You are!"

"But I'm only one person. What if everyone stays?"

"I agree with Felito," said the prettiest one. "We should all spend the night here and have a party."

"And Father will kill you when he sees you return with a couple of guys," mocked her oldest sister.

Evaristo showed up, shaking his head.

"Not so fast, young people!" he warned. "Have you considered the consequences? You are young adults, and my responsibility as a captain begins when you board the vessel and ends when you disembark. If you decide to stay, that'll be your prerogative, but I shall forewarn you: If a water spout lifts any of you a hundred feet in the air and then drops you like a rock, it was your choice, your stupidity, and your funeral, not mine."

I puffed out my chest to challenge the Old Mariner. "But you'll be breaking the law by adding two thousand extra pounds. Aren't you afraid the police will confiscate your boat? And what if we all drown?"

"What about the family of four you left behind?" interrupted one of the girls. "Was that fair? And now you're willing to carry eight extra people?"

Evaristo nodded in frustration. "You're right, it wasn't fair. But the situation was totally different at the time."

No one joked anymore. The girls murmured among themselves while Felito and I realized the predicament Evaristo was in. Surreptitiously, I led Evo aside.

"Forgive me for asking again, but aren't you risking your livelihood, prestige, freedom, and perhaps the safety of those on board?"

Evaristo dabbed at his sweaty brow. "I am applying to the best of my knowledge what is commonly known as the Good Samaritan Marine Doctrine, and frankly, son, I can't think of another way out."

Turning on his heel, Evaristo addressed Felito and the girls. "There are a month-old baby, two toddlers with their parents, and three elderly relatives on board right now, and this, my friends, is the only reason I'm risking everything I have."

Felito opened his palms. "I think the captain is making sense. Don't you all agree?"

"Captain Evaristo." I addressed him emphatically. "Please count on Felito and me to help you out."

"What if we follow suit?" the oldest girl asked her pals, and a chorus of yeses ensued. "We eight will stay behind."

"But that could be dangerous too." I tapped my forehead. "Hey, people, I have an idea. Why don't we ask all passengers to leave their heavy gear behind? We'll ask the captain of the disabled boat to store the whole lot inside his vessel until we recover it in Santa Rita."

Evaristo patted my back. "You seem to learn very quickly. Are you using your instincts?"

"Damn right I am, sir. Under no circumstance would I leave families with small children on a deserted beach exposed to disastrous weather conditions—or anyone else for that matter."

The blue horizon had changed its colors to black and gray, and we heard thunder rumbling ten seconds following a lightning strike, so I figured the storm was only ten miles away and blowing in our direction.

No one smiled, joked, or complained anymore. Evaristo informed all passengers of the precarious situation we were facing and asked everyone to leave behind every possible item weighing over two pounds.

All passengers responded eagerly, and the girls, shivering because the temperature inside the boat was rapidly cooling off, volunteered to ask the stranded captain for help in safeguarding as many things as he could possibly fit on his boat. Glad to fulfill our request, he promised to cover with canvas every single item.

The rescued passengers were the first ones to give up their strollers, umbrellas, a playpen, and shoes to Felito and the girls. Everyone on board did the same except for an elderly woman who couldn't walk without her cane and orthopedic shoes. Felito and I moved an ice chest filled to the brim with bottled drinks, food, dry ice, and shells that must have weighed at least one hundred pounds. Then we hurried to transfer umbrellas, foldable chairs, baseball bats, balls, gloves, beach toys, and radios.

Evaristo looked so confident he seemed to shine with optimism. Once the six girls, Felito, and I finished ferrying items to the stranded vessel, he ordered both mates to yank the dock lines and prepare to cast off. The mariner bid farewell to the marooned captain, who didn't want to leave, then pushed the throttle to the engine's maximum capacity. The faithful motor chugged like a steam locomotive as our vessel cut through the choppy seas.

Still concerned with the short space between the rub rail and the water line, I measured the gap once again, and found it had shrunk four inches. When I told Felito, his face went ashen, and I began to worry about sinking. Meanwhile, after applying their energy and enthusiasm to lightening our load, the girls had failed to bring along their cover-ups, so they were shivering in their bikinis. Mercifully, Felito and I played macho men, handing them our shirts, while a group of young men followed suit with their towels.

* * *

As we advanced into deeper waters, the following seas grew in size. Ominous dark clouds were approaching our area at a fast clip, and the change in temperature and atmospheric pressure created by the impending thunderstorm increased the wind speed to thirty miles an hour according to Evaristo's anemometer.

As northerly winds grew in intensity, taller waves crashed against the stern, flooding the entire aft section up to the rubbing rail. Thanks to Evaristo's boatbuilding experience, the wooden deck had metal grills that allowed flooding waters to drain down to the engine compartment, where it was automatically expelled by the bilge pumps. To calm nervous passengers who feared the boat would go under, Evaristo reassured them that the pumps were powerful enough to eject huge amounts of water in seconds.

A half-hour passed, and the low pressure center was directly above our heads. Winds grew stronger, and huge swells lifted our transom high enough for our vessel to nosedive into the backside of passing waves. This perilous situation, known as pitching, could cause the bow to penetrate vertically into the water, sinking us in a matter of minutes.

Once Evaristo ordered his mates to start distributing life jackets, everyone on board became sick and panic-stricken. Some passengers were praying, and others got so wet and cold they shook like aspen leaves on a windy day. Many couldn't stop vomiting overboard, and most grew so pale and terrified they swore never to climb onboard a ship again.

Out of the six girls, one threw up so many times

she constantly complained of stomach cramps. A young wife sitting in front of us had hiccups so severe her husband tried all kinds of tricks and maneuvers to halt the persistent attack, to no avail. The babies shrieked and wailed. Besides feeling terribly cold, I was nearly paralyzed with fear that we might have to abandon ship.

It wasn't the storm or the thought of drowning as much as the prospect of blood-thirsty sharks. I didn't want to see a shark ever again, even in a painting.

To top it all, Evaristo knew that steering the boat to continue its present course was suicidal; yet he couldn't turn to port or starboard because the huge swells, now crashing against the transom, would roll against either side of the hull, eventually overturning our vessel. We seemed to have achieved a no-win situation.

Watching Evaristo maneuver the vessel with such aplomb under punishing conditions offered terrified passengers, including Felito and me, the crucial ray of hope that keeps potential casualties praying and making deals with a higher power. I lowered my head along with many, put my palms together, and closed my eyes.

Oh my God, please have mercy. If you're punishing me for lying to my parents, I promise to never do it again. And Holy Father, if you save me, I pledge to love and respect the ocean and its creatures for as long as I live, and also to go to church on Sundays rain or shine...Amen.

I lifted my head, crossed myself, and opened my eyes to discover that not everyone was in anguish. A group of six ladies perhaps in their seventies hadn't stopped chatting during the entire nightmare. They didn't seem to mind the looming possibility of sinking and drowning. As I observed them, I wondered if being old was what made people like Pedro, my grandparents, and these women, tolerant, resilient, and willing to accept their fate.

With all available options stacked against us, Evaristo ordered his most experienced mate to move the forward anchor aft, tie it to the Samson post located at the center of the transom with a twenty-foot-long rope, drop the anchor, and let it drag twenty feet below the surface. As intended by the master, the drag created by the anchor's heavy weight would lower the stern to an angle parallel to the horizon, preventing the bow from pitching and passengers from pulling out their hair.

The strategy worked. His vessel now under control, Evaristo notified us that Santa Rita's weather station had just issued an emergency warning for all captains to remain in port until the following day. The bulletin called for gale-force winds and ten-foot waves to reach offshore waters shortly past midnight.

By the time Evaristo received this information, our floating craft was handling the heavy seas considerably more safely. Felito, who seemed to dwell in another dimension, took all the commotion with a grain of salt. Virtually hypnotized by his wristwatch, he seemed to have prevented anxiety by announcing every five minutes how much time we had left before arriving at the Santa Rita docks. My friend followed this ritual until his watch got so wet it stopped functioning. I, on the other hand, didn't have to keep track of time to realize that—God willing—we'd be docking within an hour.

I was deeply impressed by Evaristo's nautical skills, and the wisdom and common sense he displayed throughout the odyssey. I'm sure no one ever doubted the competence of an Old Salt whose unique ways with the sea made him the most respected mariner in town. But that day Evaristo carved into my heart and mind memories of what survival really means. I knew I would always remember the mulatto from Martinique with gratitude and admiration.

It was almost dark when the church on the hill, El Gato Negro Hotel, Pedro's wharf, and the railroad station across from home became clearly visible. The rain continued, the sea had a light chop, and winds were light and variable when Evaristo blew the horn to announce his arrival at the same dock we had left that morning. I had never witnessed so much collective glee and relief as I did as the mates jumped to the dock to tie our boat to the pilings.

When the girls approached us to return our shirts, Felito and I, in a genuine gesture of camaraderie, embraced and kissed each one on the cheek, to which they graciously responded in kind.

Our scary experience over, Felito and I shook our hero's hand, bid him goodbye, and left with a smile on our faces, a song in our hearts, and in my case, three solemn promises to pull off. We went our separate ways with a hell of a story to tell, a higher degree of respect for the sea and its creatures, and a load of admiration for seamen who, like Evaristo, know how to survive the ravages of nature without losing their head, dignity, and above all their sense of duty and compassion.

At home that night, Mom and Dad listened enthralled to my story. Neither had worried at all about my safety because, as Mom said, "You are a thoughtful, sensible young man incapable of doing the same stupid things some of your friends do for bragging rights and recognition."

Dad also brought up Evaristo's immaculate reputation as a responsible and knowledgeable captain and asked me how I'd come to know the man so well, but the phone auspiciously rang before I had to invent another lie to cover up my previous ones about diving with sharks.

Not that I would ever do that again—I was cured!

GOOD FRIENDS

Dinner was over, the sun was about to plunge over the horizon, and the final episode of "Raffles, the Thief with Hands of Silk" was about to be aired by CMQ Radio. It was the first Sunday in June, and one week after graduation from school.

Even though Mother considered these programs deeply moronic, there were few things in life Father and I shared with more passion than the adventures of Raffles, the modern Robin Hood who stole from the rich and gave to the poor. Mother was about to snort in derision and leave the room before it began.

But before she turned her attention to loftier activities, she tapped my shoulder.

"I saw Pedro at the hardware store, and he asked me to deliver you a message. 'Come see me when the episode is over, I'll be reading in bed.'"

I nodded automatically. But my self-absorption could handle only three issues: Raffles' last episode; fishing the following morning; and selecting with my parents the four-year Escuela Superior—the equivalent to American high school—I would be attending in Havana two months down the road.

Dad and I planned to visit several well-regarded Escuelas Superiores that summer. My parents wanted me to attend a school that promoted discipline; devotion to God, family, and country; and high-quality of education. I only insisted on attending a school with a baseball team.

I couldn't wait to visit the capital and experience what some of my friends boasted so much about—the Coney Island Amusement Park and watching a baseball game at the Cerro Stadium. Instead, Dad announced that we would promenade the magnificent Paseo del Prado, a boulevard resembling the one by the same name in Madrid. Built by a French architect during the bloody governorship of Don Miguel Tacón in 1777, our Paseo, according to Dad, was and still is Latin America's most beautiful. The handsome paving of colored marble was lined by ancient oak trees, marble benches, and solid-bronze sculptures of lions, and it ran from La Punta Castle in the renowned Malecon Drive to Havana's Central Park, only a hop and a skip from the Capitol building.

Dad was also determined we would visit the Capitol building, built in 1929 to replicate the one in Washington, D.C. He simply couldn't wait to show me one of the world's largest indoor statues—a slender woman representing the republic. This monumental effigy was laminated in 24-karat gold, he said, and at her feet rested a 25-karat diamond symbolizing Cuba's kilometer zero.

I accepted all of Dad's ideas on the condition that he would take me to watch the movie Cinerama at the Teatro Radiocentro and a baseball game at the Cerro Stadium. But in the meantime, and in anticipation of so much excitement, I'd been neglecting my visits to old Pedro.

* * *

The Raffles program over, I barged into Mom's bedroom. She frowned at me with narrowed eyes.

"What took you so long?" she asked. "For a moment I thought you didn't care about the Old Man anymore."

I shrugged. "Why do you say that?"

"Pedro said you hardly visit him anymore and that your graduation present is collecting dust."

"But Mom, what does he expect? He knows I've been busy with finals. I've also told him a million times not to spend money on me, and now he has a graduation present that I'm sure is another book."

"Don't give me that, son. You haven't stopped by the wharf in at least a month. Pedro is a caring old man who deserves better treatment, and I wonder if he's offended for not being invited to the graduation ceremony."

"Are you kidding?" I asked, arms crossed over my chest. "Pedro hates crowds, parties, and small talk, and he's saving his only suit for the day of his funeral."

Mom grabbed my arm. "You can't be serious."

"I am. He told me so."

"I'll tell you what." She pointed at Dad's closet. "Your father has a couple of outdated suits, shirts, ties, and even shoes Pedro is welcome to have. I feel so sorry for the poor man."

"But he won't accept them."

"Why not?" Mother asked.

"Because if he only dies once, why would he need additional suits?"

Mother rolled her eyes. "At times I wonder if it's mutual dementia that has kept the two of you together."

"We're not crazy," I replied sharply, "and stop feeling sorry for him. Pedro is too old to change his habits, and he's happy the way he is."

Mother gripped my hand. "Son, always bear in mind that older people are very sensitive to rejection. You two have shared a unique friendship for years, and it would be very cruel to drop him like a garbage bag."

I flushed with anger. "Why is it that you and Dad are always sermonizing at me? I'm sick and tired of the constant nagging. I'm a mature young man who is smart enough to act like an adult. Now please let go of my hand. I want to go to bed."

Mom released me, shaking her head briskly. "You've been very rude."

I lowered my eyes. "Okay, Mother, I'm sorry for losing my cool, but you and Dad are constantly haranguing me, and I can't take it anymore. If I'm old enough to attend a Havana boarding school, I should be old enough to know right from wrong."

Mom tapped her left cheek.

"Give me a goodnight kiss and promise me you'll treat Pedro with the dignity and compassion he deserves."

"I'll treat him the way I always have." I pecked her cheek.

"And tomorrow try not to be so sassy," she added. "I wonder if hormones and graduation have gone to your head."

* * *

The next morning I woke up at the crack of dawn, bought enough bait to fish till noon, and headed for the wharf.

"Buenos dias, Viejo." I threw my arm around the Old Man's shoulders. "Mom said you're upset with me. What have I said or done wrong?"

"Absolutely nothing," the Old Man said, his lips pursed in a pout.

"Come on, Pedro, stop playing games. I can see all over your face that something is bothering you."

Pedro scratched his hat. "To tell you the truth, it hurts me to think that I mean nothing to you anymore. I know you've been busy with finals, practicing for the graduation ceremony, and preparing to leave for boarding school in a couple of months—one of your life's most important moves. But if it wasn't for an accidental encounter with your mother, I'd be finding out from the grapevine that you'll be leaving Santa Rita. Perhaps you're too young to appreciate it, but when an old man is ignored by his loved ones, it causes him desolation and an unbearable void."

I cringed with guilt. "I'm sorry, Pedro. I honestly didn't mean to hurt you."

The Old Salt lowered his head. "I'll be okay, as long as you understand that feeling neglected is one of the worst torments affecting old people."

Why is he so demanding? If I don't lay guilt on my friends for leaving town without telling me, why is Pedro playing that game? Geez, what's wrong with the older generation these days?

"Sorry, Pedro," I said sheepishly. "I'll make sure it doesn't happen again."

"Did your mother say I have a graduation present for you?"

"Yes, she did. But I've asked you not to spend—"

"I know what you've asked," Pedro interrupted, "but my gift is a cheap survival kit that will last the rest of your life."

I frowned in puzzlement. "And why would I need such a thing?"

Pedro looked me straight in the eye. "It'll enable you to survive human nature and the decaying world in which we live. You're smart enough to value its message, and it will be your finest gift next to having Verónica by your side."

"Verónica by my side?" I kicked at the wharf gloomily. "I fantasize about that girl almost every day."

"I know you do, and I damn well know why." Pedro tossed a cigar butt out to sea. "Did you know that Verónica recently came to visit her parents and that she was grounded for refusing to follow her father's orders?"

I gaped at him. "But how did you know, and why didn't you tell me?"

"I accidentally saw her at the train station the day she returned to Havana, and the reason I didn't tell you was because you quit coming to the wharf."

Oh. I could have kicked myself. "Did you talk to her?"

"Not much," Pedro said, stroking his unkempt beard. "Just a simple greeting and a short exchange."

"Did she mention me at all?"

"Of course she did. And her home detention was because she wanted to see you."

I missed seeing Verónica! I thought in despair. "Please, tell me more," I begged Pedro.

"Oh, for heaven's sake, son; forget Verónica for a moment and let's concentrate on your graduation present."

I feigned a smile. "Yes...yes, of course, I'm also anxious to see my survival kit."

Pedro rubbed his hands. "Mmm...I'm sure as hell you are."

The Old Salt took me to his well-appointed quarters, kicked open the makeshift door, and from the top of his termite-burdened desk, grasped a tastefully wrapped rectangular box and handed it to me.

"Have you ever read the eight stanzas of Rudyard Kipling's poem 'If'?"

"All I've read by Kipling was *Kim,* and I was so excited by the boy's adventures, I still want to visit India someday."

"Then what are you waiting for?" Pedro demanded.

"To go to India?" I asked in disbelief.

"No, silly, to rip off the damned wrapping paper!"

Ill at ease, I yanked off the draping ribbon, the colorful wrapper, and opened the box. It held a single sheet of yellowing parchment.

"What you see," Pedro said grandly, "is Britain's most beloved poem, handwritten on papyrus paper with black India ink and in freestyle calligraphy by your old friend Pedro."

I swallowed, my mouth suddenly dry. "Gee, man, this is absolutely phenomenal. My God, look at the contrast between the deep-black lettering and the yellowish paper."

"It is not yellow paper, son, it is papyrus...same as the kind used by ancient Egyptians."

"But when did you go to Egypt?" I asked with wide-open eyes.

"I didn't have to," Pedro replied. "I purchased it from a sailor who came on a ship under that country's flag."

"It must have taken you days to finish such a stunning piece of work," I murmured, deeply moved.

"It did! And I want you to memorize the entire poem, which is the essential survival kit."

I met his eyes. "Don't worry, Pedro. I'll do exactly that. But tell me; which one is your favorite verse?"

"They all are," Pedro replied. "But the one you

should first learn by heart is the one I'm about to read. He cleared his throat and recited from memory:

> *"If you can dream—and not make dream your master,*
> *If you can think—and not make thoughts your aim,*
> *If you can meet with triumph and disaster*
> *And treat those two impostors just the same."*

I nodded, bemused. "Mmm...and why should it be the first one to be memorized?"

"Because it shows the importance of dealing with reality and keeping a level head in unusual times."

"Thank you, Pedro." Setting the poem aside, I gave my Old Friend a bear hug. "I will hang it on my bedroom wall...wherever I am, and as long as I live."

The time to leave for Havana with my Dad finally arrived. I had never visited the capital, and traveling with him would make a big difference, for he knew the city like the palm of his hand.

Prior to departure, Father had set up interviews with the principals of six private boarding schools, including a Methodist institution he had attended as a teenager; a widely known Jesuit school for boys; a secular one that admitted boys and girls; and the government-subsidized *Instituto de La Habana*—an excellent school that didn't offer boarding. Dad wasn't too keen on the latter because of student involvement in politics and because I'd have to live in a boarding house. Our trip was supposed to last a week, with two daily interviews and enough free time to visit the highlights of our beautiful capital.

The evening before our departure Mom took charge of my luggage. She began by digging from a pile of odds and ends the pigskin suitcase her mother had brought along every time she came to visit. The bag was so heavy the old woman had finally left it with us and bought a much lighter one made of pressed cardboard.

Mom laid the pigskin crate on my bed and filled it with four neckties, two suits, four pairs of shoes including a new set of Keds, a two-week underwear supply, books, a rosary to pray at night, my own water cup, a bath towel to keep the hotel's germs away, a flask of cod liver oil, and the largest tablespoon ever designed to pour the nauseating solution into my mouth every morning before breakfast. Mother packed the old pigskin bag so full Dad adamantly refused to take it, but by the time he realized its tonnage, we were already at the station, too late to remove some of the contents.

Wishing us well from the depot were my mother and our older neighbor, America. Mom had teary eyes and America held her by the shoulders, trying to convince her that all things happen for good reason.

The conductor blew his whistle, called on all passengers to board, and in less than a minute we were waving at our two well-wishers until they vanished behind a cloud of black smoke.

In two hours our train was scheduled to arrive in the historic city of Camaguey, where we would transfer to a larger one pulled by a diesel locomotive. Dad had already reserved a private compartment in one of three Pullman coaches, to spend in luxury and comfort the overnight twelve-hour trip to Havana.

"Are you looking forward to new experiences?" he asked.

"This time I am, because you're with me," I asserted. "But it won't be the same when I leave on my own."

"I understand." Dad laid his hand on mine.

"If you weren't making a decent living in Santa Rita, would you move to Havana?" I asked.

"In a heartbeat!" Dad nodded decisively. "Havana is one of Latin America's most modern and beautiful cities, and it has such an efficient transportation system, including private taxis, that you don't need to own a car to move around."

"Are you saying there are few cars in Havana?"

Dad shook his head. "On the contrary, most

citizens own American-made automobiles. The very rich have chauffeurs, the middle class drive their own, and the less fortunate have *cacharros*—older vehicles that resurrect after tinkering."

"Are there many places to eat?" I asked.

"Thousands! From the luxurious to the down-to-earth."

"And what about cinemas?"

"In Havana alone, well over fifty theaters are showing American movies at the same time as our neighbors to the north."

Swaying to the fickle rhythm of noisy tracks, the conductor stopped right by our seat. "Tickets, *por favor*!" he said, opening his palm.

Dad pulled two vouchers from his shirt pocket and handed them to the man in blue uniform.

"I see you're taking the boy to Havana," the conductor said. "Make sure you take him to the Grand Prix on Sunday afternoon. The Argentinian champion Juan Manuel Fangio will be competing against world-renowned racers, and it'll be a most exciting Formula One event. I'm sure you guys will have a great time."

But while the swinging conductor kept chatting about things to do in the big city, Dad's eyes were slowly shutting down, so I waited for a more suitable time to plead.

"Make sure he takes you." The conductor addressed me while trying to keep his balance.

Afterwards, another conductor showed up with apples and *empanadas* for sale. I bought two luscious red apples, one for Dad upon awakening and the other to nibble on while fantasizing about the big city.

Though unusual, the Santa Rita train arrived at the Camaguey depot half an hour ahead of schedule. I tapped Dad's forehead. "You slept during the entire trip. Are you all right?"

"Of course I am." Father removed his glasses. "Once the train started to sway and the tracks to squeak I couldn't stay awake—it's like being rocked in a cradle."

"Were you awake when the conductor mentioned the Formula One race?"

"Only halfway, but I knew all about it. Fangio will be racing a Mercedes SLR Formula One, and you'll be watching the event from a bench at the Paseo del Prado."

My heart leapt with joy. "Are you kidding me?"

"No, I'm not," answered Dad with a grin. "Your mother and I want you to have the most enjoyable vacation possible before you leave home in September."

"Wow, Dad, that's so nice of you and Mom...but you know something? I'm going to miss the two of you and my life in Santa Rita very much."

"We will write to each other," Dad said, dropping his voice, "and if I go to Havana on business I promise to take Mom along. Also, you'll be back for Christmas, so just try to look forward to the journey and the great opportunities at hand."

After a light snack at the Camaguey train station, we boarded the twenty-car train to the capital. Holding our two bags, a tall man in a starchy white coat, black pants, and shiny black shoes escorted us to the coach *Estrella de Oriente*. We climbed the steep stairs at the end of the car, turned right, and walked through a narrow hall to compartment number five. The courteous steward opened the door to let us in, and after setting our luggage on a narrow stand—huffing a bit with my crate—he demonstrated how to operate the toilet, the shower, and in case we wished to bathe while underway, the uniformed man drew our attention to a thick set of white towels lying on a metal shelf. Lastly, to satisfy my curiosity, he lowered the upper berth so I could feel the scented linen sheets and the goose-down pillow.

"When you choose to retire for the night," he told Dad, "just push this white button, and I'll be over to transform this compartment into a comfortable bedchamber. In the event you need ice, toiletries, or simple medications such as aspirin or Alka-Seltzer, please don't hesitate to ask. My station is at the end of the car, and I'll be up all night.

"Supper will be served in the dining coach as soon as we depart, and breakfast will be ready tomorrow morning at six. Our train will be arriving at the Havana terminal at exactly nine o'clock, and for those wishing to sleep a little longer, I'll be knocking on all doors at seven."

"What about dinner tonight?" I asked Dad.

"You just ate a bunch of snacks, son, remember?"

"Please forgive my intrusion, sir, but if the gentleman and his son wish to enjoy dessert instead of a full meal, our onboard chef has prepared delicious apple pies and homemade ice cream for this evening."

The obliging steward receded to the doorsill, and with starched correctness, stepped out of our room and closed the door.

Wow! Wait till I tell Pedro.

Our chamber was mostly lined with precious woods so polished they resembled mirrors. Impressed by its lavish appointments, I tinkered with every button and opened every drawer to satisfy my nosiness as to their purpose.

That evening Dad took me to the dining car, but it was full. The maître d' suggested we join other waiting guests in the connecting coach to wait for the next available table. That coach had a full bar with two bartenders and four waiters taking drink orders, while a young woman played Cuban and American tunes on the shortest grand piano ever imagined.

Dad spoke in my ear. "Since they couldn't fit a real grand through the door, they sawed one in half to make it work."

"You must be kidding." I paused. "Are you?"

"Of course I am, you silly goat," he said, ruffling my hair.

A bar waiter approached us for drinks, and I ordered a Cuba Libre and Dad a Guinness stout. Being the first time I'd ordered liquor from a bar, my undeveloped macho image blossomed like a thriving weed.

When the loudspeaker announced that our dining table was ready, we stood up and left our drinks for fear we might accidentally spill one on some elegant lady while swaying our way into the dining car. Draped in white linen, our designated table had enough silverware for a four-course dinner, although we only ordered two pies a-la-mode and a glass of milk for me.

Back at our sleeper we found both berths perfectly made. I begged to sleep in the top one, but Dad refused because he claimed I'd be rolling over in my sleep after so much excitement and could fall. So Dad crawled to the upper berth, and in minutes he was snorting.

In the meantime I was so agitated in my lower cubbyhole I turned on the reading light and focused on a magazine article expressing indignation at the police for brutally crushing a university student's protest the day before.

Dad was right about instability in government escuelas superiores. Perhaps I can convince him to skip that interview and have some fun together instead.

I marked the page, turned off the light, and after sheep number twenty, I was in another dimension.

As promised, our steward was knocking on every door at seven in the morning. "Buenos dias! La Habana en dos horas."

The train had slowed down considerably, and through a gap in the window curtain I read the outdoor sign: *Bienvenidos a Jaruco.*

Running parallel to our tracks, a paved narrow road burst with cyclists, automobiles, trailer trucks, and a myriad of oxen-drawn carts loaded with sugar cane heading to the nearest sugar mill. The early morning mist veiled the shrubbery along the track with pearly droplets of dew. Everything in town looked spotless, with colors so bright they seemed as though the entire city of Jaruco had been hosed down during the night.

Each time we approached an intersection, the powerful engine blew its horn loud and long, and while the clanging bells and flashing red lights alerted vehicles and pedestrians of its impending passage, the traditional wooden gate kept the absentminded at bay and the curious waving eagerly at the Havana Express. The entire town must have set their alarm clocks early that morning to greet the fireman and the engineer—superhuman celebrities who moved a roaring locomotive, hauling millions of pounds with the touch of a button.

Unlike Santa Rita, royal palms grew everywhere in Jaruco. For some reason God had been more generous in shading Jaruco from the sun than he was to my hometown. To our right was the legendary park where hundreds of men from Jaruco and neighboring towns congregated to play dominoes on Saturdays and Sundays. According to Dad, there were four players to a table. The competition began early in the morning and continued until the last surviving contestant was declared winner of all entry fees of one peso per player.

The train gradually slowed its pace until it passed the Estacion de Trenes sign. There it came to a complete stop to gather a small group of passengers. By then I was so focused on early morning Jaruco that the hissing sound of air brakes jolted me out of bed as a timely reminder that time was running short.

Dad entered our compartment all dressed up.

"I was in the dining car having café con leche and reading the morning paper when I realized it was time for you to wake up, brush your teeth, take a shower, and eat your breakfast. By the way, did you see Domino Park?"

"Of course I did, and I wondered if we should be playing dominoes instead of calling on the government school."

"We're not going to Havana to play dominoes, and you still need to pack and get dressed. I want you to see the outskirts of the city before we arrive at the terminal, so hurry up!"

I took off my pajamas and underwear, and as the Pullman slowly left the Jaruco station I grabbed one of the luscious white towels, entered the minuscule bathroom, and experienced my first thrilling encounter with a warm water shower in a moving train.

I had never imagined what "heavy traffic" meant until we crossed the big city boundaries during morning rush hour. Buses, streetcars, bicycles, automobiles, trucks, trailer trucks, and careless jaywalkers whose inanity compelled our engineer to relentlessly sound the horn, opened my wits to Havana's hustle and bustle.

Pedestrians rarely obeyed traffic lights, and the right-of-way went to whoever honked the horn first. Buses never came to a full stop when the only boarding passenger was a man. The driver simply slowed down enough for him to grab a handle and jump into the moving vehicle. Dad said the method was a tradition and that he'd never heard of an accident resulting from it.

"It's a macho thing, son," he said chuckling. "Also, men are expected to offer their seats to women and the elderly when buses and tramways are full."

"What if I don't want to?" I asked.

"The dirty looks you'll get from nearby passengers will shame you into it," Dad answered.

Santa Rita only had three buses, and I rarely saw standing passengers. Yet in Havana I saw buses sometimes with five passengers standing in the entryway and holding onto each other for their lives, and when someone sitting on the bus reached their stop, men standing on the access ramp got off the vehicle to let that person out. Amazingly, everyone returned to their previous spots without complaining, pushing, or conniving.

The train passed by a park jammed with cart

vendors selling everything from fruits and vegetables to baked goods, café con leche, newspapers, magazines, and all kinds of trappings. Blending with the hustle and bustle, nicely dressed men and women fast-walked their way to work, while boys and girls dressed in neatly ironed uniforms snaked their way to school or to board their respective school buses at a predetermined stop.

On a spot adjacent to a hydrant, a number of laborers jack-hammered into the asphalt to stop an underground leak, and lottery ticket vendors sprang from every corner, yelling at the top of their lungs the five-digit ticket numbers available for sale.

I reflected that Santa Rita's vehicles always came to a complete stop to allow pedestrians cross the street, a pothole took an act of God to be repaired, and the townspeoples' favorite pastime was visiting friends or playing dominoes. But in the big city, clocks seemed to tick at a faster pace, and pedestrians, like ants, accomplished their different endeavors by speed-walking in all directions and bumping into each other.

It took the train a good half hour to steer clear of the fuss before ascending to *los elevados*—tracks raised fifty feet above the ground that allowed trains to circumvent the booming pace of Old Havana.

I turned to Dad. "Can you look out without getting dizzy?"

"Yes, of course, why do you ask?"

"It feels like the train is traveling on a tightrope, and it's giving me butterflies in my stomach."

Dad burst out laughing. "It won't last long, I promise. In only ten minutes we'll be arriving at the terminal.

A standing line of uniformed porters awaited debarking passengers in the train-yard. "May I transfer your luggage to the main station?" one of them asked.

"*Si, por favor,*" Dad replied. "Please take our bags to the rotunda, and we'll take over from there."

As we followed the uniformed man, another train on the track parallel to ours began to load passengers traveling to Santiago. This train was scheduled to arrive in Camaguey shortly before midnight, and it didn't have sleeper coaches. Dad pointed out that our return trip would be overnight by bus to Camaguey and by train to Santa Rita the following morning. It was much cheaper, four hours faster, and it was the route I'd be taking when traveling alone.

"Come on, son." Dad quickened his pace. "Hurry up so we can catch a cab to the hotel."

Looks like the hurry-up-and-wait attitude is contagious around here.

"What's the rush?" I asked.

"There's none," Dad answered. "You simply need to move with the flow."

"Carlos! Carlos! Please wait! It's me!" A young woman shouted from behind me.

As I turned on my heels at the sound of the familiar voice, an ecstatic smile broke over my face.

"It's Verónica, Dad!"

Out of breath, face wet with perspiration, Verónica stopped in front of us and with a delighted laugh, bounced up on her toes, clamped her arms around my neck, and gave me a loud smack of a kiss. Her steamy body was such a pleasure to press against that I almost melted at my knees.

"This was all Pedro's idea," she told me with a grin. "The Old Man wanted to surprise you, so here I am!"

I pulled a fragrant handkerchief from my back pocket and handed it to her.

"Thank you, Carlos." She dabbed at her face and neck. "It is so steamy this morning."

"Wow, girl, this is what I call a terrific surprise. Have you ever met my dad?"

"I don't think so." She extended her hand. "*Mucho gusto,* señor Carlos. My name is Verónica, and I'm a close friend of your son."

Dad took her hand in kind. "It's a pleasure to

meet you, young lady. I've heard so many good things about you!"

"Thank you, Señor Carlos," Verónica replied, sounding a bit nervous. "The Old Man from the wharf mailed me a note saying that you and your son would be arriving on today's train, and since my cousin Marcos is off on Sundays, he offered me a ride—and so...welcome to Havana."

My heartthrob wore a vibrant mint-green sleeveless dress with a pink and purple floral pattern that conveyed a perfect blend of serenity and elegance. From the unusual light-peach looped collar to the carefree cutout in the back, her perfectly fitted dress and purple sandals matched her colorful personality, and her long ponytail added a touch of innocent mischief. Verónica wasn't a seventh grader anymore, but a lovely woman in the prime of her youth.

"I'm so glad to see you, Verónica." I sighed ardently. "You're beautiful as ever."

"Thank you, Carlos," she said shyly.

"What about me, do I look any different?"

Poking a finger to my chest, Verónica drove me back a couple of feet. "Mmm...let me take a good look at you. I can see that your biceps are bigger, your beard has been shaved, and your voice is much deeper."

Dad cleared his throat. "Please excuse me, but

the porter seems to have vanished with our luggage. What if I go after him and the three of us meet at the rotunda in about ten or fifteen minutes. Would that be okay?"

"That will be fine, Señor Carlos," said Verónica. "I know where the rotunda is."

Dad vanished, and my self-consciousness faded away with him.

"You told me your dad's name is also Carlos; was it okay for me to call him Señor Carlos?"

"Of course it was."

"Then how should I call you?" she asked with a coquettish grin.

"You can call me Carlitos when Dad's around, or for that matter anything you want."

"Have you missed me?" Verónica's voice quivered with emotion. "I can't wait for you to move to Havana."

With only ten minutes left of relative privacy, I grabbed her by the waist and instinctively kissed her lips—a demonstration of love that lasted only two seconds because of the crowds rushing to board the train to Santiago.

"I fantasized about you every day," I said, musing over her chocolate eyes. "Not that Santa Rita has many options, but of all the girls I've met, none has touched the memory of you. Of course, my parents think I'm too fresh and inexperienced to take a young love seriously, and Mother considers me nuts for falling in love with a Jewish girl."

Verónica shrugged. "I can't blame your parents for thinking that way. I also realize we're too young to take matters of the heart seriously, but what if we can't help it? Even if you and your parents may disagree on that issue, they will support you in the long run. But in my family, dating a Catholic boy is considered evil and a powerful reason for disownment."

I seized Verónica's moist hands.

"Do you know that when I lie in bed at night I find myself staring at the ceiling?"

"And why is that?" Verónica squeezed my hand in anticipation.

"Because it is so arousing to see you with the eyes of my heart, that I simply lie there until I fall asleep thinking of you. Plus our decision to remain incommunicado in your absence has intensified my affection by leaps and bounds."

Verónica stood on her toes and kissed me on the cheek.

"My aunt thinks that forbidden love is like a friendship set on fire," she whispered in my ear.

"That's a neat way of putting it."

"She also said that quenching the spiritual fire between two lovers might lead to a life full of ashes."

"She sounds like a very sensitive woman." I took a deep breath.

"What I'm trying to say," Verónica stepped back, "is that we should savor the present instead of worrying about the future, so let's hurry and catch up with your dad before he comes looking for us."

Damn it, she's also in a rush! Why can't we talk for the next ten minutes and still meet Dad in about fifteen?

* * *

At the rotunda, Verónica's cousin Marcos introduced himself to Dad and me, while Verónica presented us as Señor Carlos and Carlitos, which to me sounded more like an introduction of cartoon characters.

Short of stature and in his early thirties, Marcos had dark eyes under heavy eyebrows, a smooth square forehead, no beard, a small brown mustache, an obvious nose, and a well-shaped round chin.

"You must be Aunt Sarah's son, right?" I asked him.

"Yes, and the only family member besides Verónica and my mother who, in spite of being more Jewish than Moses, disagree with the archaic notion that Jews should only marry their own."

Dad looked as taken aback as I felt at this pronouncement.

"I hope you and Carlitos have some free time to visit us," Marcos told Dad. "Mother will be enthralled. And Verónica speaks of your son so often, we feel we already know him."

"We will do our best, right, son?"

"Of course, Dad, I'm all for it."

"I'll tell you what." Dad glanced at me. "After reading the article in your magazine, I decided to cancel our visit to the government institution. Mother and I would hate to see you involved in filthy politics, and this will leave us plenty of time to meet Marcos's mother."

I'm beginning to like Havana. After all, who cares about how fast people live?

With the thoughtfulness of a well-bred man, Marcos offered us a ride in his Chevrolet station wagon to our hotel in the Vedado District—a forty-five-minute ride from the train station and fifteen from Marcos's home in Miramar. Our luggage stacked in the rear, Verónica and I holding hands in the passengers' seat, and Marcos and Dad up front, we left the attractively decorated Estación de Ferrocarriles for the Hotel Presidente.

"Do you travel to Santa Rita at all?" Dad asked Marcos.

"To tell you the truth, Señor Carlos, I don't get along with Verónica's father. When she was much younger, Mother and I visited them several times a year, and we always returned in anger and frustration because of Benny's conceit and Olga's intolerance. Under the circumstances, and to maintain family ties without aggravation, we presented them a good excuse to quit driving to Santa Rita.

"In the meantime we begged them to let Verónica spend most of her summer vacation with us. Benny and Olga didn't mind because it would offer Verónica an excellent opportunity to expand her horizons and cultural literacy in our historic yet modern city."

Dad turned to Verónica. "Forgive me if I am prying; but has your dad always been so difficult?"

"To be honest, Señor Carlos, he's gotten much worse with time."

"Years ago Benny wasn't the arrogant slave driver he now is," added Marcos. "Something must have poisoned this man's soul. Now Olga and his two mastiffs are the only creatures who can live under the same roof with him."

Marcos glanced at Verónica and me in the rearview mirror, then turned to Dad. "Allow me to speak frankly, Señor Carlos. Mother and I love Verónica as daughter and sister, so knowing she would be attending school in Havana, and aware of the abuse and humiliation she's endured during the last few years, we've invited her to stay with us instead of a boarding school."

"And how do you feel about that?" Dad asked Verónica.

"I will never repay them for their generosity. I miss the days when our entire family gathered in Santa Rita or here in the capital, but like Marcos said, my father has changed into sort of an ogre, and Mother, who has no backbone, tolerates his tantrums and degradations." Verónica knit her brows. "Please understand, Señor Carlos, he has no right to destroy my life. It was becoming dangerous for me to stay there."

"I am so sorry, Verónica." Dad shook his head in disbelief. "But you're absolutely right; your father has no right to ruin your life."

Dad turned to Marcos. "Forgive my intrusion, but were Verónica's views on dating and marriage what fueled her father's rage?"

"Frankly, Señor Carlos, only God and Benny could answer that. But when Verónica first challenged her father's convictions, he grew vicious. He beat her, screaming and raging. You may not believe it, but she was threatened with house imprisonment unless she agreed to follow his beliefs."

My jaw dropped in shock, hardly able to bear the thought of her suffering.

"Why is Olga so submissive?" I asked.

"She is afraid of her husband's tantrums, I guess," answered Marcos, "so she simply ignores his cruelty. That's why Mother and I decided that the only member of that clan worth saving was Verónica."

"Gee, girl," I said tightly, "I never realized how horrible your life in Santa Rita was until now."

Father tapped Marcos's shoulder. "Tell us about your dad?"

"Papa wasn't Jewish," Marcos said. "So when he married my mother, she was disowned by her entire family—another example of cultural and religious intolerance.

"Even worse, Señor Carlos," said Verónica, "when Marcos was a young boy, his father died suddenly of a heart attack."

"Oh, I'm so sorry, Marcos."

"Thank you, señor. It's been years since his passing, but I still miss my old man; and I don't think Mother will ever recover from the loss."

"How old was your dad when the tragedy occurred?"

"He was only forty-three...an awful waste!"

"It certainly was," Dad replied. "Were you and your father very close?"

"He worked long hours seven days a week, slept little, ate little, and devoted his few hours of free time to Mother and me. Papa did everything in his power to be with us, but I'm convinced he succumbed to self-neglect, excessive work, and a stressful lifestyle. Paradoxically, he left us a considerable fortune at the expense of his own life."

"In my opinion," Dad said to Marcos, "your father's crucial mission was to produce enough wealth to keep you and your mom financially independent from your mother's relatives. Unfortunately, your dedicated dad became so obsessed with that thought that eventually he reached the point of no return."

"Truth being told, Señor Carlos, I never saw it that way, but you might be absolutely right. On the other hand, I thank God every day for Dad's family being so compassionate and supportive all along."

* * *

Upon our arrival at the Hotel Presidente, a bellman removed our luggage from the wagon and set it on a two-wheeler while Dad and I exited the car.

Marcos rolled down his window. "Señor Carlos, I look forward to seeing the two of you again!" he called.

"We'll give it a good try." Dad waved as their car pulled away.

"Hey, Carlitos," Verónica shouted. "Call me on the phone so we can talk!"

Shortly after lunch, Papa hired a cab to take us to the Paseo del Prado to watch the Formula One race. It took longer than usual to arrive because, according to our driver, the main arteries were already closed for the occasion.

The entire city must have decided to watch the event from the same spot, because by the time we arrived at the Paseo, the benches were already taken and the sidewalks on both sides of the promenade were packed with spectators of all ages, some sitting on the curb, others on folding chairs. For those who arrived late, standing room was the only option.

I shot two Kodak rolls with my Brownie camera of Fangio's Mercedes zipping by our intersection. Dad and I both found it exhilarating to join hundreds of warm-blooded fans cheering for the first Latin American contender to win the Havana Formula One race.

In my excitement at being in the midst of such a world-class event, I ate two hot dogs, three popsicles, a bag of potato chips, cotton candy, and an ice cream cone. As expected, by the time the race was over I was so full Dad suggested a brisk walk to the

Capitol, and from there, a cab to the hotel. What a great way to end a Sunday.

Wait till I tell Pedro I saw Fangio win the race!

Monday after breakfast, a cab took us from the hotel to the suburb of Marianao to visit Father Basilio, the heavyset principal of the Jesuit boarding school. But as it went, the priest was having such a busy Monday that our campus tour started an hour late.

Accustomed to the yardstick of a small town, to me this center of education was of monumental size. The stone and brick three-story building occupied an entire block. Inside the complex were classrooms, offices, a chapel with a magnificent German organ, and a wing reserved for dormitories. Surrounding the building were a ship-shape baseball field, a gymnasium, a spic-and-span Olympic pool, basketball and tennis courts, and a mile-long track. Also connected to the main structure, a one-story compound housed a large dining room with a fully equipped kitchen.

After touring the campus, the heavyset priest escorted us to his office on the third floor. For a moment I thought Father Basilio wouldn't be able to make it without gasping for air or suffering heat stroke, especially given the brown woolen habit he wore in the midst of a hot summer. But to our amazement the man climbed the marble staircase like a young athlete in boxing shorts.

He asked us to sit on voluminous leather chairs across from his oversized mahogany desk. The room had no air conditioning, and there wasn't a drop of sweat on the man's brow.

After a short chat, he handed us an inch-thick brochure with color photographs of campus facilities, a description of student life during the previous academic year, and sufficient propaganda to motivate the prospective student to register on the spot. Dad asked the priest how much a brochure like that would cost and he replied they were not for sale, but if we wanted to take one home, a minimum donation of twenty pesos would help defray the publishing costs.

As I asked about their baseball team, Father Basilio haughtily claimed to have the best intercollegiate set of players in the entire city.

"We have dominated the sport during the last twelve years, and we shall continue to do so."

"Which team is next in line?" asked Dad.

"The Methodist School lineup, as long as they keep the same coach," answered the priest. "Those players have been trying to defeat us for years, and even though they came dangerously close during the last season, our institution, as always, ended up on top."

Father Basilio smoothed his glossy scalp. "So, son, I take it you're interested in baseball?"

"Of course I am," I said eagerly. "I play a strong first base, and my batting is way above average."

The principal crossed his arms over his barrel chest. "We'll be delighted to add you as another family member, and perhaps—just perhaps—as part of our baseball team, but before we get ahead of ourselves, I'd like to ask you a series of questions that may or may not qualify you to become one of our students."

This sounds easier than I thought. Thank God I brought along my grades and the principal's letter of recommendation.

"First question!" Father Basilio pounded on his desk to stress a series of hurdles. "Are you and your parents active members of the Catholic Church?"

"Yes, Father, we are, and we attend services almost every Sunday."

"Have you been baptized by the Holy Catholic and Apostolic Church?"

"Yes, Father, soon after I was born."

"And where was that church?"

"In Santa Rita, Father," I replied.

"Have you taken your First Communion?"

"Yes sir, about eight years ago."

"Again, in what church?"

"Also the one in Santa Rita, sir," I said, askance. *Why isn't Father Basilio asking about my grades?*

"What about confirmation?" The priest scrutinized me from head to toe. "Have you been confirmed, and if so, can you provide a certificate?"

"No, Father, I have not been confirmed." *I think I smell trouble.*

Stooping over his desk, the cagey principal proclaimed: "Sorry, young fellow, but you cannot be accepted in our school."

Dad's voice rose, along with his eyebrows. "You mean my son is not worthy of your institution just because he hasn't been confirmed?"

"Let me remind you, señor," Father Basilio stood up like a soldier at attention, "that rules are made to be followed, and for our organization to excel and continue to lead in our community, it must scrupulously adhere to the Holy Sacraments."

I interrupted in self-defense. "But Father Basilio, I can take confirmation classes from our priest in Santa Rita, complete my studies in a couple of weeks, and mail you a signed certificate within a month."

"Sorry, boy," the priest declared. "You'll have to come back in twelve months and ask Father Gilberto to prepare you for confirmation."

Dad flushed purple as if about to detonate. "In plain Spanish, Father Basilio: you only seem to accept boys who are confirmed a year in advance, and the rest don't count. Doesn't it bother you that my son will lose an entire year of school when he can be easily confirmed in Santa Rita's church long before registration?"

"Look, señor." The priest impassively paced the room. "The tenets of our consecrated institution must be followed exhaustively and without favoritism. Either the young man takes the confirmation course with Father Gilberto next year, or you must pursue another alternative."

Hands on his hips, Father Basilio stopped in front of us. "Ten years have passed since your son took the first communion, and for us to ensure that the young man is up to our holy standards, he must train with trustworthy Father Gilberto and not with an unknown run-of-the-mill priest who may decide to rush your boy through the course simply to make him and his family look good. We've seen this travesty before, and I won't let it happen again. I trust Father Gilberto, but he's vacationing in the Pyrenees until the end of summer. Therefore, your son must wait until the next academic year to take the course and pass the exam with Father Gilberto...no exceptions!"

Holding my hand, Dad confronted the priest: "Father Basilio, you are the most pedantic nitpicker ever to cross my path. I suggest you grab your bible and reread Matthew 19:14, where Jesus said, '*Let the children come to Me and do not hinder them, for the kingdom of heaven belongs to such as these.'* And for the record, Father Basilio, even though my boy is no longer a child, to this day the Word of the Lord stands indisputably fresh."

Dad rose from the awkward leather chair. "Come on, son. Let's register somewhere else. Perhaps the Methodist school I attended will admit you without pretext. Besides, you may be able to join their team and help defeat this man's pride."

"I-I didn't mean to offend you," Father Basilio stuttered, red as a pomegranate.

"No, Father Basilio, you know it wasn't my son or me you have offended."

In a sanctimonious expression of piety, Father Basilio pressed his palms together, closed his eyes, and said, "I cannot believe you're accusing me of offending the Son of God!"

Dad shook his head and without further ado, we left the principal's office, utterly outraged. I'd never been prouder of my father.

On our way back to the hotel, Dad asked the cab driver to stop at a delicatessen known all over Havana for preparing the most luscious Cuban sandwiches in town. He bought a couple, dropped them in a sack, and asked the same driver to take us to Malecón Drive, a couple of blocks from our hotel.

We sat on the concrete retaining wall, watching large waves crash against the rocks below. White as cotton, clusters of foam soared into the air puffed

by the wind, and even though the annoying sea spray continually fogged my father's glasses, we shared an exceptional moment eating the world's best sandwich on one of America's most dazzling ocean drives.

"What are we doing tonight?" I asked with the surreptitious hope of visiting Verónica.

"I bought tickets for the New Orleans Philharmonic Orchestra. They'll be playing Tchaikovsky's Fifth Symphony at the Auditorium Theater."

"I already know that piece. Felito's father plays it constantly on his high-fidelity record player."

"You know, son? I think this is the perfect time to mention other values that are linked to a well-rounded education."

Dad took a deep breath. "One of many objectives regarding your personal edification is to develop an avid hunger for knowledge and an endless curiosity for God's Creation." He turned to meet my eyes. "Even against your wishes," he continued. "You have read book after book concerning a wide range of topics that will eventually make you an enlightened and accomplished man. Quality music—like that we will hear tonight—is an integral part of cultural literacy, yet I must admit that music was the most anemic part of your home education. I listened to it occasionally but we don't have a record player like Felito's father, and so your ears are not yet polished to appreciate the beauty of harmonized sound. I hope you will use tonight's opportunity to redefine your sense of values while feeding your spirit with the magical sounds of a symphony orchestra performing a Russian piece impossible to forget."

I nodded, dubious. "Felito's father said that classical music is the speech of angels. Don't you think he's exaggerating?"

"On the contrary, he's absolutely right; but I'll describe it in a less idealized way: Music is the common language of mankind."

"Your description makes more sense," I said emphatically. Then I paused. "Dad, this may be a stupid question, but how do you define quality in music?"

"Well, in the opinion of many, quality music moves you from the waist up and popular music from the waist down."

"I like your definition; but you seem to have issues with popular music."

"No, I don't," Dad said firmly. "But how can you enjoy eating pheasant if you've never tasted chicken?"

He wagged a finger at me. "But don't take my advice as snobbish. Mother and I are proud of your standing against the widespread mediocrity that oozes from society's deepest crevices, and we're delighted to know that your impeccable mores rise above the standards of ordinary men."

"Come on, Dad, for heaven's sake—you're embarrassing me! I'm like all my friends, except I know about things they never heard of. Please stop seeing me like some enlightened Buddha." I gazed out at the waves.

"On the other hand," I added, "thanks for your words of support. I shall always do my best to avoid being judged under a dimmer light."

Dad kissed my brow. "We believe in you, Carlos, and before you leave home we wanted to express our gratitude for making us proud." His arm around me, Dad's eyes glimmered against the warm colors of the setting sun.

"Dad...are you sure we'll see Verónica again before we leave?"

"Of course we will."

"But when?"

"Well, let me see...tonight is the concert, and tomorrow morning we'll be visiting an old friend and former business partner. In the afternoon we'll be heading to the Cuban Coney Island, and after dinner

I have tickets to see the world-renowned ballerina Alicia Alonso performing *Swan Lake* at the Teatro Blanquita."

"What about Wednesday?" I asked.

"If you're accepted by the Methodist school," Dad replied, "it won't be necessary to meet with other principals, so we can rearrange the next three days enjoying each other and having fun in this beautiful city."

"Then what about Wednesday?" I insisted.

"Wednesday afternoon will be ideal to watch the movie premiere of "This is Cinerama" at the Teatro Radiocentro.

"Can I invite Verónica?" I asked hesitantly.

"That sounds like a great idea," he replied. "Why don't you call and see if she wants to join us for the matinee at two o'clock?"

Beaming with elation I grabbed and hugged Dad with all my might. "Thank you, thank you. Wow! I can't believe you agreed. That's what I call a top-of-the-line dad."

We walked back to the hotel to phone Verónica, but by the time we arrived, Dad realized it was getting late for the concert and we still had to dress up and grab a taxi to the Auditorium Theater. In view of the limited time, we'd be having snacks in the foyer instead of a full dinner at a restaurant.

Few times has my father been wrong about quality, and the concert that evening was no exception. I knew I would never forget the velvety sounds of the violins, the brilliant timbre of the brass instruments, and the impressive reverberation coming from the percussion section. Dad was right: Felito's father's record player couldn't come close to the glory of a live performance. But most of all I loved the last movement, and I whistled and hummed its melody all the way to the hotel.

On Tuesday we overslept till mid-morning. Tired after three days of perpetual motion, Dad decided to visit an old business acquaintance instead of going to the amusement park. The lunch with Señor Puente lasted three hours—three solid hours of laughter, because in spite of being old as Methuselah, Dad's friend had such an inventory of jokes, some clean and some not, that time and the local beer simply flew by. Plus, the engagement offered me a chance to do something important to my father, even at the expense of missing the widely known amusement park.

After lunch we grabbed a bus downtown to buy Mom a present, then rushed back to the hotel to change. I wore a more elegant outfit that barely fit in my suitcase. We ordered sandwiches to our room instead of eating at a restaurant, then raced to the

Teatro Blanquita, the island's largest theater with a seating capacity of six thousand people.

This was also the first time I'd seen a ballet, and Miss Alonso danced so brilliantly it seemed as though she defeated the law of gravity. The production was long and void of words, so I had to use my imagination and Dad's undeniable ability as a prompter.

My only objection in those days was seeing effeminate men in tights. But Dad, always on the side of the fine arts, told me to forget that issue because while some were not, most male dancers were solid men.

"Think of these male dancers as top athletes with refined manners and forget homosexuality."

At the hotel that night we called Mom to tell her about our comings and goings, including the unfortunate incident at the Jesuit School. We talked for a while, and when we hung up I felt like a slice of my heart was still in Santa Rita.

Wednesday morning we had an early breakfast at the hotel and an appointment with the Methodist school director at nine. At eight I called Verónica.

A lady answered: "Good morning, this is Sarah. To whom am I speaking?"

This must be Marcos's mother, I realized. "Buenos

dias, Señora, this is Carlos, Verónica's friend from Santa Rita." I took a deep breath.

"A very pleasant morning to you, young man. I'm so happy to meet you, even if it is over the phone."

"Señora Sarah, I'm delighted to have met you over the wire as well." Drops of cold sweat rolled down my spine.

"Thank you, Carlos. You seem to be such a polished young man. I assume you wanted to talk to Verónica?"

"Si, señora...if I may."

"She went to exchange a pair of shoes and won't be back for another hour. Would you like to leave her a message?"

I conveyed to Verónica's aunt the reason for my call and assured her that Dad and I would be more than willing to pick Verónica up in a taxi and bring her back home as soon as the show was over.

"Verónica talks about you all the time," said the polite lady, "and that's the main reason I would also like to meet you in person."

"Señora Sarah, do you think Verónica will accept my invitation?" I asked.

"In a heartbeat, young man, if not sooner. But may I extend you and your father a personal invitation?"

Oh, dear, the lady is complicating things. "Naturalmente, Señora, it'll be an honor," I replied.

"What if you and your dad join Verónica and me for a poolside lunch before the show?"

Oh my God, this is going to bring down my sand castle. I'm sure Dad will hit the ceiling.

"But of course, Señora Sarah." Sweat dripped into my eyes. "Just tell us at what time."

"Try to be here before noon, but the sooner you arrive, the better we'll get to know each other. In fact, you have no idea how much the friendship between you and Verónica harks back to the idyllic times my deceased husband and I dated each other."

Sarah told me their address, and I promised to be on our way as soon as our meeting with the school principal was over.

"Verónica said she likes to call you Carlitos. May I also call you by that name?"

"Of course, Señora Sarah," I said, incapable of staying still.

"Then you must call me Sarah, and forget the señora attribute."

"Thank you, madam, that's very sweet."

Once I hung up the phone, I told Dad about our lunch engagement. To my surprise, he didn't complain.

Unlike the Jesuit principal, Doctor Perez, the Methodist school director, was expecting us in his office, ready to serve. He began by escorting us to the sport facilities, including the baseball field, which had newly covered bleachers behind the home plate. We also visited their new basketball stadium, which they rented to other institutions for special events. In general the Methodist school was much smaller than Father Basilio's, and no classroom ever exceeded thirty students.

Doctor Perez had gone to the same school five years before my father, and so they engaged in an animated conversation while we walked back to the office. He asked us to sit, called his secretary to bring a form for Dad to sign, asked for my Santa Rita transcript and a down payment to guarantee room and board, and in virtually no time I was registered at the same school Dad had attended when he was my age.

In the end, the friendly teacher asked my father how good a baseball player I was, to which Dad replied, "Absolutely terrific." Dad was so pleased with the outcome of our visit he shook the director's hand three times before we left.

A taxi took us to Verónica's address.

"Are you sure we are in the right place?" Father asked the driver.

"Señor," he said, opening the passenger door, "this is exactly the one!"

As the driver left, we stood in awe before one of the most beautiful mansions on Miramar's Fifth Avenue.

"Wow," I said softly.

In the center of an impressive courtyard and surrounded by geraniums, a fountain stood thirty yards from the mansion's main entrance. Under the hot tropical sun, one of three gardeners added the final touches to a chain of oleanders encircling the entire complex while another clipped rosebushes alongside a narrow path that led from the fountain to the front door.

Ample balconies surrounded the two-story residence on every floor, all supported by Italian marble columns enfolded in blooming bougainvillea. We climbed three steps from the narrow path to the lower balcony to reach the front door.

"La señora Sarah los está esperando!" the oldest gardener yelled from afar.

"How does he know she's waiting for us?" I asked Dad.

"According to Havana's grapevine, gardeners have rabbit ears, that's why." Dad rang the doorbell.

"Aren't you a bit nervous?" I asked.

He shrugged. "Why should I be?"

"I'm not sure why," I replied, "but my stomach has been in knots since we left Doctor Perez's office." I did know why, though. I was worrying that Verónica might soon lose interest in me, given her family's obvious wealth.

In a matter of seconds we heard the cavernous barking of a large dog, followed by a woman's command to quiet down. A maid in uniform opened the door.

"Buenos dias, señora." Dad bowed lightly. "My son and I are—"

"No need for introduction." The neatly dressed servant pointed to a large brocaded sofa. "Please come in and have a seat. I'll tell the ladies that the two Carloses have arrived."

"Muchas gracias!" Dad and I harmonized.

"What's the dog's name?" I asked, pointing warily at the huge beast.

"His name is Capitán, and he belongs to Señor Marcos, who had him trained as a guard dog."

The maid left, and Capitán sat at attention in front of me, ears pointing up and eyes locked on my own.

Ahead of the spacious living room was a dining area with a fully stocked bar and furniture of the finest Cuban mahogany. The floor was of white granite so polished it reflected the room, and an oil portrait of a neatly dressed man in his mid-forties hung above the dining room fireplace.

"He must be Marcos's father," Dad remarked.

"Why would they need a fireplace in tropical Havana?" I asked, bemused.

"Perhaps someone suffers from occasional chills or Sarah needed some sort of pedestal above which to hang the painting." Dad gave me a wink.

From our lovely sofa and through the glass doors and windows separating the dining room from the back grounds, we could see a manicured garden with coconut palms and cypress trees surrounding a cascading swimming pool. We discovered before long that the swing door located toward the rear of the dining area connected to a kitchen so large and well equipped it resembled that of a hotel. To our left, a marble staircase curved upward to the second-story bedrooms and their connecting bathrooms.

"What a wonderful surprise!" A lady perhaps in her mid-sixties appeared at the top of the staircase. "Verónica and I have been anxiously looking forward to your visit." Holding tightly to the handrail, she descended to the first floor with extreme care and difficulty.

"Please forgive my sluggishness, but I suffer from severe bouts of arthritis in virtually every joint."

Dad and I extended our hands to greet the gracious lady.

"No handshakes, please," she expressed with

open arms. “I like to hug people. Handshakes are good only in the business world.”

The silver-haired woman was so affectionate and her manners so pleasant that she made me feel at ease. But I still wasn’t sure whether she was Verónica’s aunt Sarah or someone else, so I held my tongue.

“Señora Sarah,” Dad addressed her assertively. “It is a pleasure to meet such a warm and thoughtful lady.”

Thank God Dad cleared the air. He must be a good judge of character or simply took a chance.

Following a short conversation, Sarah asked one of the servants to fetch her walking cane and to instruct the cook to prepare lunch and serve it on the patio.

“Señora Sarah, where is Verónica?” I asked after a mental debate.

“Verónica has been trying on different dresses all morning, and when I left her room she still hadn’t made up her mind.”

I hoped her indecision meant she wanted to look her best for me—but maybe it was her creative strain trying to express itself. I didn’t know enough about girls to draw a conclusion.

As Sarah opened the glass door leading to the manicured patio, she summoned the maid to bring a cooler with sodas, cold beer, and a bottle of French

Chardonnay inside a bucket-full of ice. "And please remember to let the wine breathe before bringing it to the table," she added.

During our conversation, Sarah confirmed that the portrait above the fireplace was of her beloved husband Marcos, who had insisted on building the fireplace, even though in Havana it was considered a ridiculous whim.

"My husband didn't care about public opinion," Sarah said, "and when he wanted something done to the house, only God could stop him. Besides, Marcos worked so hard throughout his life, we felt he deserved to do with the house and his money exactly as he wished."

"Buenos dias, Señor Carlos and Carlitos!" Verónica swept out to the colorful courtyard, followed by Capitán.

My heartthrob wore a turquoise and white retro polka-dot dress with halter straps, crinoline, a white belt, and white high-heeled shoes, and another girlish ponytail. Stressed as I was, I didn't know whether to kiss her in front of Sarah and Dad or shake her hand. I was a shy boy when it came to public demonstrations of love, and that was that. But since Verónica didn't mind showing affection in the middle of a crowd, she stood on her toes, held my face with both hands, and gave me a big smack of a kiss.

"I'm so excited to go out with you and your dad to see Cinerama!" Her great dark eyes twinkled. "Also, I'd like to invite you to ice cream after the movie."

"But Verónica!" Sarah exclaimed, hands on her hips. "I thought you'd do it as a surprise."

"I know, Sarah, but I'm too excited to wait that long!"

We had lunch, the taxi arrived, and an entourage of well-wishers gathered at the front entrance. Sarah stood leaning on her cane, Capitán didn't cease barking, the short Chinese cook stood atop a bench, and three maids waved as if we were to cross the Atlantic on a sailboat. Farther back, to make sure no one noticed his presence, the old gardener with rabbit-ears waved and waved until the taxi turned around the block. Why this group of people from different backgrounds was such a hospitable bunch, I had no idea.

The theater was totally full on a Wednesday afternoon, and I wondered how long the lines would be on Saturday night. The Cinerama screen wrapped around us as if we were right inside the movie. And that movie was such an experience, especially during the harrowing roller coaster ride, that in spite of the visible three-segment screen, I could see why it had taken over Havana moviegoers like a storm.

The three of us got along so well that anyone

seeing us leave the gorgeous Radiocentro theater with so much cheer would've thought Father was a teenager struggling with premature aging.

After Verónica's charming ice cream invitation, we hired a taxi to take her home, and upon arrival Dad waited in the car while I escorted my girlfriend to the front door. Auspiciously, the balcony light that was supposed to stay on all night wasn't, so we did what most novios do under such conditions; we concealed ourselves in the darkest corner and went on to hug and kiss like in the movies.

Back at our hotel room, we noticed a red light blinking on the telephone.

"Mmm...I wonder who sent us a message." Dad picked up the receiver and listened attentively, frowning.

"Bad news!" he said when he hung up. "Mom left a message stating that Julia, our store manager, suffered a broken hip after falling from a ladder while dusting the upper shelves."

Damn! I thought. *Just when everything was going so well.* "That means we should be heading back, right?"

"Yes, son, that's correct," replied Dad. "Otherwise our store will remain closed until I get back, and no one will be taking the weekly inventory."

I felt as though someone had poured a bucketful of ice on me.

"I'll call the bus station to reserve a couple of seats for tonight...if possible. I'm really sorry, son."

I sighed with resignation. "That's okay, Dad. I know the store is our livelihood. I'll call Verónica and let her know."

"Thank you, Carlos." Dad nodded sadly. "I'm so proud to see how mature you have become."

"Thanks, Dad; I know you're disappointed too. At least I'll be back in Havana in less than two months. I can see why you love this city so much."

Dad called the inter-province bus station and reserved two adjoining seats for the bus leaving for Camaguey that evening at ten, then called his favorite restaurant in Havana for a dinner reservation to celebrate our last supper in the big city.

"Carlos, please sit by my side. I have something important to share with you," he said solemnly.

I sat at the edge of his bed, waiting for more bad news.

Father massaged his brow, then laid an arm on my shoulder.

"My dear boy." Dad's voice shuddered. "It never crossed my mind that the two of us, in spite of our age difference, could've enjoyed this amazing venture so much. You know that as a father I have been more autocratic than the regular dad. Well, after almost four days of camaraderie and inner scrutiny, I have discovered that my past inability to share a more down-to-Earth relationship with you created a chasm that has separated the two of us for the last sixteen years.

"You see, Carlos, I've mistakenly maintained that it was impossible for kids your age to relate to older folk with maturity and wisdom, and it never crossed my mind that relaxing my self-imposed disciplinarian role would've promoted the quality of friendship you and I have enjoyed during the last four days.

"This trip has opened my mind to new horizons in our relationship. Therefore I shall renounce my hardheaded past and dedicate more effort to nurturing the precious bond you and I may enjoy for the rest of our lives. Because in the end, Carlos, equality, patience, and love are the foundations of long-lasting relationships.

"And in closing; your mother and I are proud of your dedication to academic excellence, moral integrity, respect for human values, and for exhibiting a sincere sense of compassion among your peers. I, for one, shall be thanking God the rest of my days for holding you in the palm of his hands."

We hugged tightly, and I held back tears, but deep

inside, my heart knew I was embracing my life's everlasting friend.

Dinner that evening was casual so I didn't have to wear another coat and tie outfit. Servings were generous, and I also had two desserts, *dulce de leche* and a mango shake.

"I'm so full, I'm about to burst," I complained to Dad.

We went back to the hotel to wrap things up. Dad called Mom to inform her of our next-day arrival. I also phoned Verónica, who sobbed incessantly throughout the call. We promised we would write often, always bearing in mind that in less than two months we would be seeing each other again. We also agreed that in the event she visited her parents in Santa Rita during this time, she would disregard my existence for everyone's sake. She reluctantly agreed.

I also said goodbye to Sarah and Marcos, who was home at the time, and thanked them both for welcoming me and my father to their home.

What a great experience, and how enlightening I found our trip to Havana. Yet, when I boarded the bus that evening, the first thought that came to mind was: *This is my turn to tell Pedro a hell of a story.*

COMING OF AGE

"Wake up, Carlos, it's eleven-thirty. You're not planning to stay in bed all day, are you?" Mother removed a pillow from my face.

"Gee, Mom, instead of being so pushy, why don't you let me sleep a little longer?"

"But you never sleep past eight o'clock. What's wrong?"

"Nothing—I'm just still exhausted after a dreadful twelve-hour bus ride and two more hours in an old jarring train."

"But your dad just went to work without complaints, and you're much younger. How can you feel so lethargic after having such a great time in Havana?"

I sat at the edge of the bed, holding my head. "You'll understand after I tell you."

Mom sat by my side, wrapped an arm around my shoulder, and kissed me on the cheek.

"My back hurts; do you mind rubbing it a bit?" I pleaded.

"Of course I don't mind. You've enjoyed back-rubs since you were a child."

"You know, Mom? You're so sweet," I mumbled.

"Thank you, son, that's very nice. But let's make a deal: I'll massage your back while I listen to your painful experience, and then you'll zoom out of bed and take a shower."

"All right, Mom." I gave her hand a squeeze. "With that in mind I'll stretch the yarn as much as I can." I sighed like a purring cat as she kept her side of the bargain, then began my tale.

"You know we were called home suddenly, so the lady who reserved our bus seats could not put us together. Dad sat next to a young woman wearing earplugs and an eye mask. Suffice it to say, minutes after the driver closed the door she was sound asleep and so was Dad.

"I, on the other hand, had to sit next to a pachyderm who must have weighed at least three hundred pounds, stunk like a gorilla, coughed and sneezed without mercy, and to make it worse, he smoked cheap cigars that reeked like a blazing garbage dump.

"The bus was so full I couldn't change seats, and the lady behind us was so furious she complained boisterously to the steward, who in turn offered the human whale a drink of icy water to soothe his throat, then asked him to quit smoking inside the bus. The man obeyed, but the coughing and the smell continued to suffocate me to where I had to leave the bus at every stop to breathe fresh air."

"Wow, it sounds like a trip to hell," said Mother.

"But that's not all," I continued. "I had eaten so much at a Havana restaurant shortly before we left that my stomach was on fire. As you can imagine, I couldn't sleep at all, and when we finally got home last night I felt like a freight train had run me over. That's why, even though I slept well last night, I still couldn't gather enough energy to jump out of bed this morning."

"I'm really sorry. It must have been a nightmare!" Mom lowered my t-shirt and quit rubbing my back.

"But I'm not finished," I grumbled. "My biggest concern is that Dad wants me to travel back and forth to Havana by bus because trains are too expensive."

"But Carlos, can't you see he wanted to treat you to a first-class trip as a reward for good grades?"

"I know, Mom, but could you try to change his mind so I can travel in comfort?"

"Heck no, and don't you dare ask!" Mother shook her head fiercely. "Dad will get so upset he'll regret his generosity, so plan to take the bus like a good sport and forget living a luxury life on a pauper's pocket."

Mom turned me to face her squarely. "When

Dad and I first settled in Santa Rita," she said, "all we had was a little cash and a small savings account to open a clothing store. Your father went back and forth to Havana regularly in search of new patterns. Those trips were uncomfortable, unreliable, and in smelly buses without air conditioning or shock absorbers. He traveled for years under those miserable circumstances, and while in Havana he slept in cheap hotels, and instead of hiring taxicabs he used public transportation to move heavily loaded boxes from one warehouse to the next."

I felt chastened. "He never told me any of that," I said.

"By the time you were born," Mom continued, "our family was financially sound, and it has been good ever since."

"What about you, Mom? How did you survive the difficult times?"

"Well, I don't want to bore you with the details, but it was harsh. I mended socks, sometimes to the point they were embarrassing to wear, recycled the same food two and three times so it never resembled the original recipe, and I pressed our clothing with a kerosene iron worthy of an antiquities museum. But as my mother said, every new baby brings a loaf of bread under his arm, and so did you. Following your arrival things began to change for the better, and sixteen years later we have a debt-free, solid, and lucrative business. But we're not in a position for you to travel in luxury, my boy."

Mom stood up, hands on her hips. "So for your own sake, get your butt out of bed, call Felito, and enjoy the beautiful outdoors with your buddy. Act and think as you did before the trip instead of finding excuses to do little and gain much. Struggling with adversity will strengthen your character and determination, and in the end you'll climb above the heap by your own boot straps."

"Okay, Mom, I'll get out of bed and call my friend, but not without first telling you what I think, and *por favor*, don't share this with Dad."

"Okay, I won't, but please keep it short."

"If I ever have a family," I said, nervously wringing my hands, "and my financial status is up and growing, I won't force my children to walk over burning coals to replicate my experiences. I totally disagree with your outdated Victorian norms, and if I ever become wealthy, I will shower my children with all the comforts and luxuries life has to offer."

"Are you kidding?" Mom shrieked. "Can't you see you'll be raising spoiled brats instead of productive citizens, and lazy beggars instead of respectable men and women? For Christ's sake, how could you be so stupid?"

I shrugged. "It's in the bible, Mother, and the words of the Apostle Paul will prove me right: 'From those to whom much is given, much is expected.' Therefore I'm planning to share my wealth with my descendants and together enjoy the good life."

Pale as a corpse, Mom wagged an admonishing finger at me. "Okay, Carlos, I won't tell your father, but I shall warn you: There are half-truths, truths, and timeless truths, and I blame your immaturity and naïveté for failing to appreciate the latter ones."

I kissed my mom on the cheek. "Come on, Mother, can't you see I'm kidding?"

"No, you were not!" She shook her head. "How can you leave home for six days and come back with a different head?"

"All right, Mom, to tell you the truth, I was so impressed by Verónica's lifestyle I haven't being able to give up the notion of being well-off. Her aunt Sarah gives her all she wants—a palace with maids, a closet full of expensive clothing, and the promise of a Mercedes-Benz as soon as she's old enough to drive, compliments of a relative with money to burn. I love my life as it is, know exactly where I stand, and why I must use my own resources to become the respectful and well-bred man you and Dad deserve. But on the other hand...I can't wait to drive Verónica's Mercedes."

Mom threw up her arms in dismay. "Are you still joking, or are you telling me the truth?"

"Of course I'm telling you the truth! I love my parents too much to disappoint them, but then again—wouldn't you enjoy driving your own Mercedes all over Santa Rita?"

"I don't know how to drive, and I don't have a license," Mom snapped, "so get off your butt, take a shower, and move on. You're too smart to stay in bed daydreaming about Verónica's Mercedes. And always remember that God has placed difficulties between man and everything he wishes to have, for a reason."

I went straight to the bathroom, opened the cold water faucet, and shivered under its icy flow in an attempt to regain lost energy. While the trip to Havana had opened my eyes to a million possibilities, my heart still gravitated toward Santa Rita's mundane lifestyle.

On my way to visit Pedro the following day, I stopped briefly at Felito's to show him pictures of the trip, but since he wasn't home at the time, I stayed for a moment to chat with his parents. For starters, I told Don Rafael about the influence his favorite musical composition had wielded on me, and the memorable experience of listening to a live symphony orchestra.

"I'm so glad you told me," exclaimed Felito's

father in his deep Castilian accent. "The reason I play music rather loud is to spread the seeds of beautiful sounds so that at least one may fall and bear fruit on fertile ears. So, my dear Carlos...all I can say is thank you for making my day!"

"I'm the one who should be thankful," I replied to Don Rafael. "After listening to good music day in and day out, I figured your son would be an expert in the classical genre."

"No such luck!" said my buddy's mother, Carmen. "Our son only listens to cha-chas, boleros, merengues, and American rock and roll. Felito claims his father has weird taste when it comes to music and feels embarrassed when his buddies listen to Dad's favorites."

"Mmm. That's surprising," I mumbled.

"Have you heard the Spanish proverb: 'In the house of the blacksmith, guests eat with wooden knives?'" asked Carmen.

"No, señora, but I understand what it means."

I stopped at home on my way to the wharf to visit Pedro.

"Your father came from work for a short nap, so be quiet." Mother tapped her lips. "I didn't know whether you'd be home for lunch or eat at Felito's."

"I like to eat here, but please let me help you."

Mom handed me the basic ingredients to make

two ham sandwiches, which I prepared on the kitchen counter and presented on a plate garnished with lettuce, radishes, and other veggies. While I worked on the sandwiches, Mom fixed me two oversized crackers topped with chunks of guava paste to be chased by my ubiquitous glass of milk. We sat across from each other at the kitchen table, and I spent at least an hour telling her about our trip to Havana, especially our encounter with Verónica, which she didn't take lightly because she knew I had a crush on the Jewish girl. As I spoke, I wolfed down my sandwich. "Boy, I'm sure going to miss lunches like these at school," I said.

"But you'll have a great time in Havana," she answered. "The food is delicious in the big city."

"And you know something?" I stood up to leave. "Dad said he'll be taking you along to visit from time to time."

"Yes, he told me. Won't that be great?"

"It'll be wonderful!" I kissed her brow and headed off to ride my bicycle to the wharf.

"When you see Pedro, please say hello," she called, "and remember he's older than a week ago, so be kind to him."

"Yes, Mother. I still remember your sermon from before I left town."

I looked all over for the Old Man, feeling quite frantic.

"Are you after Pedro?" asked Gonzalo, a seven-foot, three-hundred-pound Haitian who worked at the wharf on weekdays and repaired heavy equipment on Saturdays and Sundays. "He hasn't been out of bed for an entire week."

"What's wrong? Is he sick?"

"No one thinks so. Everyone feels Pedro is back to his worn-out 'I'm about to die' scenario."

I shook my head in disbelief. "I'll go see him right away."

"Please wait!" Gonzalo grabbed me by the arm. "You should realize that in spite of your age, you're the only person he listens to and trusts, so please be careful what you say."

"I wish he wasn't so dependent," I grumbled.

"Quit avoiding responsibility; you're not a child anymore." Gonzalo fixed his huge black eyes on mine. "You simply must accept certain obligations, so stop looking for excuses."

I crossed my arms over my chest. "But how can I help Pedro when I'll be gone most of the time?"

"I'm not talking about spoon-feeding the man or caring for his physical needs. All you need to do is to show Pedro that you care," said the heavyweight.

"Write to the Old Man, and when you're back in town pay special attention to him."

"Mmm... I can always mail postcards and write letters, but again, why only me?"

Gonzalo spoke after a short pause. "Young man, since you were a small boy you've become something of a mascot to our group, but Pedro in particular has played a significant role in your growth. And frankly, you've been blessed for having the wise Old Man as a mentor, playing the role of Jiminy Cricket in your life. I suppose you know who Jiminy Cricket is, don't you?"

"Of course I do. I've read 'Pinocchio' many times and saw the Walt Disney movie. He's like a conscience that can sit on your shoulder. But since you fellows are also his friends, shouldn't you share some of the responsibility?"

Gonzalo scowled at me. "And who says we don't? Whether the Old Man feels or fakes he's at the verge of death, we're the ones taking him to the clinic. All the workers keep an eye on his health and do what needs to be done on his behalf. But we cannot substitute for the joy and companionship you provide, and as some higher-up once said, 'Man cannot live on bread alone.' Now, in simple terms—since no good fortune should be taken for granted, and everything in life has a price—the time has come to pay your debts."

Gonzalo's words shocked me. Never before had I felt the heaviness of heart caused by assuming responsibility for someone else's wellbeing.

* * *

"Hey Pedro, it's me, Carlos. Please open the door."

"I'll be right over," yelled the Old Man. "Just wait till I put on my pants. Wow! What a pleasant surprise to have you back from Havana in one piece."

Pedro finally opened the makeshift door. "I haven't had a drink since you left, and this morning I took a shower and sprayed my armpits with a stinging lotion Gonzalo gave me," he announced, throwing his arms around me.

Somewhat hesitantly, I responded in kind. The notion of being morally responsible for the Old Man's unconventional behavior made me feel awkwardly entrapped.

"What's that gift-wrapped box under your arm?" Pedro pointed at it.

"Oh, er...well, I brought you a present."

"But why did you spend your money on me?"

"I just wanted to smell the aroma of a good cigar when I'm around you."

A smile shimmered in Pedro's face as he opened

the aromatic cedar box. “Partagás cigars? Wow! I was working part-time for the railroad the last time I smoked cigars like these! What a nice surprise! But let’s get out of this hole and sit on a bench under the morning sun.”

Shaking my head, I followed Pedro’s spry steps to the dock. *This man had the audacity to announce his imminent death to those workers? How can he be so callous?*

At the end of the wharf, we sat with our legs hanging over the water. In the corner of my eye I saw Gonzalo walking toward us.

“Come on, Viejo!” He shook the Old Man’s shoulder. “How can you be sitting on a cold and humid dock, smoking an expensive Havana cigar, when just this morning you were a dying man?”

“Thank you for asking, Gonzalo, but I truly feel much better.” Pedro sighed deeply. “But don’t entertain false hopes. I’m here because this damn kid actually forced me out of my deathbed to deep-fry under the morning sun.”

Gonzalo gave me a surreptitious wink. “Why did you let him dictate what you can and cannot do? If you’re about to die, no one should be bossing you around.”

“I totally agree,” said the now cheerful Old Salt, “but then I realized that by exposing my skin to the healing properties of the morning rays, I may live a little longer."

The giant Haitian shook his head, turned around, and left.

"Why do you lie to your friends like that?" I asked.

"Because they're constantly giving me a hard time, and I wanted to retaliate by threatening to die."

"But that's preposterous," I said. "In the end you'll be making a fool of yourself, and when death really knocks on your door they'll think you're crying wolf again."

"But I'm gaining notoriety, young man, notoriety in retaliation for their ignoring my afflictions."

"What afflictions?" I asked, confused.

"Loneliness and insignificance, among others," Pedro replied, puffing on the aromatic cigar. "All these workers define me as a cantankerous creature who doesn't understand the present, has no memory of the past, and doesn't care about the future. Like the pyramids, I may be full of history, but I'm still old, dusty, and partially dilapidated on top."

"What about me, Pedro?" I asked somberly. "Do I also cause you misery?"

"On the contrary," said the Old Man. "I feel important when you're present because you bring meaning to my life!"

"In what way?" I asked, truly perplexed.

"To answer your question, let's first talk about the significance of meaning." Pedro adopted his professorial tone. "You seek me for knowledge and guidance because I possess the erudition and experience that only a man who has walked the Earth for almost a century can offer, and this means a lot to me.

"I have read virtually every book yet written, and have suffered the ravages of human greed and the devastation brought about by bigotry and hatred. I know better than most what true love is really like. I've witnessed the desolating forces of nature and the beauty of its reawakening. I have seen time after time the destructive powers of man and their resulting grief, and thanks to the miracle of faith, I have felt the joys of giving and forgiving—virtues that led me to the doorstep of our Maker."

Pedro's voice quivered. "Despite your young age, your thirst for knowledge adds meaning to my life, and the reason I pursue meaning is because absolute truth I'll never find."

Pedro fixed me with a gentle gaze. "Through the years I've been planting in your mind seeds that are beginning to bear fruit..."

I kicked my feet in the water. "What kind of seeds?"

"Moral values, loyalty, and the ability to exercise

common sense. In fact, some workers contend that through the years, a fragment of my own humanity has merged with yours. As far as I'm concerned, nothing on Earth could be more inspiring."

"What about loneliness, then? Are you always bothered by it?"

"Not when you're here." Pedro wiped his sweaty brow. "How can I feel lonely when you're constantly bugging the hell out of me?" Pedro shook his head. "I'm getting kind of weepy; let's talk about something else!"

"I totally agree. Wait till I tell you about Havana!"

"And Verónica—did she contact you?"

"Of course she did! And I thank you for being so thoughtful. You can't imagine how much I enjoyed her company in such a different setting."

"Naaa...you don't have to thank me. I just wanted to lift up your heart and spirit, especially when your new school is so far away from home."

"In all honesty, Pedro, I can't get her off my mind, and God knows how much I've tried."

"Don't be a fool!" Pedro knocked on my head. "Why would you want to?" You can herniate your brain for trying so hard!"

I shared our Havana experiences with Pedro until late afternoon, when I realized it was time to leave. "Old Man, it's getting late and I must go, but before

I do, I wanted to reassure you that regardless of distance, you'll be always a part of me. I shall keep you current on my life's comings and goings, and I also promise to continue bugging the hell out of you, even if it is by mail, or by long distance...that is, if I have money to burn."

I shook Pedro's tough, leathery hand and left, knowing I'd be seeing him again soon, for I still had forty-five days left in Santa Rita.

I felt as though my summer vacation was the shortest ever, and the closer my departure drew, the more I wanted to stay in Santa Rita. In my deepest thoughts I had never entertained the possibility that missing my parents, Pedro, and my buddies, would bring tears to my eyes, but it did, for after all, I was a happy and fulfilled young man whose only incentive to leave town was an awaiting girl. Otherwise I would've given anything to stay another year, one in which schools, homework, and tests were nonexistent and playing with friends was a daily routine.

At the time I didn't fully appreciate my parents' efforts for sending me to one of Havana's most prestigious boarding schools, partly because I knew deep inside that my days of freelance joy were about to be bartered for a life crammed with stark realities. I often found myself drowning in self-pity—an aberration that only kids who have everything are prone to display. Known by adults as growing pains, I had begun to comprehend that like the sun and the moon, human existence also undergoes complex phases, and I was about to leave the most pleasant for a more demanding and unpredictable one.

As I aged further into adulthood, I attained a period in which I yearned to kiss my parents' feet in gratitude for their love, support, and dedication, and as I continued to expand my horizons, one night I took them both out to dinner at the world-renowned Tropicana nightclub with a mission in mind: to celebrate their devoted parenting and to thank them with all my heart for the man they helped to carve.

But before that time, I could only think about my imminent departure.

Since Mother had vanished the old pigskin trunk from service upon our return from Havana, jamming two new suitcases with stuff I may or may not need became her last-moment obsession.

"Are you sure you know where to call a taxi?" asked Dad the day before I was to leave.

"Oh dear," Mom interjected. "I forgot to tell you that Señora Sarah sent me a note asking for permission to drive our son from the bus terminal to school."

"That's very nice of them," said Dad. He patted my coat pocket. "How much cash are you carrying?"

"Close to a hundred pesos. Do you think that's enough?"

"That's plenty for a while," he said confidently. "We'll send you more via Western Union in a week or so."

According to Alberto Guzmán, Santa Rita's radio station owner and official weather seer, Friday, August 26, my departure date, was expected to be the rainiest on record. Local weather freaks, however, claimed that no Santa Rita meteorological post had ever existed and that Guzmán, after climbing to his rooftop every morning before sunrise, arbitrarily decided the town's weather history and pattern for the day.

Friday morning we arrived at the train station one hour before departure. I wore a brand new suit, shiny black shoes waxed and polished by Dad the night before, and a necktie Mom took from his armoire. Though overdressed for a long bus trip, I wasn't going to take off my coat and tie at that moment. But even though the bus had air conditioning, I knew I wouldn't fall asleep wearing a woolen coat and a painfully constricting tie. Besides, I didn't want to single myself out among passengers in casual wear and summer shorts. As soon as the train left, I planned to cram these garments into a suitcase.

We didn't expect many well-wishers at the terminal, but surprisingly, numerous friends and relatives rose to the occasion on that sunny Friday morning. Once again, Doña América stood by my mother, handkerchief in hand. This time the lady came accompanied by Rivero, the disfigured hunchback who, after being bullied and mocked by the town's idiots, still carried his cross with the dignity of a saint.

My austere grandfather came with Grandma, the dignified lady who wore white talcum powder on her face in lieu of cosmetics. Also present were my friend Felito and his parents, Carmen and Don Rafael. Evaristo, the gutsy sailor from Martinique, showed up wearing his familiar canvas shorts and a colorful shirt. Gonzalo, the giant from the wharf, came, along with my friend Alfredito, the young shark teaser who ended up in the hospital following an attack. Also Tio Jorge came, the uncle who argued that tradition is what we resort to when social issues are not based in reason. To my surprise, Verónica's friend Chucho was there and called me aside to inform me that Verónica was madly in love and waiting for me.

Pedro showed up in his funeral suit, for as he said, "Why wait to wear it inside the box, when the outfit already has pinholes drilled by insects?" His black tie looked more like a silk scarf because of its width, and his once-black Ingelmo shoes, an expensive wedding gift presented by a friend two generations before, were now sage-green from mold and had visible cracks on top.

"So those are the shoes you intend to wear at your funeral, eh?" I asked.

"Yep!" Pedro replied. "But I decided to wear them at yours instead."

The train arrived on time, and I only had five minutes to hug, kiss, and shake hands with everybody. Last in line except for my parents, Pedro hugged me so tightly it seemed he would refuse to let me go.

"You make me proud, Carlos," he said categorically. "Buena suerte, y acuérdate de mi."

"Good luck to you as well, Jiminy Cricket!"

"And son, don't forget to send me a handful of Partagás cigars once in a while, okay?"

"You can count on it, Old Man."

I boarded the train, escorted by my parents, who wanted to make sure I found my assigned seat. Once I was settled, they left the car somewhat reluctantly. Our conductor blew the whistle, the sooty old engine belched steam all over herself, and the four-car train began to crawl slowly and with conviction. I stuck my head out the window for a final look at my well-wishers, and all I could see was a grayish blend of smoke and steam.

Out of the blue, Grandpa's words came to mind:

"No place on Earth offers a merrier life than a little town, the only locale in which the joys and sorrows of one become the business of many."

Farewell, Santa Rita.

ABOUT THE AUTHOR

Andrew J. Rodriguez is a student of the human condition who views the writer's craft as a means to enrapture the mind and touch the heart. *Santa Rita Stories* is his fifth book following *Helen's Treasure: Odyssey of a Ladies' Man, The Incredible Adventures of Enrique Diaz,* a finalist for both the Book of the Year Award sponsored by Foreword Magazine and the Best Books Award sponsored by USA Book News. His second book, *Adios, Havana: A Memoir,* won the prestigious Colorado Independent Publishers Association EVVY Award in 2005, as well as the Allbooks Reviews Editor's Choice Award. His first novel, the highly acclaimed *The Teleportation of an American Teenager,* is a time-travel adventure that moves from Mongolia to medieval Venice along the fabled Silk Road. The author and his wife live in Colorado and Florida.

CPSIA information can be obtained at www.ICGtesting.com
Printed in the USA
LVOW12s0231140614

390008LV00010B/46/P